SALVATION'S KISS

TALES OF MYTHON BOOK 1

KATHRYN JAYNE

Copyright (C) 2020 Kathryn Jayne

Layout design and Copyright (C) 2020 by Next Chapter

Published 2020 by Sanguine– A Next Chapter Imprint

Edited by Lorna Read

Cover art by CoverMint

This book is a work of fiction. Names, characters, places, and incidents are the product of the author's imagination or are used fictitiously. Any resemblance to actual events, locales, or persons, living or dead, is purely coincidental.

All rights reserved. No part of this book may be reproduced or transmitted in any form or by any means, electronic or mechanical, including photocopying, recording, or by any information storage and retrieval system, without the author's permission.

Let your imagination soar and carry you to places unseen, for only there exists a world with no limitations.

PROLOGUE

There is no denying it. Hearing it is the year 224 can be quite confusing, especially if you don't know the real truth of history. But I am not talking B.C. or A.D. No, I am talking O.D. or Óla Dei, meaning 'all seen'. It's also, quite aptly, the abbreviation used for an overdose, which is something we all experienced a few hundred years ago, an overdose of the unseen. Our world forever changed, but you won't find that in your history books.

Before our year counter reset, your time ended, or at least it did for us. You continued on, unaware of what actually happened, and if my tales make it out of this region, then no doubt they will be passed over as fable, but this is our truth, this world is our truth.

As with most ends, it came as a complete force of devastation. The Doomsday clock leapt to midnight and the world as we knew it ended. But it wasn't missiles flying or chemicals assailing the sky, it was those who had existed unseen amongst us since the beginning, stepping into the light and making themselves known. These creatures, beings thought only to be spun from the minds of fablers like myself, had grown weary of living in the shadows, hiding their true nature, and Mankind fell to them in the blink of an eye and a new order was forced upon us.

But things changed too quickly, and the devastation was too great. That was when the Perennials came. Remember the story of how man obtained fire? Remember the gods of old? That was actually the Perennials. Invoking their powerful magics, these beings sacrificed themselves to rewrite history, turning back the clock for many minds and reaching into the great source of all to ensure no one your side would remember the truth.

They took it upon themselves to banish our land, remove it from sight and history, and seal within it as many of the creatures from your myths and legends as they could gather. Certain people in your history have worked alongside them, hunting these beings and directing their fate accordingly, sometimes relocating them to the island of Mython.

The problem is, Mython is a big island, and those of us here still have tales and books detailing the true history in all its horrific glory. Having seen how creatures had ravished the land, suffice to say our beginning was not an era of peace and harmony.

While the world outside had forgotten we had ever existed and moved into their new century, we eventually, through wars, rebellions and negotiations, found our own balance of sorts; one that is maintained by the most powerful of each race, those with Elder blood coursing through their veins.

Our country is divided into territories, each with its own elected leader who reports issues of note to the council, a collection of thirteen species predominately consisting of Elder bloodlines from the main preternatural lines such as shifter, fey, vampire, magical innate, elementals, celestials and so on. Humans were of course included, but we elect our own representatives just as any clan without such a sovereign did. The only missing faction is the Perennial, because none exist any more, at least none that we are aware of. After creating order, in our world and yours, it is said they invoked the last of their magic to seal our land from discovery.

Over two hundred years have passed since the wars died down and an uneasy truce was formed. The balance appears to be working. Now, life has returned to normal, or at least a manner of normal only possible here. Humans and preternatural are sharing space and resources, and the council are doing what is needed to maintain peace.

As I mentioned before, I am a fabler and it is my calling to tell the tales of our people. My name is Kathryn Jayne, and the tale here is just one of the many lives that call to me. Hopefully, what limited powers I have will guide it to your hands. Be it fiction in your eyes or not, these stories must be told.

CHAPTER 1

Good riddance, Conrad thought, snapping his visor down as he tore down the street on his bike without casting a backwards glance towards his old academy.

Six months ago, if his mother had told him she was taking an assignment in a different territory, he would stayed here and completed his discipline. But now, he would welcome a fresh start, a fresh academy where no one looked at him with vehement hatred. Where no one knew what he was.

Everything had been going fine. He and Rei had been happy, or at least he thought they had been. Sure, he had known she was a banshee; in fact, that had been part of the allure that drew him towards her in the first place. He had accepted her without question, without hesitation, and she had hung on his arm savouring every party invite and social escalation that came with being his girlfriend. Maybe that was all he had been to her, a way to rise through the social ranks, but if that was the case, why did she have to ruin him?

'*Horrific, unlovable, monstrous.*' The words echoed through his mind as he drove past the park where they used to walk hand in hand. He hadn't realised she didn't know what he was, that it would have made such a difference. That day, when she asked to see his other-self, she had destroyed him.

His friends, even those he had known for over twenty years, turned against him in the blink of an eye, joining in with her vicious slander, shunning and shaming him, until everyone kept their distance. The last six months had been hell. A fresh start was exactly what he needed and he certainly wouldn't make the same mistake again. He would finish his discipline, maybe even make a friend or two, but he knew now no one would ever fully accept him and his internal harmony had forever been disrupted.

He revved the bike, taking the corner too fast. *Breathe*, he reminded himself. *It's over now.* But he knew that wasn't true. He had once been proud of his heritage, of who and what he was. Now, where that pride had once been there was only shame.

Rain poured from the sky, obscuring almost everything from view. Small islands of visibility, cast by the amber shades of streetlights, created the illusion of falling silver as the fat, speeding droplets streaked past. With the recent string of abductions, even drivers thought better than to be out alone at this time of night, especially in such a torrential downpour. Ashley breathed warmth into her hands, her breath misting as it escaped her darkening lips in an attempt to blow the sodden rusty strands of hair from her face. Spring was only a few months away, but even with thoughts of summer's heat, the rain still penetrated her thin uniform with icy precision, despite the protection of her not-so-waterproof jacket.

The forty-minute walk home after her shift was exhausting, especially after spending the day in lectures, but there was little choice. Not if she wanted to pay the bills. Her brother helped where he could, but, as one of those selected to venture beyond the barrier and keep order, keep the unseen in their place, relocate them here, or dispatch them, he had more than enough to contend with. After their parents' death he rarely returned, and yet in some ways they had grown closer, still finding time to correspond across the distance between his assignments.

When Ashley had been adopted at the age of six, her new brother, Alex, had always seemed to be frustrated at her about one thing or another. She was always in the wrong place or touching the wrong things. It was only when he held her close as she sobbed at their parents' graves that she realised how much he actually cared… that the constant ribbing and tormenting was nothing more than a healthy sibling relationship.

Their life insurance had just cleared the remaining mortgage on their three bedroom home, which had been left to the pair of them. Alex insisted they kept the property, that she lived there and saw to its upkeep in his absence. It was a small house, but big enough to hold a lifetime of memories and for a single person to rattle around in, lost to the dark thoughts of the past.

Small slivers of light, escaping from between drawn curtains, began to appear as she left the rain-obscured park she often cut through. Her pace quickened, her sodden shoes squeaking with every step as the water, already soaked into the soles, squelched between her numb toes. The screeching protest of the rusty gate, marking the end of her journey, berated her for not having managed to treat it yet. It was one of the many small jobs she could do herself, but lately, between her classes and the extra shifts at the care home, free time had become something of a distant memory.

Stifling a yawn, she thrust her trembling hand into the pocket of her saturated jacket, the sodden tissues and receipts within it yet another reminder of a job left undone as she probed for the small key ring. Alex had given her a set of keys to call her own after finding a key chain and earrings that almost matched the tree of life pendant she always wore. The platinum pendant had once belonged to her birth mother and this, along with a small case, had been the sum of her belongings on the fateful day when she had let go of her mother's hand and lost her forever.

She hadn't meant to let go. They had been returning to their seats, but the crowds of people filtering in and out of the train had knocked them apart. She had fought her way through, back towards their seats, but when she arrived her mother was no longer there. The police had searched for her, but as she didn't know her mother's name, or their address, or even their destination, there was little that could be done. No matter how hard they looked, they found no record of Ashley, not even her birth. It had been raining like this on that day. The growling of thunder as it rumbled across the sky always brought these memories back.

Key in hand, she opened the door, pulling the handle towards her slightly as she wiggled the key in the stiff lock. Another job for the list. Inside was no warmer than out, but at least it was dry. Shutting the door, she kicked the bottom panel to force the swollen wood back into place before securing the bolts and shedding her shoes.

A quick glance at her watch revealed it to be a little after midnight. The nursing home often requested her to stay to help the night shift until eleven when any of their regulars called in sick, knowing she needed all the extra hours she could get. Peeling her wet coat from her bare arms, she reminded herself to visit the sick carer. With the most recent outbreak of what the government were calling Pyrexia Blight, or PB for short, many people were becoming sick. But Ashley knew there was more to this disease than the factions admitted. They had to call it something, but she knew its true source and it was unlikely to ever be disclosed, not unless mass panic was the intention. Even she hadn't shared the truth with anyone outside her circle.

Flicking the radiators onto timer, the boiler rattled into life, groaning in protest at being made to work. The sodden clothes clung to her stinging skin as she peeled them off, placing them inside the washing machine before grabbing a towel from the laundry basket to wrap around herself. With a slight sigh, she picked the basket up, propping it on her hip as she navigated the narrow staircase. The protesting of her limbs as she made the climb only served to confirm she was too exhausted to put it away; if it was upstairs, at least it was a little closer.

The warmth from the shower soon turned her pale skin red as it returned heat to her frigid body. Exhausted, she relished in the soft sensation as her pyjamas teased her flesh with their whisper-soft touch. With a dry towel placed across her pillow, she huddled into bed, not even bothering to comb her rust-coloured locks as she surrendered herself to the warmth of the blankets before taking a look at the picture pinned to her wall. A few more weeks and the bicycle would be hers. Granted, it wouldn't be the flashy one she looked upon to remind herself why she was saving her extra pennies, but Ethel Huston—the owner of the second-hand and curio store—had been taking payments on the one now reserved in the back for months.

No sooner had her head touched the pillow when a small vibration at her wrist startled her. Her heavy eyelids raised as her gaze turned to her watch, a smile lifting her tired features as she saw a message from Tess, asking if she was home safe. Sending a quick reply, she looked to the slimline watch again. It was easily the most expensive thing she owned, a gift from the very person who had just checked up on her. With thoughts of her closest friend, her eyes finally succumbed to the tired weight of another full day and she drifted into a restful sleep.

The lunch hall was crowded, as usual. Small tables were shoved aside and pulled together to segregate people into their cliques and clans, while the sounds of rumbustious laughter and the latest gossip and trends mingled with the undertones of study. Ashley had entered through the alcove, spying Tess seated in their regular corner as the heavenly aroma of freshly cooked delights assailed her senses, reminding her it was only a few more days until she could once more stock her cupboards. Living on a shoestring budget was hard, but every saving, no matter how small, brought her closer to the bike. She could live a few more months on dried noodles and canned food, especially if it meant she would find herself with some free time again.

Weaving her way through the mob of lingering students and gathering lunch crowds, she found herself once more savouring the delicious aromas, inhaling deeply as if doing so would sate her burning hunger. With a smile, she dropped into the seat opposite her fair-haired friend with a heavy sigh.

"Late night?" Ashley asked, watching as Tess's perfectly manicured nails glistened as she raised her hand to stifle a yawn, all too aware that her own tiredness was more evident from the dark circles beneath her satin-grey eyes, circles no amount of makeup seemed to hide.

"Someone has to make sure you get home safe." Tess grinned, taking a sip from her hot drink. "How was class?"

"Honestly? If I have to hear *Mister* Baker talk about the clan divides for much longer, I won't need to worry about not sleeping. Seriously, the man could make dragons' rising sound dull. I mean he must have slept through the whole thing." Ashley cleared her throat, adopting the nasal, monotone speech of the only teacher on campus who insisted on being addressed as Mister. "While it is important to consider the effect the clans have on legal jurisdictions we must also keep in mind the emergence and recognition of the preternaturals' called for a new order to be established. One which protected everyone."

"Oh, come on, you do him a discredit, there's no way he sounded *that* interesting." Tess laughed, flicking her silky hair behind her shoulder. Ashley, feeling self-conscious about the pillow-dried, tangled birds-nest she was trying to pass off as a messy bun, adjusted her scrunchy slightly before blowing the loose strands from her eyes.

"Honestly, we grew up listening to this. The clans came about before we were born and the government became nothing more than a collaboration of Elder blood leaders, vampires, shifters, celestials, mages, and whatever. We probably know the ins and outs better than he does. After all, it is all we've known."

"Speaking of our glorious leaders." Tess lowered her voice, her vision scanning the surroundings for eavesdroppers. Surprise lit her features when she saw Jack. Standing, she lifted her arm, beckoning him over. With a quick, awkward wave, which turned into him pushing his hand through his light-brown hair, he made his way towards them, his freckled face breaking into a smile. "Did you hear the latest? Another person's gone missing. There's talk among the lecturers about handing out panic alarms."

"Same as the others?" Jack questioned. Every time anyone seemed to look at their device these days, they were greeted by another image of a grinning face, the happiness of the victim now a distant memory while the abduction notice pleaded for anyone with information to contact the Blue Coats. Often this held a promise of a small reward for any information which helped with their ongoing investigations. Following each new abduction, another message would circulate from Overton Academy containing the territory's guidelines on staying safe.

"Yeah, Papa says their chip was disabled at the point of abduction," she confirmed. Tess's father was ushering the field of technological advancements into a new era, and was often called upon for assistance when things took an unprecedented turn, such as tamper-proof chips suddenly failing. Over the last few decades it became required to be able to identify people, species, and track movements to ensure compliance to the new preternaturals laws. It was as much for protection as it was a deterrent. Normally, when someone went missing they could be located within minutes.

The chips contained all of a person's data, from blood type and inoculations, to location tracking and personal details. They were even used to provide secure access to accounts and emails, ensuring hacking data and identity theft became a thing of the past. There had been much protest at first, but now it had become a natural part of society, especially after being readily embraced by the students and trend setters due to the scan and pay functions reducing the need to carry currency, and the cross-compatibility meaning anything they needed was at their fingertips, as forgotten assignments saved on the home network could be accessed as easily as lecture schedules. All you needed to do was pick up and access any device. Ashley found herself unconsciously rubbing her wrist, where even now the faint scar from the implant she received at the time of adoption was visible.

"How's that even possible? Didn't you say your dad thought they were hack-proof?"

"That's why he's been working late. They are trying to ascertain what it would take for the tracker to be corrupted. That's just between us though, okay?" she whispered, learning in towards them.

"You know it," Ashley and Jack agreed in unison.

"Speaking of secrets," Jack began, his gaze flicking to Ashley, "I hear our territory's PB affliction rate is far below the prediction. Do you really think they don't know what's causing it? I mean, we can't be the only ones who've figured it out, right?" Jack hooked a chair with his foot, pulling it out to join them sitting. "I understand why they can't announce the reasons, it would cause unrest among the population, but I hear it's got pretty bad in other places."

"They might not know," Ashley intervened. "The Atelís don't really cause much harm and, aside from some flu-like symptoms for the first week or so, they go on as normal. It's when they're awakened they'll see a problem, and one thing our chips don't do is update our blood status. They may genuinely believe it's a virus. Besides, it's not like I can just go to someone and say, 'Hey did you know PB is actually caused by the vampires expanding their sleeper ranks?' I have no way of explaining how I know. The factions could be unaware that it is even happening, and there's no way to know if it is a rogue clan or a precision movement."

"But you can see it."

"I still can't explain how, I just..." Ashley shuddered, her gaze panning across the cafeteria until her eyes rested on a blond-haired young man who was casting his lecherous gaze in their direction.

"Want to place a bet?" Ashley asked—loud enough for those around to overhear—while rubbing her arms in an attempt to dispel the goose pimples which had chased across her flesh when her eyes had met with the distant figure's.

"Him?" Jack announced, nodding his head towards the place her eyes strayed to. With an exhausted sigh, she nodded, pushing herself to stand. "I've got a five if you're successful," he offered, producing the note.

With a nod of acceptance, she smartened her appearance and sauntered, as best she could on weary limbs, towards the crowd. She hated this part, but it was necessary. She didn't care what people said about her behind her back. None of them realised what it was like to be her. When she saw the young man again, his gaze followed her every move, his eyes raking her from hips to lips, pausing there as she drew her tongue seductively across them. As their eyes met he stood wordlessly, invading her space. With a glance back towards her friends, she noticed Will had joined them and was watching her intently with a dark expression. Turning her gaze away quickly, she grabbed the man's collar, pulling him down to meet her lips in a sultry kiss that was met by the sound of wolf whistles from his friends. She felt heat ripple from her core, turning the cool metal of her necklace warm, as he became consumed by the kiss. Releasing him, she placed her hand on his chest, easing him away as the all too familiar look of confusion washed over his features. Before a word could be spoken, she had once more vanished into the cafeteria crowd and knew neither he, nor those in proximity to him, would recall what she looked like.

Lowering herself back into her seat, she turned her gaze towards the soft glow of the lighting above, aware that the pale shade would highlight her washed-out pallor even more than it had before, when she had been merely tired. Jack, in a flamboyant gesture designed to attract the attention of those who had just witnessed her act, presented the note. She snatched it from him unceremoniously, tucking it in her pocket, knowing he would get it back later, and the near silence around them returned to normal volume.

"Alright, you win again," he acknowledged. Ashley flashed him a smile before resting her head on her arms as fatigue caught up with her. Jack glanced across towards the figure, no doubt recalling the time when her lips had met his in such a way. For some reason, he was the one person who remembered what she had done. Perhaps it was because they were already friends, but there were times when she believed it may be something more.

"You finished for the day?" Will asked, when she hadn't moved after a few moments.

"No, we've still got Cryptobiology. Then I've a few hours before my next shift."

"When was your last day off?" Will questioned, nudging his plate of chips closer towards her. She felt the unmistakable caress of Tess's touch on her back, and lifted her head, glancing at her watch. With a weary smile, her fingers sneaked out, grabbing one of the hot sticks of temptation from almost beneath her nose.

"My birthday." She flashed a quick smile at Will, helping herself to another chip. "You're late today," she began, only to be cut off by Tess's concern.

"That was eight months ago, you can't keep this up, not with your—"

"Anyway, we should probably head over," Ashley interrupted, before words were spoken that could not be unheard. She loved her friends. She had known Ashley and Jack almost all of her adopted life. At some point during their senior year in high school, Will had inserted himself into their small group, but there were still things about her he did not know. Things the rest of them had sworn never to reveal.

∼

Will watched Ashley stand, his lips lifting as she threw him a wink and pinched another chip from his plate before walking away. He watched the subtle sway of her hips, noticing the way the small heels of her shoes scuffed the floor, suggesting she was more exhausted than she let on. He knew her tells, he had been watching her for years. Watching her whore her affections for lunch money, trade kisses for change. The worst part was that it was her own friends who encouraged it.

When she had vanished from view, he glanced towards the young man she had kissed, recalling how she had parted the crowd to bring that man's lips to her own, and once again he felt the pang of jealousy burning in his stomach. For years, he had tried to get her to notice him, to realise he would always be there when she needed someone. Just once, he wished she would notice him, that her fingers would weave their way through *his* hair as she pulled him close and finally saw all he was, and all he could be for her.

He pushed the plate aside, his appetite ruined. Besides, he'd only bought them because it was the last Wednesday of the month, the one day he could guarantee she had scarcely eaten a morsel.

"Don't mind if I do." Will felt himself flinch as the seat opposite him drew out, scraping the floor in a way that caused him to shudder as Devon turned it. The dark-haired figure of Devon Prescott cast a daunting shadow across the table as he pulled the plate towards him, devouring the remaining chips. "You got my money?" Looking up, his eyes met with the almost black irises of the man before him. His hand extended, his gaze piercing Will as he made the money gesture with his hand.

"Yeah, I got your money," he grumbled, producing a small wad of notes, tossing them on the table.

"Good job," the figure snarled. Standing, Devon snatched the payment, counting the notes before rubbing his hand through Will's tousled hair, much as one would a toddler. Then again, to a vampire, that was possibly how he appeared. He touched the extended device, accepting payment and Will's thumb print beside his own to mark the transaction as complete. "Same time next month." Devon gave something resembling a salute with the money in hand as he walked away, a wicked grin on his lips.

As the tension drained, Will let his head fall against the table. He hated vampires. They thought themselves above everyone else. They had a secret monopoly on the town and no idea what a 'mere mortal' would have to do to come up with the protection money they demanded. He couldn't afford for his gran to lose the store, it was her way of clinging on to the memory of his father. Yet she refused to pay anyone for protection.

When she had taken over the curio business, everything seemed to go wrong at once. Windows were broken, stock would go missing, the furnace broke. The Blue Coats said it showed signs of sabotage, but were never able to uncover the perpetrators. Someone was playing with her, leaning on her grief in order to terrify and exploit her, but she refused to be intimidated. Even now, she believed standing her ground was why the torment stopped. She had no idea that, fearing for her safety, Will had approached Devon, and asked for his clan's protection. It was no secret he made money on campus through less than savoury activities, and he was known to be in the service of Vincent Masters, one of the most influential clan leaders in Overton.

Within a week, Devon reported they had found and dealt with the perpetrator, but part of him wondered if they had been responsible. He could never prove it, but knew that all small business owners paid tribute to one clan or another. The problem was, the payments were high—too high for a student secretly supporting a failing store. Lifting his jacket sleeve, he scratched tentatively around the angry-looking Y-shaped wounds tracking down his arm. Rubbing his fingers together, he felt the warm tingling of his healing energy before he focused it towards the inflamed areas, while glancing around to ensure no one was paying undue attention.

Will's family came from a long line of healers, but when his father didn't possess the gift they assumed the talent had become extinguished. Will had kept it secret when the gift had manifested in himself, covertly charging for small healings to desperate parties. He knew better than to use his own name, especially when his main clients were seeking the removal of tell-tale signs of infidelity. His name and services were passed along through discreet whispers alone.

These services, along with blood-letting at the local Taphouse, were the only way he could afford to pay to ensure his gran's safety, but the payments were becoming draining and, if his luck didn't change, next month he would fall short. His last blood-letting had flagged him as Tapped-out, meaning he would not be allowed to donate any more blood until his count had increased and, as it was the main source of his income, it left him in a dire situation.

He passed a hand through his golden hair, his honey-coloured eyes seeking out someone who would pay for his skills. It was then he spotted her. The young woman wearing the blue scarf. The way her hand kept adjusting it sung of her secret, and if the sheepish look of the young man sitting opposite her was anything to go by, he was the one responsible. She wound her fingers in her boyfriend's hand, shrinking away when he moved in for a kiss. Again adjusting the scarf. He was willing to bet it hid a mark, and their removal was a speciality of his. Logging onto the school profile, he accessed his secondary account, sending her a quick student message about the services he offered. The way she glanced around on reading it suggested her interest and, sure enough, seconds later the arrangements were made and she was excusing herself to go to the bathroom.

Keeping his abilities a secret was difficult, although it was about to become easier. His last client had not been seeking his services, but when he laid eyes upon her battered figure as she nursed a drink in the coffee house, he knew he needed to help her. She wouldn't speak of how she came to be injured, although, with two broken ribs, a fractured wrist, bruising up the length of her forearm, and a black eye, he had drawn his own conclusions.

He had known she wouldn't be able to pay for his services even before he reached out to touch her moth-eaten cardigan. As he stood to leave, sliding over a note with the address of a local coven who would take her in and help her, she grasped his hand, pressing a metal bracelet into it. He had accepted it gratefully, knowing it was likely the only thing of value she had, and to refuse it would be to insult her pride.

He didn't realise the true value of what she had given him. When he placed it on his wrist, its magic snaked through his body, seeking permission to connect with his own energy. Granting it, he found a mental image appearing in his mind, and realised she had given him a glamour charm, an item that allowed someone to change their appearance to whatever degree they desired. This enchantment had but a single memory, so he created his new self with care, relieved to find a way to be more open about his abilities without it being linked back to his family. He had his own future in mind, and reigniting the Huston healers was not on his agenda.

Emily hurried down the deserted road. She was cold, wet, and work had been a nightmare, an endless string of calls and complaints that had only caused the migraine she had been nursing all day to worsen. She hadn't felt quite right since she had visited the Taphouse last night. It had been a dare, a group of young women out for a little adventure and danger, while knowing they were perfectly safe. The fact they had been paid for their donations had been a bonus, as it allowed them to continue their night of drinking away the tension of the day.

She had cried off tonight's birthday party drinkathon. As the newest of the group, she was able to excuse herself with very little objection, especially since the pain in her head had been escalating throughout the day. At one point, the throbbing in her temples had been so bad she had almost requested to go home sick, but doing so would only have increased the burden on her office friends.

All she wanted to do was get home and slip into the bath while her mum cooked her a light snack. Leaning against the wall, she massaged her temples, the deep, resounding beat of her heart almost akin to footsteps. Squeezing her eyes closed, she pinched the bridge of her nose, grateful for the wall's support as her shoulder rested against it. The moment it passed, she would call her mum and see if she could pick her up.

She was so focused on the pain, on remaining upright, she didn't notice the dark figure emerging from the shadows. Turning, determined to press on, she tried to scream as a coarse hand reached out to grab her. The pain behind her eyes exploded as her legs gave beneath her. Before she could even fight, her awareness faded into darkness.

CHAPTER 2

*C*ryptobiology class had a scarce attendance on a Wednesday. Such was often the case, as many of the students optioning this as part of their studies found this was the only class of the day, and often just borrowed the dictations from someone in attendance. Many took this class to fill out a resume aimed towards research and development rather than a medical career.

Everybody knew vampires made the best surgeons, due to their aptitude for the body's systems, being able to anticipate the chance of bleeds and complications, and their speed. It was for this reason the profession was being dominated by them. Whereas shifters and their sensitive noses were able to find trace changes in body chemicals and the scents accompanying ailments, which made them perfect doctors, able to find illnesses in their patients often before symptoms were shown. That's not to say non-preternaturals couldn't make the grade, but the employment records favoured those able to execute their role to perfection, and it was no secret that most preternaturals had an extended life and thus amassed more knowledge and skills during the course of their service. Of course, many who would go on to this profession tended to be privately educated in leading-edge medical academies, meaning most academies, while offering the course, found its students took it out of necessity, since it was offered as an extra-credit course which was favoured alongside the R&D Degree.

After an accident involving some over-enthusiastic chemistry students, the science wing had been closed, and the temporary classroom assignment saw them shifting from the frontward-facing science benches to standard desks. The seats and tables traced the room creating a U-shape, with the digital board on the remaining wall. This was a classroom geared more towards participation than study, but it had been the only one available for their continual use.

Cryptobiology was taught by Adele. This sandy-haired woman was once rumoured to have worked in one of the leading scientific research facilities in all of Mython. Her hair was always tied back in a no-nonsense ponytail, complete with perfect ringlet at its tip, and whilst looking upon her conjured images of a strict school mistress, she was actually a rather soft-spoken, warm-hearted mentor to anyone who had the desire to learn.

Adele currently possessed a distinctive gait due to the recent upgrade of her cybernetic leg. The clipping of her heels was audible down the tile-paved corridor, instilling a ready silence within the class. Cryptobiology was one of the more popular topics for students hoping to be adopted by one of the top research and development companies that could be found on the outskirts of Overton. Since the revelation that preternatural beings existed, the frontier of science had changed, becoming barely recognisable, and everyone wanted to possess the upper edge.

When the first fragile alliances on Mython were being developed, the preternaturals sought to offer an olive branch in the form of new insights into science, medicine, even technology, and whilst a time of fear and panic had threatened to consume the nation, the latest upgraded technology was released and figure-headed by the Elder-bloodlines of the newly formed council, to show what magic and man could accomplish together. The older generation sought shelter, fearing their new position on the food chain, even after the conflicts had calmed and an order—which would grow and adapt to become the measures seen today—emerged. The youth, however, revelled in the inventions brought forth. The latest trends in technology became a buffer to fear as consumerism won over instinct, and from this, order emerged.

A low murmur of approaching conversation could be heard outside, stopping abruptly as it reached the classroom door. Already waiting in silence, all eyes turned to Adele and the young man who had accompanied her. He passed a hand through his ear-length brown hair, his cheeks flushing slightly as he realised he was now the centre of some curious expressions.

"Very well, be seated there. Partner with Tess's group and we can arrange an orientation after. We can discuss the other matters later." Adele gestured towards the empty seat beside Ashley. "Tess, can you give Mr Mendel this term's notes since he will be joining us."

Tess nodded as the young man took his appointed seat and flashed Ashley a guarded smile. His gaze seemed to linger a little too long, causing her face to flush and an unnatural warmth to spread through her core as her vision fixed on his lapis-lazuli-shade eyes. This unnatural heat was a new sensation, clean, not like the cold pressure she felt when she was near an Atelís, or the icy caress of a vampire's gaze. A warm sensation was something new, something she had felt from no one else her path had crossed. For a moment, she found herself drawn into his eyes, noticing the flecks of gold burning like embers amidst the brilliant blue as he looked upon her with something that seemed akin to recognition. A new heat flushed through her as she wondered if their paths had crossed before.

"Conrad," he whispered, nodding his head in introduction as he took his seat, breaking the tether between them.

"Ashley, Tess, Jack," she introduced, as Adele began to load the lesson into the digital screen. "Have you transferred from another session?"

"No, late enrolment. We just moved here last week." She could see him studying her profile in her peripheral vision, but when she looked at him he lowered her head towards his notebook, a slight frown furrowing his brow.

"What do you think of our city so far?" Ashely whispered, her attention split between Conrad and the digital board, where the lecturer had launched into an explanation of cell mutations. There was something about him she couldn't place. Whenever she felt strange feelings around someone, she always tried to discover what was behind them. Something told her being aware of who she was around was the only way to keep herself safe.

"Different to what I'm used to."

"Yeah, it can be a bit much here sometimes. If you've no other lectures, I could give you the tour and transfer class notes. I'm free after this until work," Ashley offered, glancing down at her digital notepad, making sure she had captured all the key points on the diagram.

"Sounds great," he said, but she heard the slight hesitation in his voice.

"Lucky you. I've been pestering for months for some girl time," Tess teased, flashing a smile that showed she knew her friend had sensed something unusual from this stranger.

"You're welcome to come," Conrad said, a little too quickly. "Far be it from me to come between two ladies."

"Pass. I've got engineering mathematics after this. Next time, though." Tess turned her focus back towards the lecturer as Ashley, while making notes, was still trying to formulate an opinion about the newest member of their study team.

Conrad smiled as he watched Ashley close her eyes with delight as the rich flavour of ice-cream teased her tongue. He had insisted, in thanks for her showing him all the best places in Overton's city centre, that she allowed him to treat her at the dessert parlour. His offer seemed to spark a small internal battle within until finally, she nodded her acceptance.

"You weren't kidding, this place is amazing." He broke the silence almost regretfully, seeing how much she was savouring this treat. The way her eyes seemed to sparkle suggested this was something of a rare indulgence for her. If this was all it took to earn a smile so vibrant, he would bring her here every week. Except he couldn't. For his own sake, if not for hers. Even if there was something about this rusty-haired beauty that stirred his other-self, as if that part of him called to her, knew her, he couldn't allow it. He knew better. Besides, she was simply human, and that one fact ensured that no matter how he felt, they could never be more than friends. *Never*, he asserted. His stern thoughts didn't change anything, though. His temperature still rose a fraction whenever their auras crossed, but no matter how desperately he tried, he could scent nothing on her that was causing him to react this way.

He needed to know more, understand the hold she seemed to have on him. It wasn't right, it wasn't fair. He should *not* be feeling this way. From the moment her eyes had met his, and shifted from their beautiful grey to the stormy shade of rain clouds, it was as if a tether between them had been formed. Her gaze was mesmerising, inviting him to reveal his every secret, and having been caught so unaware he had almost complied. His mother had a name for eyes like hers—witch eyes—although he tasted no magic from the air around her.

"So, what brought you this way?" Ashley asked. He found himself smiling at her innocent pleasure as her finger traced around the edge of the ice-cream glass carefully to ensure she removed every trace of caramel.

A shiver passed through him, his gaze imagining her touch upon his flesh for a moment before berating himself silently. What the hell was he doing? He was not one to be infatuated with another, and that's all this was, infatuation towards the first person to show him any kindness after the hell he had suffered for so long. A relationship was the furthest thing from his mind, but she had only smiled at him and he was already in trouble. *No,* he asserted. He wasn't willing to be make himself vulnerable again, to face another rejection, especially not from her. Not from the person whose disarming smile had made him feel as if he had finally come home.

He realised he was staring, and her question had gone unanswered.

"Mum's work," he admitted, tearing his gaze from her to the dessert before him. "She's received a research grant from one of the centres outside Overton. It was too far a commute from our old territory, plus the place they're renting us is amazing. She can work from home most days, it has everything." He cringed, knowing he had overcompensated for the silence with too much information.

"She must be talented to be offered something like that."

"She's renowned in her field." Conrad turned his penetrative gaze towards her again, watching the subtle undertones of her eyes shift as if they mirrored her every thought. "Why don't you ask me what you really want to?" He instantly regretted asking, wondering exactly what he could tell her, why she filled his thoughts with such confusion and contradictions.

"I don't know what you mean." The blush that chased across her cheeks would have put the stars to shame.

"I've seen how you're looking at me, how you're trying to see me." There was no other way to describe it; the intensity with which she beheld him felt as if she was trying to peer into the deepest region of his soul, to see everything he was. Everything he kept hidden. Worse still, that part of him responded to her scrutiny in a way he had never before experienced and he knew if she were to see him so completely, look beyond his defences, she would not like what she found. Maybe that was the answer. Perhaps he should let her; do away with the charade, scare her away. But then, why bother moving here at all? He closed his eyes, envisioning her gentle features twisting into hatred and disgust the way Rei's had. His resolve faltered. Besides, she was only human, they were incompatible. Everything he was feeling now was because she smiled, because he had gone too long without an ounce of kindness from his peers. It would soon pass.

"I look at everyone like this." She shrugged, tracing her finger around the glass once more.

"I noticed. What is it you're looking for?" He inhaled, once more trying to sense any power she exhibited, but the only scent from her was the soft aroma of lavender clothes powder and the delicate fragrance of honey released from her hair as she shook her head softly.

Ashley looked at her watch, her eyes widening. "Gosh, is that the time? I should get going or I'll be late for my shift." Seeming flustered, she gathered her things together, slipping on her jacket. He glanced at the clock behind the counter. Six o'clock. How was it possible for four hours to have passed so quickly?

"Is it okay if we talk tomorrow? I may need some more notes since it seems we're studying along the same lines." There was no hesitation in her answer, and yet he felt as if he had held his breath indefinitely.

"Sure. Tomorrow then." The promise left a brief tingle of electricity hanging in the air between them. He wondered if she felt it, too, or if it was a torture reserved only for him.

Conrad watched as she left, finishing his ice-cream. He had never seen anyone so invested in their surroundings before. It was as if she kept vigil on everyone around her. He was certain even she didn't realise the extent of her observations. As she reached the door, she held it open for a young couple, their eyes briefly meeting in thanks. He felt it again, the change of pressure from within himself as she glanced back and his whole self begged to be revealed, causing a dull ache behind his eyes as he forced it back down, back in its place where it would stay hidden. "What are you doing?" Conrad scolded quietly as he caught himself watching her walk past the window. He shivered, running his hands up his bare arms. He never normally felt the cold, so he wondered why it was that when she left, a chill had raced through him.

Glancing at his watch, he reached for his device, sending a quick message to his mother, confirming his enrolment had gone smoothly. She had been unnecessarily distressed about this move, but the anomalies here warranted further investigation. Not to mention they had been summoned; the pull of the dead had been too much for his family to ignore.

Emily strained against the thick leather cuffs, attempting to shift her body. Tears streaked her face as she fought, causing the single-framed bed beneath her to vibrate and its locked metal wheels to grind against the concrete floor. Her skin felt warm against the metal at her back, as it reflected back what little body heat still remained.

The scratchy sound of a hoarse whisper was all that remained of her desperate screams for help. Every muscle burned under the stress of her constant resistance. It could have been hours or days since she had awoken, time here had no meaning. She scanned the small concrete confines, deliberately trying not to focus upon the thick bindings securing her, yet still seeing the heavy-duty cuffs strapped to the thick belts around her waist and securing her to the bed. They reminded her of how she had seen her aunt restrained after her violent breakdown.

Tears escaped the corner of her eyes, while she forced herself to take in her surroundings, to look for something, anything, that could help her escape. Walls surrounded her and the only light came filtering through the single cage door on the furthest wall, although from what she could see, this room had lights, too. They were just off, creating a dismal image of being forgotten, abandoned, and alone.

Trying to focus on thoughts other than her own helplessness, she wondered if her parents were looking for her, if they had even realised she was missing yet. The thought caused a glimmer of hope to shimmer through the darkness. As soon as her parents realised she hadn't come home, they would contact the Blue Coats, and this nightmare would be over. She needed only to survive until she was found. Help was coming.

A chuckle from the darkness behind her startled her. Its deep, resounding tone echoed through her body, causing the fine hairs on her arms to stand. "I see that glimmer of hope a lot in you wretched creatures," came a gravelly voice from the shadows. Her strangled whimper seemed to please him, his lips turning into a smug smile as he moved from the shadows so she could look upon her captor. "You are falsely contemplating the notion that the Blue Coats will find you. Do you think we would go to such measures as to stage an abduction if we didn't possess a way to deactivate your identity chip?" The words struck her like a physical blow, stealing what little breath remained. "Devon, add this one to our Black Card Menu for now."

Another figure approached, entering the concrete confines through the steel door. Her body grew rigid in response to his eyes meeting hers. For a moment, everything was still, her body ceased its protest. For several long seconds as he walked around her, she felt nothing. Not the sharp pricking of her finger, or the probing of his fingers as he examined the area on her wrist where her chip had once been.

"FB+NM64V." Devon read the figures from the device before discarding the tab he had affixed to it.

"We have had ample interest in the training and acquisition of a Lightning Flash. Let us see what we can do with this one."

"Patch or pipette?"

Emily felt the moment Devon released her from his thrall. Her muscles strained as the resistance in her renewed.

"Patch. Start with micro doses and increase from there. We don't want a repeat of the last Tabu." The one called Devon nodded, casting but a dismissive glance in her direction as she felt the warmth of urine pool beneath her, soaking the off-white gown. "Have one of the underlings get the hose and attend to that first. It won't do to have such odours lingering."

CHAPTER 3

The weeks flew by and, to both his pleasure and distress, Conrad found himself studying alongside Ashley for many of his lectures. Those not with her seemed to, by some fortune, have either Jack or Tess in attendance, and so he had quickly found himself welcomed into their small group. A blessing and a curse. His infatuation had not passed as he hoped. If anything, her grasp on him increased as she became a shadow in his every thought, always present, haunting him.

Seeing Ashley each day was sweet torture. Every time her witch eyes locked on him he lost a little of his resolve to stay hidden. To his frustration, he adored her, everything about her from her messy rusty locks to the way she always found a smile. She worked hard and most days seemed on the verge of being burnt out, and yet she never once complained. She was everything his old friends were not, and part of him wondered if she would be able to accept him as easily as she did everyone else. He banished the thought as soon as it surfaced.

A silky voice beckoned him as he stepped from the faculty lounge, where he had once again refused Adele's suggestion that he should consider changing his discipline. Everyone, in this academy and his last, thought he should follow in his mother's footsteps, but that was not the future he wanted. He knew what he wanted—an image of Ashley surfaced in his mind—"No," he growled almost silently before turning to see who had called him.

"A group of us are getting together at Michaela's house tonight, will you come?" The brunette knew she was attractive; whether it was the nymph in her or just her own confidence, he couldn't tell. But Conrad knew her type. She belonged to the popular cliques, just as he had in his last academy. He had been just like them, confident, outgoing, and always engaged in one activity or another, that was, until Rei had turned everyone against him. What had happened to her hadn't been his fault, he'd had no part in it.

"So are you coming? I can send the invite through the—"

"Can't. Sorry, excuse me." He hurried past, head down. It was not the first invite he'd had to one of the social events; in fact, they seemed to come in an endless stream. No one seemed to realise he preferred his current companions, the genuine kindness. He would not repeat his past mistakes. His old friends had been popular, too, part of the clique everyone craved to be in. Friendship didn't matter there, not really, or his childhood friends would not have turned on him so readily. Something had altered in him the day he saw their once-friendly expressions marred by hatred.

He had always been proud of what he was—proud of their heritage, their calling—but her words had cut deep and were echoed on everyone's lips. He was a monster, an abomination, disgusting, unlovable. He had trusted Rei so completely. Yet she destroyed him and he had never quite found balance since. It was one of the reasons he was finding his growing attraction to Ashley so distressing. She haunted his thoughts, rekindled everything within him he thought he'd lost. He felt whole, complete, at ease whenever she was near and such a pull terrified him. She was human, it could never be, and even if there was a way, he couldn't face such rejection again, not from the person who had possessed his heart with a single glance, from someone who felt like home. To see her look upon him as Rei had, as his friends had, would be his undoing.

In a country where preternaturals were accepted without question, he wondered why what he was earned so much ire amongst his so-called friends. He had sworn never again. Never again would he reveal himself to another, never again would he be judged in this way. He could still see the fear in the eyes of those he had called friends before they turned on him. The popular crowds were fickle. This time, he would make certain he could truly trust the people he chose to associate with and even then, he would never show them his otherself.

He sped into the lecture room, not quite as early as he'd intended. His face brightened as he saw his friends deep in conversation, and the pang of disappointment on discovering Ashley wasn't amongst them was buried before it could be noticed. Even he tried to ignore it. As he pulled his seat around to sit opposite them, his gaze flickered to the corner as his hackles rose and he recognised the heavy aura belonging to the vampires. They were part of the reason his mother had moved here. Not this group per se, but she had uncovered something interesting about this locale. Of all the country, this one territory had the lowest reported numbers of non-consenting preternaturals and PB affliction statistics, with the highest rate of missing persons. His mother was investigating if there was any correlation, while his father, a renowned Blue Coat, looked into the missing persons. The call of the deceased had been loud, impossible to resist. His parents had agreed to share information given that the chances were, with such combined statistics, there was a dark angel at work putting those suffering from unwanted transitions out of their misery. Together, they were certain to find an answer. His parents made a formidable team. His smile faltered as he caught the tail end of Jack's sentence before his words stilled mid-word, as if not wishing to share his conversation. Normally, he would have pleaded ignorance, but the topic intrigued him.

"Counter-vampirism?" he echoed in a whisper. Jack clasped his hand across his mouth, his eyes darting to Tess as if to question how much he could have overheard. "How could you hope to accomplish such a thing?"

"We were speaking hypothetically," Tess interjected, casting a berating look towards her friend. Conrad was part of their group, but there was still a lot about his friends he didn't know.

"Of hypothetically contaminating water?" Conrad pressed.

"If there was a cure, would this not be the best delivery method?" Tess proposed. "It was discussed in Jack's ethics and philosophy class today. You can't think we were serious."

"I suppose, but—" Conrad began, shedding his thin jacket to reveal one of his almost sculpted short-sleeved t-shirts.

"How are you not cold?" Jack questioned, smoothly changing the topic, pulling his own jacket tighter as if to emphasise his point.

"Hot-blooded, I guess." As he answered, a warm sensation enveloped him, its familiarity now more like a soft embrace than the discomfort he had once felt. Raising his vision towards the door he felt the smile illuminating his features as he watched Ashley skilfully balance two trays, while using her elbow to push the door wider. Just as he stood to help, a female student rose, holding the door and earning herself a smile he wished he'd been the recipient of.

As usual, the tray contained a number of hot drinks which she distributed to the small group in attendance. In the few months he had been here, Conrad had quickly realised this was a ritual that not only he looked forward to, even the lecturer enjoyed this regular treat courtesy of their student. Ashley made the best hot chocolate he had tasted, and everyone seemed to agree as they thanked her for their boon.

"Why is it that the school cafeteria allows you to use their supplies?" Conrad questioned, eyeing the metal cups suspiciously. It was a thought that had been playing on his mind, but he had never thought to ask. He placed it to his lips, breathing in its scent before taking his first sip.

"My supplies, their utensils," she corrected, with a playful wave of her finger.

"Have you not noticed? She doesn't leave with the rest of us," Jack commented, as Ashley took her seat beside Tess after depositing the final cup in the place where the lecturer would stand. "She stays behind after hours to help clean in exchange for use of the kitchen."

"You *really* can't be trusted with secrets, can you?" Ashley sighed, turning her reflective eyes towards the ceiling. Conrad had seen first-hand how they altered slightly in shade depending on her mood. The light shade they adopted now suggested she was more amused than annoyed. "Until I can replace my cooker, it's helping me out more than them. Besides, it saves me waiting around for my shift, and everyone is feeling the recent strain of absences." Ashley lifted her cup, not quite managing to disguise her yawn. He felt his lips twitch, thinking the fact she had tried was adorable.

As they settled down to the lecture, Conrad felt his vision being drawn towards the vampires. They were eyeing him with an all-too-familiar contempt; their kind were often wary of his. Then again, this group seemed to show the same kind of animosity towards the few other preternatural beings in attendance. Oddly, he thought, they didn't appear to hold any contempt towards Ashley. They even graced her with a smile as they accepted their drinks. Then again, although part of him wanted to believe she was something more than human, he wasn't sure if she was anything more than enchanting, and their lack of reaction served only to confirm what his senses told him. She was human, normal—*except for those witch eyes,* he added to himself.

"You can tell, can't you?" Ashley whispered, nudging him lightly with her elbow. He hadn't realised he'd been staring. In his last academy he had always had to be alert, especially around preternaturals more prone towards violence. One of the young men blew him a kiss, causing a fit of chuckles from his friends. "How?"

"Maybe the same way you can?" he ventured, quirking an eyebrow in the hope to tease some information from her. He hadn't missed the way her eyes altered when she recognised someone who wasn't human. There was no judgement, no prejudice, just recognition. He wondered how a human could sense something so intricate. Most preternaturals were aware of others, but identifying the species was something few could do, and a trait he was thankful for.

"Hey, Ash," Tess interrupted. "Dad got some comp tickets to the movies, wanna come?"

"That would be amazing." Tapping on her phone, she brought up her shift rota. "How's tomorrow? I have the day off."

"Lies," Jack hissed, comically feigning heart pain.

"You know I never work spring equilux," she said, and there was something in the way her vision shifted to her drink that he couldn't quite place.

"Equilux? I never pegged you as superstitious," Conrad said, glancing at the date on his watch, double-checking it. With so much happening over the last few months, he had missed the approach of the Spring Equinox. It had slipped his mind completely until she reminded him that the time of equal night and day was almost upon them. He glanced at her again. Few humans attached any relevance to the genuine time of equality. Most didn't even realise the equinox was not it.

"Are we going back your place after?" Jack posed. "Sleepover?"

"Of course! Don't we always?" She glanced towards Conrad, as if weighing her thoughts. "You're welcome to join us if you don't mind the couch."

~

Conrad wasn't sure what movie they had just watched. Sitting beside Ashley had been his first mistake. The scent of her hair had tormented him, the sweet honey aroma more appetising than any of the snacks they had purchased. He had never seen her with her hair down or straightened before. The way it cascaded down her back like a waterfall of liquid fire, shimmering in the light of the film, begged him to reach out and touch its silky texture. While her gaze remained transfixed on the screen, her expressions altered with whatever occurred, her emotions on display, unfiltered for all to see.

Occasionally, she would turn towards him, giving him the most brilliant smile, often as his fingers brushed hers within the popcorn bucket he had brought for her. The way she glanced at him made him want to shuffle closer and execute one of those clichéd moves from the old-fashioned films, allowing him to embrace her. He had almost done it, but every time he worked up the courage he reminded himself of his past. If he were to hold her, he knew he would want more, need more. To try to change their friendship would be to risk himself again. The part telling him it was worth the chance just to feel her lips upon his, to explore the ever-present tether, was growing louder, more difficult to ignore. But even with the best intentions, they could never be. His very nature meant they could never be together. His love would consume her.

"So, what is it about the equilux that sees Miss Workaholic take a day off?" Conrad broached, breaking his thoughts away from the torturous adoration as he fell into step beside Tess to filter into the foyer. He turned to Ashley, noticing her steps had frozen as her eyes caught a glimpse of a stranger across the foyer. Something akin to reluctance seemed to flash across her features, gone in the blink of an eye to be replaced by an empty smile, lacking its normal warmth. Conrad studied the figure for a moment. Vampire, his senses warned, typically handsome, with dark curls fell to his shoulders emphasising his jawline. His eyes held something like longing as he looked towards them, towards Ashley, he realised.

"Taking a bet?" Jack interrupted. Ashley glanced around before nodding and disappearing amidst the crowd.

"What? Did I miss something?" Conrad glanced around, his vision panning the surroundings until his sight rested on her warm aura. He froze, his heart lurching as she saw her grasp the back of the vampire's head, pulling him down into a sensual kiss. In that instant, it was as if his world turned to grey. He watched as the figure's arms wrapped around her possessively, his slender fingers threading themselves in her hair in the same way he had longed to. He glanced away, a hand to his chest as he struggled to breathe and kept his vision anywhere but there as the seconds seems to stretch into hours. "Bathroom?" he questioned weakly, as his wandering gaze encountered Tess, earning him a curious look.

"Just over there." She gestured towards an alcove to the left of the stairs that led down from the screens they had just exited.

"Thanks." His legs could barely move him quickly enough through the crowd. The door swung shut with silent swish. Breathlessly, he placed his hands in the sink, breathing deeply before scooping his palms beneath the tap, trying to wash away the disappointment he knew he had no right to feel with the ice-cold water. He had spent so much time with the small group that he had failed to consider Ashley might have a boyfriend. The realisation struck him harder than he had expected. It should have been a relief that she was taken, as now he had another reason to deny what his soul cried for. A reason not to ask if she would consider sharing dessert again one evening, alone—an invitation that had been on the tip of his tongue more times than he could count. It was a blessing she worked so much that the opportunity had never arisen, that she was in another's arms. It would save him the hurt that was sure to follow this detestable infatuation. Yet the pain of seeing her in arms that weren't his felt far worse than any past betrayal.

He thought he had settled for admiring her, for refusing the yearnings and protecting himself, but the image of her kissing that vampire plagued him. Why did his heart and his other-self keep insisting they could make it work despite the fact she was only human? He felt as if he lived in a state of consent contradiction, needing her so desperately he would risk anything, while needing to protect himself from the rejection that was sure to follow. Massaging his chest slightly, he tried to return his breathing to normal. He should be happy, relieved. So why did he feel that the very breath had been stolen from his lungs? He glared at himself in the tarnished mirror, startling as he realised he was not alone.

"You okay?" Jack stood watching him, a look of genuine concern etched deeply into his brow.

"Yeah, just a little light-headed. I think the heat in there got to me." Conrad dipped his hands in the water again, allowing its freshness to wash over him as he attempted to gather himself, guard his treacherous emotions.

"Tell me about it. I know it's still officially winter for a few days yet, but it was like a sauna." Jack fanned himself, blowing out an uncomfortable breath before coming to stand with him beside the sink.

"So, is Ashley's boyfriend coming tonight?" he ventured, using the paper towel to cover the disappointment he knew was visible.

"Sorry?"

"The guy she was with a moment ago."

As a look of realisation crossed Jack's face, Conrad realised, in that moment, that his friend had seen right through him. Perhaps it was the slight tremble in his voice that had given him away, or the telling look he hadn't managed to conceal.

"Oh, you..." He glanced towards the door, as if his vision could penetrate the barrier to focus upon their friend.

"Please don't say anything."

Jack pushed a hand through his hair, flustered, fidgeting slightly as his gaze turned to meet Conrad's directly. "Look, Ashley... well, it's... complicated."

"What about her isn't?" He forced a smile. If there was one word he could have used to sum her up, that would have been it, if only for the reason that she made him feel so confused. She was his complication, one he couldn't seem to work past.

"You're still coming back with us, right?" Jack must have sensed his hesitation, his discomfort.

"I—"

"Please. There's some things she needs to tell you, important things that have no place beyond our circle. Just give her—"

"Jack, Conrad, you guys in there?" Tess's panicked voice echoed alongside the pounding on the door. "Jack, get out here now. Ash collapsed!"

Conrad's heart began to pound. His feet seemed frozen in place but all he wanted to do was to run to her.

"Shit." Jack glanced towards Conrad. "I gotta—" he gestured towards the door. "Damn it," he cursed, dashing from the bathroom. It was a few moments before he could follow, and he froze again as he saw her, his beautiful source of anguish. She sat upon the vibrant carpet, her skin deathly pale, her gaze fixed blankly ahead while Tess fussed around her, stroking her hair, speaking softly while Jack attempted to dispel the crowd.

"It's okay, she's my sister," Jack announced, his arms waving as if to shoo everyone away. "Diabetic. She'll be fine." He tossed his keys to Tess. "Grab the car," he commanded, before moving to sit beside Ashley. He broke off a piece of chocolate from a bar stashed within his coat pocket before placing it in her hands and guiding it towards her lips. "Come on, *sis*," he almost growled as Ashley sat there looking dazed. When she didn't respond, he passed a hand through his light-brown hair quickly, his glare enough to dispel the remaining people who were still lingering, whispering. Red lights illuminated the outside of the cinema and before Conrad had time to register what he was doing Ashley was cradled in his arms.

"I'll carry her to the car," he said, before any objections could be voiced. His stomach churned as she nuzzled her head against his chest. He frowned as Jack held the door. There was a little too much familiarity with her friends' actions to sit well with him, and the story they had just woven was an obvious lie. The question was, why. Why would they leave her in this state when the best place for her would be in hospital, being checked over? People didn't just collapse for no good reason.

He glanced around, questioning why her boyfriend had abandoned her, a protective annoyance creeping over him as he wondered if his sudden disappearance was because he was to blame. He pushed the thought of him away, the image of her locked in his embrace, as her warmth against his chest caused his own temperature to rise, and he heard a whispered warning as clear as if it had been in his ear. '*Mine.*' He paused, hoping the voice had only been within his mind and not escaping his lips.

Jack grabbed the door, ushering them quickly into his car. Conrad glanced behind them, expecting to see her boyfriend make another appearance, but was more than a little relieved when he didn't. Although such a realisation sent him into turmoil. How could someone just slink into the shadows, leaving the person they cared for to fend for themselves? Even if he was a psychic vampire, if he had taken too much—losing himself in the moment as was so easy to do in her presence—it was his responsibility to make sure she was safe. That had to be it, the reason her friends knew what to do, why they seemed so well versed and unfazed. It was far from the first time this had happened. It could even explain his absence. If he were to be caught causing such damage, the P.T.F or Blue Coats would need to step in.

"Ash, you with us?" Tess called back over her shoulder. When she didn't respond, Jack opened the glove compartment of the car, rummaging through before pulling out a small tube.

"Get her to drink this." He tossed it back to Conrad, who pulled at the tab, placing the liquid to her lips. She seemed to suckle instinctively, swallowing the sugary gel.

"What *was* that back there?" Conrad asked, squeezing the remaining fluid into Ashley's mouth before glancing at the label—an isotonic energy gel, a quick way to replenish energy. He was liking this less and less. "I've seen her eat. No way this is diabetes. Is it something to do with that *vampire* back there?" He failed to hide the bite in his voice, but hoped, by proving he already knew what her boyfriend was, it would encourage them to be honest with him.

"Yes. But now's not the time," Tess called back.

"Clearly you're too familiar with this. Don't you see he could be doing lasting damage? Why won't you let someone look at her? Report him? Something?" Suddenly, her constant exhaustion made sense. She wasn't just overworked. Her boyfriend was slowly killing her and for some reason everyone was turning a blind eye.

"Trust me, hospital is the last place she wants to be, especially tonight," Jack added, seeming to angle himself towards Conrad in an attempt to stop his foot pressing on the imaginary brake.

"What's tonight?"

"The worst day ever, twice," Ashley whispered, blinking slowly as her confusion seemed to wane. Conrad wondered what she meant, putting it down to the lingering confusion. "How bad?" she croaked, her hand moving slowly to squeeze Conrad's leg in what he thought was intended as a comforting gesture. "Sorry," she whispered, just loud enough for him to hear.

"Small crowd, no familiar faces."

Ashley nodded, relief seeming to transform her tired face from worry to relaxation. She closed her eyes shuffling slightly to lean her head on Conrad's shoulder.

"I owe you an explanation... but can we leave it for tonight and just watch some movies and order pizza?"

"One condition," Conrad whispered, lifting his arm so she could rest more comfortably. "The takeaway's on me." He looked at his arm cradled around her, wondering why he was doing this to himself... why he was savouring this moment of closeness and the soft fragrance of her hair, while knowing it could never be. He relished the feeling of her warmth against him as her breathing slowed and allowed his own head to fall back to gaze towards the car's roof despairingly. She would be his undoing, of this he was certain.

∼

Refusing movie night had left Will with a hollow pit in his stomach. It had pained him almost as much as discovering Conrad had been invited. He knew it was a difficult night for Ashley, one she hated to spend alone. This one night they always had a sleepover, watched movies, cooked disastrous foods, and ordered takeaway. Anything to ensure the night was a good one. It was a painful anniversary for Ashley for more reasons than one. Not only had it been the day she became an orphan but, by some cruel fate, many years later it was also the night the accident had happened.

Ashley had stepped away from the car only moments before the collision occurred, propelling the vehicle down the small embankment. The driver had sped away, not caring for the devastation he had left in his wake. Will knew she still had nightmares, although not as frequently as before. She had survived only with minor scratches caused by the debris from the initial collision, and despite her phobia of hospitals had stayed by her parents' bedside, but after weeks of false hope, they had both succumbed to their injuries. The doctors had said the burns had been too severe for beings of their nature to survive. The accident had been a tragedy, but, if he were honest with himself, it had also been the excuse he had needed to insert himself into her life. They shared a pain, one of loss.

His level of understanding had been something neither Jack nor Tess could offer, despite their age-old friendship. He knew she still blamed herself, and had suffered with survivor's guilt for years. It was their common ground, the one thing they talked about alone. Their secret. This time every year, she would surround herself with those she loved and, in her own way, both celebrate and mourn the lives of those she had lost. It was a night she never wanted to spend alone, and one he could never imagine not been a part of. There was nothing that could have kept him away, except for this.

Tonight, as much as he wanted to join in, to find joy within her presence, he couldn't. He was in trouble, and the less time he spent in their company at the moment, the better. Slowly, he had been pulling away, watching his friends from afar, knowing the ones he owed money to watched him for signs of any weakness they could exploit.

He had not quite scraped together enough for the payment this month, and now he had to repay them in other ways.

Often vampires were known to bleed someone owing such a small amount. He was short of less than the price of a meal, but because he had been using the Taphouse to supplement the payments, he was, literally, tapped-out, a phrase they assigned to regular donors who couldn't safely give again until their blood count rose. Given his abilities, he replenished quicker than most, but the test still showed he was not suitable. So he had to do something far more excessive. It was his first warning. If he defaulted again, things would only escalate and people he loved could be hurt.

His entire body trembled as he held the coarse metal key in his grasp. It still showed the rough edges from the less than perfect mould it had been cast from. Not for the first time, he was grateful for the glamour charm. If the apparently disabled cameras did detect him sneaking into the faculty head's office, they would find no trace of the person existing before tonight.

The metal rattled from the force of his trembling fingers as he inserted the key into the lock, turning it with more ease than expected. Quietly, he crept to the desk, his heart pounding as he fumbled through the room from memory. The academy was submerged in darkness, only the occasional flicker of torches from the outside patrols breaking the unnerving blanket. He ducked behind the desk, expecting, like happened in so many movies, for a guard to happen past the door, shine the torch within and investigate further. It didn't happen. He connected the small device the vampires had given him to the faculty data storage device. The tiny, blinking, red light was almost undetectable, yet to him it felt like a beacon announcing his presence.

Time seemed to stretch on endlessly and he focused on his surroundings in an attempt to distract himself. The sickly odour of smoothies brought his focus to the small bin that hadn't yet been emptied, another complication he hoped had been taken into account. When the blinking light finally turned green, he snatched the magnetic device away, securing the door behind him, leaving no trace he was ever there. Or at least he hoped this was true.

He sped to the agreed meeting point, shedding his glamour as he pulled off the black sweatshirt. Any who saw his change would have thought it nothing more than a trick of the light; after all, a face and hair colour didn't change when someone pulled a jumper over their head.

The vampires had chosen his regular Taphouse near the cinema for the exchange. He opted to donate here because it was one of the calmer locations he had visited. The interior was maintained to a high standard. Low level lighting, easy on the eyes, flickered almost like candlelight from large chandeliers and mounted sconces. The aroma of delicious, if not slightly undercooked, meats wafted around with the mingling of the patrons. Food was served here from opening until closing, with their more favoured vices available to order. The menu changed daily depending on shipments and who came in to donate. Everything from blood to magical essence could be consumed here, but such treats were handled solely as a dessert.

The night was young, and the Taphouse had only been open for around an hour, meaning the customers were few in number. Everyone knew the interesting desserts never arrived until after ten. His eyes wandered the expensive wooden furniture, padded with luxurious fabrics and cushions. Seeing an open booth far from the regular path of foot traffic, he slid in, placing a card upon the table as he had been instructed. Apparently, this was to ensure his safety until Devon arrived. A human this side of the Taphouse was usually something of a hustler, seeking to peddle their wares without the safety and commission of the Taphouse.

As he sat waiting, he saw a familiar black car pull alongside the cinema's exit. His skin bristled as Conrad emerged, carrying Ashley in his arms. Something was wrong. For the last few years, he knew she had been suffering from dizzy spells and fainting, but never had he seen her unable to walk. The thought of her being so close to Conrad made him seethe. If anyone should be holding her it should be him, not some stranger who followed her around like a lovesick puppy.

Why she never sought help for her condition was beyond him. Perhaps she assumed that whatever it was would cost her her job. For a long time, he had intended to heal her, confess about his gift and lift the curse from her. He had played the scenario over in his mind so many times. It was at this point that she would notice him, look at him the way he'd seen her look at Conrad. He'd been waiting for the right moment, a time when she was in desperate need and he could be her knight, offering her salvation through his touch and earning her affections. He snarled at the thought of her within Conrad's embrace. It should be him there, holding her, comforting her. But since *he* had come to their academy, everything had changed.

Will had been working so hard to get Ashley to see him that it bordered on insulting that she seemed too intent on analysing everyone else to notice him. That would end now. Tonight, he would take her from Conrad's arms and be her saviour. He rose to his feet in determination, but a strong hand seized his shoulder, shoving him down.

"Going somewhere?" the dark voice questioned.

Fumbling for a reason, Will glanced around. "Thought you were a no-show."

"As if. You got it?" Devon asked, a sneer twisting his lips as he ran a hand through his light-brown hair.

"Yes." He revealed the small device in his hand, loading the debt tally on his own device, where Devon pressed his thumb to strike the latest payment as complete.

"Now there's a matter of interest." He could see the vampire's hunger as he slid in beside him. "Don't worry, I know you're tapped-out, but if I let you go without at least a taste, it would reflect badly on our arrangement."

"I thought my job covered it,"

"It did, but our contract says if you default, I must take at least a portion of the outstanding dues in blood. Don't worry, I've no plans to turn you. After all, your blood is too good to pass." Will felt alarm fill him. "Oh yes, I've been here when you were letting, you've a taste of magic in those veins. We don't have many MI letters these days. Worth a lot. I hope you're getting well compensated."

Will heard himself gasp as Devon's tongue extended, the leech-like sucker piercing his flesh as the three jaw plates within closed. It was more shock than pain that caused his reaction, but he could see it had pleased the vampire.

The tongue released him, allowing the blood to flow freely into the awaiting mouth as it nuzzled and suckled at his wrist. There were three kinds of vampires he knew of, Will reminded himself trying to focus on something other than what was happening. There were the ones with fangs, the ones whose tongues pierced the flesh, and psychic vampires, who fed on a person's energy rather than their blood.

Those from the blood-sucking clans released an anaesthetic and sometimes an anticoagulant, too, depending on how long they planned to feed for. It was said the different types evolved in this manner due to environmental differences. He tried to think of their names to keep himself focused as the room began to sway around him. For a moment, his vision fixed upon the grey-coloured text upon the menu, triggering images of Ashley's smoky eyes. Thoughts of her gave him strength to hold on to his consciousness. He imagined her expressive gaze turning towards him as she smiled, welcoming him into her embrace. Just as her image began to fade and a cold darkness took root, he felt the pressure upon his wrist ease. "All settled, until next month. By the way, if you want to skip the middle man, I'll give you a good price to bleed for me. Think it over. You know how to reach me."

As Devon left, Will let his head fall back against the soft, padded seat, all too aware of the danger of being caught on this side of the bar. Blood-letting was very strict in order to protect clients and donors. They were assigned a number which rated their blood attributes in type, properties, and purities. He was MA+MI60, where MI stood for magic innate, meaning his blood had magic in it, and its overall purity was 60%. It was rare to find anyone with a score higher than 60%. Even virgins only pushed the balance up to 70%, although they were said to taste purer than their stats, thus were gifted with a V at the end of their statistic. Then there was his Letting ID for people who favoured a certain person; this was like a brand, used to identify regulars since the properties could change depending on the donor's diet and health.

"You need to leave," whispered a voice. Its soft, honeyed tones were familiar. It took a moment for him to place its owner as Whitney, one of the servers who was assigned to remove the syphons—the leech-like creatures that harvested blood—from their donors and deliver them to the appropriate customer. She slid into the booth beside him, her hand carefully stroking his arm as she looked upon him with concern.

She always seemed to have a radiant smile, no doubt from the many hours she spent practising for the patrons. "Sitting here is an invitation for others. Come on." He felt her arm supporting him as she led him towards the back. His balance faltered, causing him to stumble, almost pulling them both from their feet. "I'll get you something to eat and drink. Devon's bad news, better if you steer clear from personal dealings. He's not one to play by the rules." She sat him in one of the many empty donor booths, fussing around him and repositioning the cushions until he was comfortable.

His eyelids flickered closed for a moment, his heavy limbs unwilling to respond to even the simplest command. He had not heard Whitney leave, so when she shook him gently to place the sweet drink and snacks on the small, swinging side-table, it caused him to startle. The glass cup steamed, its fragrance of honey and chocolate causing a small amount of saliva to pool in his dry mouth. He struggled to straighten himself as she unclipped the table, swivelling it until it rested before him. "You can stay here until you're recovered. You know the drill. Don't disturb the donors. I'll be about, just don't leave until you're ready."

"What do I owe you for this?" he asked, his weary arms extending towards the glass.

"This one's on me, as long as you promise not to make a habit of what you did tonight."

"Deal." She seemed to eye him critically as he agreed to her demands. Obviously seeing that he was earnest, she gave a curt nod before returning to her work.

As promised, she left the door open, and Will allowed himself to sink deeper into the soft cushions, enjoying the way they supported his weight so perfectly. These booths were made for comfort; after all, a donor could be here for hours. The thick glass separating them from each other was a measure to ensure they felt safe, and whilst they were kept separate during donations, they never felt truly alone. Entertainment was provided and was displayed on one of the glass partitions near the door, where the opacity of the glass altered to allow it to become a monitor. A donor could also register for chat and either type or talk to other willing participants. While they were in isolation, they were never alone, and seeing others offered a feeling of security to everyone.

He glanced towards the booth next to him, seeing a young man with several syphons on his arm. Syphons had been specially bred to draw an exact measure of blood from their designated host, and they tasted delicious, much like the sugar shell of a rich, expensive chocolate, and were served on a platter and eaten like candies.

Feeling a little steadier, he slowly rearranged his energy in order to replenish his reserves and stop the fading in and out sensation of his vision. As soon as he was able, he would leave. He knew better than to loiter here longer than necessary. He sighed in frustration, knowing that in his current state, there was no way he would darken Ashley's door, as it would invite too many questions and bring a serious tone to what she needed to be a pleasant evening.

CHAPTER 4

Ashley stifled a yawn as the cool night air greeted her, stinging her damp face. Her eyes were still reddened from the tears she had shed. One of the worst parts of working with the elderly was when they lost someone. For three days she had sat at Ada's bedside as she took one laboured breath after another, until finally tonight, her exhausted body had surrendered to death's embrace and her soul returned home. The doctor had arrived on site twenty minutes ago, and Ashley had clocked out, making her way home.

Over the years, she had grown close to the small number of residents in the nursing home. They were more like her extended family than patients and she loved them all. Losing any of them hurt.

Glancing at her watch, she quickened her pace. While the days had become warmer, the night air still bit, especially on a night like tonight where the stars shone brightly and were rarely masked by the scant skittering of dark, wispy clouds. She was looking forward to her next pay cheque when finally the bike would be hers and the forty minute walk would become a fifteen minute ride.

As she walked, an uneasy feeling crept over her. With a quick glance at her surroundings, she pulled her jacket tighter as her fine hairs rose. Darkness engulfed the path before her, swallowing the pale walkway where the lamppost's mechanics lay in tatters, coiled around their stone plinth like a nest of snakes, hissing and writhing as their once-working gears churned. In the distance, the flickering welcome of the bandstand's solar-powered illumination beckoned, with a promise of light beyond the darkness. Passing each broken lamp, she counted aloud, reminding herself how many remained until the comfort of light would once more embrace her. She tucked her right hand into her pocket, caressing her device, wondering if she should call Tess to keep her company during the walk. A glance at her watch dispelled the notion. Besides, if there was someone lurking, any speaking would only serve to alert them of her whereabouts.

Stopping, she crouched to fasten the lace on one of her black, low-heeled shoes, using the time to steady her breathing, slowing it down into long, controlled breaths while taking the opportunity to better survey her surroundings. Her heart hammered as each rustle set her nerves on edge.

When the light from the bandstand washed over her, her shoulders visibly relaxed as she released a breath. The small, winding passage beyond was bathed in the dappled illumination of the lampposts, their orange glow welcoming to her weary vision.

The sound of gravel crunching beneath her shoes counted the paces as she walked the decorative garden. Even in its pale illumination it was a sight to behold. Flowers that worshipped the sunlight bowed their head in tribute to the night, as the garden's night bloomers revealed their own beauty. Day or night, this was a mesmerising place.

A sudden chill encompassed her. Her instincts told her not to look behind, to keep her head down and continue walking, and she succeeded, her ears straining to hear any other footfalls upon the gravel. She paused again, swearing she heard a sound buried within the noise of her own movement. Instinctively, she glanced over her shoulder and yelped to see a figure barely a breath away from her. Staggering forward, her mouth opened to scream but, before the sound could pierce the air, a calloused hand clasped around her mouth, dragging her back as his other arm snaked around her torso. Sinking her teeth deep into his hand, she pierced his flesh, drawing blood. She prepared to run, but instead of loosening his grip he held her tighter, a low chuckle growling within his throat as he seemed to press his bleeding hand harder into her mouth, causing her to choke and retch as the salty, bitter fluid slid down her throat.

A shrill whistle pieced the air as she kicked out, thrashing backwards and forwards, hoping to connect a blow, hoping to free herself from his crushing grasp. The gravel underfoot slid as she thrust her weight one way and another until a second figure appeared as silently as the first, grasping her. Bucking, she used all her strength, managing to free one of her legs. The sound of tearing fabric echoed almost as loud as her muffled screams, as the attacker at her legs sunk their teeth into her exposed calf with more aggression than was needed. Her flailing momentum tore his exposed teeth through her flesh, splitting her skin like a hot knife through butter.

The warmth of rapidly flowing blood was only felt for a moment before the limb became numb. Sickness rose within her as she heard the hungry slurping sounds of the creature feasting upon her, draining her life one overflowing mouthful at a time. Her head began to swim as a deep, burning sensation from her core began to engulf her. She heard a scream, one she believed to be her own, escaping from the firm, silencing grasp as her vision became overpowered with darkness. As if fearful of this sound, she felt her attackers' grip release. She landed heavily, her forehead striking the stone steps of the bandstand where they had been attempting to drag her. Small fragments of light filtered through the consuming darkness that swam across her vision. Her trembling arm rose to clamp her hand around the enormous slice down her leg. She knew that if she couldn't staunch the bleeding, she would lose consciousness and her chances of being discovered alive would be slim.

Tugging her coat free with her teeth, she attempted to wrap it around her leg, to fashion a tourniquet. But her strength was failing.

She lay back, panting, her mind screaming at her to move, lift her arm and tie the knot, and yet she found she no longer possessed the strength to control her heavy limbs. Her fading attention shifted towards listening for her attackers' return. They had to know she was no longer strong enough to fend them off, and when they realised this, they would no doubt return to finish what they started.

The sound of hurried footsteps upon the gravel turned her mouth dry as her mind swarmed with all the things she had left unsaid, and thoughts of the one kiss she wanted more than anything to have. Conrad's image filled her mind, teasing a weak smile from her lips. As her body began to cool, she imagined herself in the warmth of his embrace, melting into her first real kiss, a kiss with no hidden agenda or any necessity other than answering her own longing.

"Relax," whispered a suggestive voice as the sound of footsteps stilled. She flinched as she felt warm hands upon her exposed flesh. "If I don't help you, you'll bleed out. Rest." His voice echoed around her mind as the darkness claimed her before her vision could clear enough to see his face.

∼

Tess transferred the lesson plan from her home network to her device, ready for tomorrow. It had been a long day. Then again, lately they all had been. Part of her was tempted to drop one of her lectures to give her more time. She had thought she could do it all, attend lectures, refresh basics, plan lessons, teach, and study, but it was becoming more taxing as the year progressed and her class required more of her support.

The creaking leather of her chair protested against the sudden movement after hours of being still as she slumped backward, relishing the relief as its thick padding supported her aching muscles. Casting her eyes to the carefully moderated lighting, a tired smile played on her lips as she thought back to how she and her father had worked on perfecting the exact frequency that was conducive to study, without being so intense it strained the eyes. She felt terrible that she hadn't found the opportunity to tell her friends her news, and it was killing her to keep something so enormous from them. Things had been too busy lately, and every time an opportunity had presented itself, something else had interfered.

"Hey, kiddo." Her father knocked on the door, poking his head through cautiously, ready to duck back at a moment's notice if he had disturbed something important. "Thought you could use a drink." He stepped inside, placing the mug on the side, earning a smile. Although it wasn't the thoughtful gesture and reversal of roles that made her smile, it was the extreme angles in which his hair splayed out. If mad scientists were to elect a visual figurehead, they would use her father's image after a night of work. His black hair showed signs of his frustrated hand passing through it as he tried to solve the next problem. "How are the lectures going? Everything you wanted?"

"It's a little strange being the same age as everyone else," she confessed, taking a sip of the malted drink only for it to stir her hunger, causing a loud rumble in her stomach.

"That's what you get for being a prodigy." He grinned. "On that note, I thought your friends were going to be coming over to celebrate. I know you wanted to wait until you settled in to tell them, but it's been six months."

"I know, Papa. At first, I just wanted to make sure it was what I wanted before saying anything. I mean, their offer came as such a shock—until then, I always thought I'd come and work for you. Besides, Ash has been so busy."

"Surely you know she's drop anything for you? You know she'll be thrilled. It's not every day a student steps straight into the role of lecturer. Surely they must be wondering why you're still at the academy now your studies are concluded?"

"Not really, Papa. I'm still studying, too."

He perched herself on the edge of the desk before leaning forward to kiss her forehead. "Don't overdo it, kiddo. I remember when I used to lecture. It's more time-consuming than you think. Besides, I'm missing my tinkering buddy!"

"Papa," she sighed, a grin spreading across her face, "I think what you mean to say is you're missing not having to do the maths."

"You know me, kiddo. I love the ideas, I love the creation, and I love having you by my side and not just for the calculations, but that brain of yours is something else!"

"How's the prototype coming along?"

"Something's not quite right, it should be better. I'll crack it eventually, maybe quicker if I had my favourite assistant. Anyway, I'm heading to bed. Don't stay up too late."

"Okay, Papa, I'm just about finished up here." He kissed the crown of her head before letting himself out.

Finishing her drink, she stifled a yawn, her attempt to stand morphing into a stretch. A quick glance at her watch caused her to freeze and a sickening warmth spread throughout her as she saw the small red notification dot—that illuminated to signal Ashley had left work—had not yet extinguished. She had been so absorbed in finalising the lesson plans for the remainder of the month, she hadn't noticed its warning.

When she had given Ashley the watch for her birthday, she'd had an ulterior motive. It was true she wanted her friend to have something special, especially since she struggled so hard to ensure her bills were paid, but she also wanted to make sure she was safe. It was no secret how hard she worked. Since Tess's father had been the lead engineer on this latest model, it meant he was able to secure the watches months before their release and just in time for her friend's birthday last May, a full three weeks before their official launch.

What Tess hadn't told her was that she had adjusted its programming slightly, so it paired with her own to notify her when Ashley left work and reached home. She hated that her friend worked so much, but she refused any offers of aid. Tess had even attempted to rent her spare room to help cover the bills, but Ashley was proud, committed to doing everything alone.

Opening her device, she loaded the location data, her stomach contracting as she saw her friend had not moved for the last forty minutes. Drilling into the information, her frozen breathing released as she found Ashley's current heart rate and respiration data. But something was wrong. After a sudden spike in activity, her stats had dropped—in fact, looking at the figures, she wondered if her friend was even conscious. Surely she knew better than to risk collapse when she was alone. Then again, Tess still wasn't certain if Ashley's need to interact with unwilling preternaturals was within her ability to refuse. It had always seemed more like a compulsion than a choice once her eyes had met with a target's, but still, they had devised so many plans to avoid her being alone that Ashley knew she must let either herself or Jack know before approaching anyone.

Tess grabbed her jacket from the coat-stand, slipping it over her pyjamas as she dashed outside. The cool air made her shiver, but her rising panic acted as a buffer, surrounding her in a sickening warmth. Fumbling with the lock to her car, she berated herself for not realising the danger sooner, for not noticing that the small *ping* that signified her friend had reached home had not sounded.

The park was only a few minutes' drive away from where Tess lived, yet everything seemed to be too slow. Abandoning her car at the gate, she grabbed her taser. Its comforting weight in her hand eased her fears as she passed through the wrought iron gate.

Her loose laces struck against the floor as she ran, her heart pounding as she cut every corner possible, feeling the dampness of the grass as it crushed beneath her trainers. When the bandstand came into sight, she found an energy she thought she had already expended, her pace quickening further as her gaze trained upon the figure slumped upon the steps. For a moment, she swore she saw movement, someone slinking away into the shadows as she approached. Grasping her taser more tightly, her hands began to tremble as she glanced around before moving to sit beside her friend.

Even in the pale light, she could see the darkening of Ashley's temple and cheek where an angry bruise was beginning to form.

Placing her hand tentatively on Ashley's arm, she wondered how, exactly, she planned to get both of them out of here. If she waited for the Blue Coats—who patrolled the parks every third hour—they would insist Ashley was checked into hospital, and she knew her friend would rather freeze to death than wake up there. Ashley had always avoided hospitals and it was a resolve that had only strengthened when her parents had both died within the sterile building. Knowing all she did, Tess knew that, no matter how bad things looked, hospital would never be an option. Not given her friend's unique skills. In an environment dominated by preternaturals, the risk of them realising what she could do was too great and would only paint a target on her back.

"Ash, can you hear me?" she asked softly, as she felt her friend stir beneath her touch. As she moved, Tess saw the fabric of her trouser leg part, affording her a glimpse of a large scar she knew her friend had not possessed before this night. Before she could examine it further, Ashley moved again.

"Tess, what...?" While her had eyes fluttered open, Tess could see they weren't really focusing on anything.

"Come on, let's get you up. Patrol must be due soon, let's get you to the car. Do you remember what happened?"

"I collapsed." She raised her hand to her face, feeling the swelling beneath her tentative touch. "Hit my head on the step, I think."

Tess eyed her suspiciously. She could always tell when her friend was lying as her face always betrayed every emotion. Besides, a fall did not tear clothing or create a scar. Thinking better of voicing her observations, she remained silent, focusing instead on helping her friend put one foot before the other.

∼

Ashley's nightgown clung to her burning flesh as she tossed and turned on the leather sofa. Sweat trickled across her exposed skin, spurring into movement by the rapid heaving of her chest with each unsatisfying breath. Her arm peeled from the damp leather to cover her face in an attempt to nurse the throbbing behind her eyes. Along with the night-time fever, waking nightmares had haunted her, delirium in which her attackers returned for her. She retched as she recalled sinking her teeth into one of the attackers. Bile burned her throat as her mouth turned sour at the rekindled memory of his blood sliding down her throat, causing her to heave.

She still couldn't understand why they had fled. But leaving her alive had been a curse in itself. She knew what was coming and it was her own fault. She had bitten him without thinking. When the morning alarm vibrated on her wrist, she groaned, peeling herself from her makeshift bed, half-crawling upstairs to the shower, a feat that had seemed impossible these last few nights, when she had surrendered herself to the sofa.

As the warm water massaged her aching limbs, she turned her leg, blinking back tears as she examined the savage scar and bite mark on the inside of her thigh. Whoever had done this to her had not been gentle, they had torn her flesh, leaving a jagged scar down her leg. Their intention had been to kill, but the blood tag near the place the razor-sharp teeth had pierced her spoke of a different fate now awaiting her. She would not become Atelís; consuming their blood had ensured she'd make a full transition. Tears streaked her cheeks, mingling with the lukewarm water of the shower as it rained down upon her, never quite making her feel cleansed. It would have been better if she had bled out before the blood had fully entered her system. Death would have been better than the fate awaiting her. How she came to survive was still hazy. She was certain they hadn't sealed the wound before fleeing, they had dropped her too abruptly for such consideration.

Placing her head under the stream of water, she washed away her tears. In a single night they had stripped her of everything she was, everything she was destined to do. She only had a few more days left among humanity; a few more days to figure out what needed to be done. She did not want the change being forced upon her. She did not want to walk alongside a clan. Thoughts of ending her life mocked her. It was too late for death now. All such an action would do would be to hasten the curse's activation.

Stepping from the shower, she felt a little better. The sound of her hand wiping the condensation from the mirror threatened to rekindle the persistent headache. Over the last few days, she had discovered the fever and pains were worse at night. As the sun rose and the day began, her discomfort almost faded into the background. Her vision fixed upon the fading bruise across her cheek. The fact it had started to fade slightly only served to reinforce the curse's grasp on her.

"They were careless. If I don't help, you'll bleed out." The unknown voice echoed through her mind, as she stared at herself. A new realisation flooded her mind as the distorted memory of this voice returned. The person who sealed this hadn't been one of those who had attacked her. She felt the questions rising in her again, wondering why her attackers had seemed to vanish into thin air when they clearly had possessed the advantage. She had been at their mercy, but they had dropped her and fled. Perhaps they had been scared of whoever had saved her.

Her eyes still burning from tears, she passed her brush through her wet hair, tying it back before dressing. It was a short day today, something she was thankful for. She had fought her way through lectures this week, fending off exhaustion and fever in silence.

A vibration drew her attention to her watch; it was the care home, once again notifying her not to report for her shift. Accessing her own biometric data, she saw her temperature was still elevated and gave a sigh. Since the attack, she had not been allowed to work. She had agreed to give them access to her health data when she took the job, and anyone thought to be a risk to the vulnerable residents was notified not to report for their duty. Unlike them, she knew what she had was not contagious, although eventually it would be the end of her.

Hastily dressing, she made herself presentable. Checking her funds, she sighed, weighing the choice between putting a request on

Companionate—and paying to have another student nearby collect her on their way to the academy—or stopping by the pharmacy and using the money to buy some pain relief for her throbbing head. Settling on the medicine, she pulled her hiking boots into place, her muscles aching, unsoothed by the fire which chased through her body. After grabbing the drawstring bag filled with her special supplies, she began the journey knowing this would be the last time she could use her talents to save others who were in the very situation she found herself in. She would have to make this one count. The phial within her bag contained the last of her saliva from before the incident, so she would see that as many people as possible received her boon today. Especially since it had no effect on her.

∽

Time for Emily moved in a blur. Her heart was finally starting to calm, the panicked gasps now only short, sharp bursts. Never had she been so terrified in her life. She had prayed the things swarming before her vision weren't real and, now that a calmer reality began to return, she knew it was just as horrific as the hallucination caused by the Lightning Flash she was being administered.

Over the last few weeks, they had began treating the pressure sores on her head, shoulders, buttocks and heels. She thought they would have hurt, but her body felt numb almost all the time now. The numbness was preferable to the cold torrents of water when they hosed her down. The discovery of her wounds had led to her being laid face down. No longer being able to see her body made her question if its existence—if the memories of walking and running—had been nothing more than the dream of an imprisoned mind. While they were treating the pressure sore at the back of her head, she remembered sobbing as their hands came away with clumps of her hair attached as her once beautiful locks began to fall out.

She was almost grateful when the master came to hack it off. His hand had caressed her shaved scalp, the first touch she had experienced since her outburst. She had sworn not to disappoint him again, but she knew she had to earn his favour. To accept the punishment as he cast violent and terrifying images upon her. She wouldn't disappoint him again. She could barely remember when last he allowed her dreams and visions to be those of euphoria and beauty, but she would earn his favour, recapture the lost sensations.

Hearing the approach of footsteps, she braced herself for what would follow. After each punishment had ended she was hosed her down, washing away the amassing bodily fluids. Her breath froze as the bed tilted vertically and the icy torrent battered her, chilling her to the bone, causing her racking cough to echo around the small confines.

The bed swivelled again, the rough texture of a towel causing her to flinch. It had been a long time since anyone had dried her. There was a moment of relief as her arms were worked free from the bindings and her sodden gown was cut from her. The almost unbearable roughness of the towel caused her to flinch, yet she felt herself leaning into the contact, grateful for it regardless of the pain. Fresh dressings were placed upon her wounds, binding the raw and festering blisters torn into her flesh from her struggles.

"There now, isn't that better? You see what happens when you're a good girl?" Her master stroked her cheek and someone continued to dry her and he smiled as she pressed her face into his hand, seeking his affection. "I think you've learnt your lesson, haven't you?" For a moment Emily wasn't sure what lesson he was referring to, then she recalled the last time they tried to change her clothes, her shameful behaviour as she clawed and fought. She nodded frantically, praying he would forgive her indiscretion. "Very good. Then I see no reason why your next dreams can't be filled of wonder. But do not cross me again, or you will find yourself forever trapped in the realm of nightmares and horrors."

Wincing as the cuffs were re-secured, she nodded her head, her voice too raw from the terrors of her last trips to even attempt an answer. "Good girl." Disappointment masked her gaunt features as he left her alone again, her heart fluttering as she heard him speak in a world that seemed to exist beyond her own. "Devon, this Lightning Flash has learnt her lesson, see she is appropriately rewarded."

"Yes, sire, anything else?"

"Begin the pneumonia treatment. We will require her to be in better form. I think this Tabu will fetch a good price on the auctions. If she shows herself subservient, we could even consider removing the restraints and begin a more salubrious regime."

"Do you think she's ready to be moved out of here?"

"It has been a month since her last indiscretion and she is aware of what will occur should she disappoint me again."

CHAPTER 5

*A*shley gave a weary a smile as she offered one of the drinks from the tray to a young lady who caught her eye. With a promise to return the cup to the cafeteria, the stranger moved on, unaware of the second chance she had just been given. The scent of the hot chocolate upon the trays almost overpowered the acrid chemicals wafting from the chemistry labs she passed on her way to Cryptobiology.

Weaving her way carefully through the crowded corridor, she cringed as her uncoordinated steps caused small measures of the drinks to pool upon the polished trays. Blowing a strand of hair from her eyes, she slipped through the open door before it had a chance to close, depositing the trays at the front of the room, knowing everyone would help themselves. She was too tired to make the rounds.

"Oooh, biscuits!" Jack grinned, grabbing one from the tray before joining her. "What's the occasion?"

"Sugar." Ashley smiled. She hadn't missed the lingering glances being cast her way by Tess and Jack. The way their brows crinkled in silent conversation confirmed she still looked as exhausted as she felt. Jack sat staring at her, the cookie motionless between his teeth as he paused in mid-bite, a faraway expression drifting across his eyes. "Jack, you okay? Jack?"

"What? Oh, sorry," he mumbled, pulling the intact cookie from his lips. "I just had the weirdest daydream, sealed tombs and gasoline. I'd ask what you put in them but I don't think anything is that strong." He gestured to the cookie, taking a bite before shuddering.

"You hadn't even bitten it." Tess briefly turned her gaze towards the ceiling, shaking her head in amusement, causing the two perfectly curled locks left loose from her impressive up-do to swing.

"Exactly," he muttered around the mouthful of cookie. "Nana said I'm descended from psychics, maybe it's a secret power," he jested, pulling out his sketchpad and digital notebook.

"Okay, oh oracle, who's going to come through the door next?" Tess teased.

Jack closed his eyes. "The devil!" He waved his hands, reminiscent of the flamboyant gestures of the carnival fortune tellers, yet there was something serious about his expression as he turned to the door, waiting expectantly, his hands autonomously sketching.

"A handsome devil maybe," Tess teased lightly, nudging Ashley as Conrad entered.

The comment chased fire into her cheeks she couldn't hide, almost making her wish she hadn't confided her interest to her best friend. Not that she hadn't realised for herself. Tess said she had never seen two people so obviously compatible trying so hard to keep their relationship platonic. Her words had made her realise that was exactly what she had been doing, that she didn't want to miss out on something that could be extraordinary. She was determined to wait for him to realise what she had, that there was a pull between them that was impossible to ignore. She had waited too long. Her fantasies of what could be no longer mattered.

He circled behind them, tracing his hand across her back lightly, the gesture barely kindling a smile as she silently mourned what could never be. She attempted to hide the bitter regret that looking upon him caused. She had recently committed herself to telling him everything, and now there was no point, no reason to see if their kiss would ignite the fires promised by her dreams. His touch caused heat to rise as if her body welcomed him, and more than anything she wanted to have one kiss, one *real* kiss that was her own choice, and it needed to be with him, the only person who had stirred such thoughts and longings. But that couldn't happen now. It was better she simply disappeared silently rather than creating further complications that would only make her decision more difficult.

"Are you staying behind again tonight?" he questioned, drawing his chair opposite, as had become his habit. She could see the concern in his eyes and was more than a little relieved that Tess had shown her how to cover her bruise. It was one less thing to explain.

"No, I've got an early shift at the home," she lied. She had already decided not to cause her friends any more worry than was needed. Tomorrow, she planned to speak to Tess about visiting her brother. That way, when she didn't return they would just assume she had chosen to stay closer to him. She had no intention of living as a vampire, so her only option was entombment followed swiftly by a fiery death. She already had the details planned, and her friends would be none-the-wiser. She glanced at Jack, his words about sealed tombs and gasoline weighing on her mind. There was no way he could know.

"I have to stay late tonight, but you're welcome to borrow my bike. You have to be careful. My dad was saying another person went missing yesterday. You should try to avoid walking alone, especially since the number of Atelís is on the rise across the country." The three friends exchanged a quick glance, not unnoticed by him. "Don't tell me you were buying into the PB malarkey?"

"Not at all, but we didn't think anyone else had realised its cause," Jack interjected, before anyone could stop him.

"They tried to pass it off as PB in my last academy, too. I don't see why anyone would fall for it. I mean, you just have to look at the tongues." He licked his out as if in demonstration. Without pause for thought, the three of them mirrored his gesture. Ashley saw his face pale and drew her tongue in quickly, her eyes growing wide as they locked fearfully with his. She felt heat chase through her as his eyes smouldered with anger.

"You okay, Ash?" Tess questioned, seeing the sudden change in her friend's demeanour. Flustered, Ashley moved quickly, cramming her belongings into her bag, her elbow colliding with her drink, sending its contents spilling across the tabletop. Jack produced a bundle of tissues from his pocket, frantically mopping up the expanding mess.

"I just need, I... erm... excuse me, I'm not feeling so good," Ashley whispered, snatching up her bag as she rushed from the class.

～

As Jack mopped up the spilt drink, Conrad grabbed his things, hurrying after Ashley. He questioned how he could have failed to notice. All things preternatural had a scent or a pressure about them which made them easy for him to identify, but he had sensed no change in her, none at all. It hadn't taken long for him to realise Ashley only ever wore make-up to the academy when she was exhausted. It was her way of hiding some of the more obvious signs of her fatigue. This week, she had worn it every day, but that had not been all he noticed. She had been quieter than normal, withdrawn, and now he knew why.

He could hear her footsteps in the stairwell and quickened his pace. Reaching the landing between floors, he grasped her wrist, invoking a startled yelp as she turned to face him. There was a fear in her eyes that had no place there. She flinched from his touch, but not before his skin was enveloped with the familiar heat that came from contact, and with it came the realisation that something was *very* wrong.

Having moved back and forth in his mind about what he should do about his growing feelings towards her, he had decided it was safer to keep her at a distance, but that didn't prevent his body from betraying him. His hand would reach out, tucking away a stray strand of her hair, stroking her arm, squeezing her hand, or brushing her fingers with his as she lifted a drink from his grasp at lunch. Any excuse to touch her and his body would betray his wishes and exploit it. His mind raced back to every time he had laid his hand upon her for the last few days, and with a sudden chill he realised all contact had been absent of the warmth associated with touching her, and it was only now he realised why. He hadn't actually been touching her. Sure, it had felt like his hand had rested upon hers, that his fingers traced across her back, but the pressure was from her aura not her skin, as if it were shielding her.

His heart sank as he saw the tears streaking her face and the unmistakable hint of a bruise once concealed beneath the layer of running make-up. He placed his fingers to her face, tilting her chin to bring her gaze to his. He was trying not to display the anger burning in his core; it had no place here, she had no cause to see it.

"You're..." She nodded, there was no reason to voice what they both already knew. "How?"

"I was attacked," she whispered. Without a thought, Conrad felt himself take her within his arms, holding her close. She rested her head upon his chest, her voice never rising above a whisper. "I don't think they knew what I'd been doing. It was just random." She choked out a strangled laugh. "I always thought someone would realise and deal with me, but I... I never thought I'd be like this because I was in the wrong place at the wrong time."

Conrad eased her back, his hands on her shoulder so he could study her face as a flicker of understanding passed through his eyes. He couldn't believe what he was hearing. His beautiful witch really did possess some magic beyond the spell she had over him.

"You're the reason the PB figures are low, why this territory has fewer unwanted transitions. How? I mean..." He breathed in her scent again, tasting the air around her and still finding nothing. Ashley crossed an arm across herself protectively, her gaze not lifting from the floor as they resumed walking.

"I found out in high school. Me, Tess and Jack have always been close. One day, there was this air about him, sullied, wrong. He'd been jumped a few days before and they took more than his money, they made him Atelís. I don't know why but something told me I should kiss him. A day later, his fever broke and he was back to himself, with no trace of the change. Even the bite tag had been removed. The funny thing is, no one ever remembers it was me who kissed them, except Jack. After that, the three of us decided to use what I could do to help as many people as possible."

"That's your bet," he whispered in understanding, feeling more relief than he knew was appropriate. "You use it as a precursor, a dare in case you have to explain yourself." She nodded, confirming his suspicions. "But"—he circled her, studying her throat, collar bone, wrists, all the normal places a tag would appear, but her skin was perfect, unblemished—"I don't see a bite." He studied her shoulders, once more noticing how she recoiled against his touch.

"It's not there," she whispered, and he saw her eyelids droop towards the floor, the tears threatening to spill from her heavy eyelashes, and he understood.

"Come home with me, now," he commanded, growling as he grasped her hand and led the way, leaving no room for argument, no chance for her to object, and to his relief she simply followed. He didn't trust himself to say any more. His temperature was rising, his blood boiling as his other-self demanded justice, vengeance, and blood. He would hunt down anyone who had laid a hand on her and deliver them personally to hell.

∼

Conrad had thought many times about bringing Ashley to his home to meet his parents, but never in any of his imaginary scenarios had it been for this reason. His parents didn't harbour the same caution about what they were as he did, and he knew under normal circumstances he couldn't have risked bringing her here, not before telling her the truth of his origins. But none of that mattered now.

He had spoken to them about Ashley covertly, probing to discover if there was any way a human and one of their kind could become anything more than friends. He had seen the pain in his mother's eyes as she broke the news to him. In all their history, never had one of their kind been able to partner safely with a human, or many of the preternatural species. His love would destroy her. It ran too hot, too deep for something so frail to survive. They had told him, for both their sakes, that he should turn his focus to creatures of a sturdier composition.

Ashley had hopped on the back of his bike without reservation, sliding the spare helmet on and pressing herself against him in such a way that, had this been any other day, any other situation, he would have taken the long road home just to spend a few more moments so close to her. He imagined his presence offering her strength and warmth, reassurance that whoever wronged her would be destroyed, and purged from existence. As if sensing these powerful feelings of protection, she seemed to relax, leaning closer, holding him tighter, and all too soon the mechanical clanking of the gate's gears were opening.

The home they lived in was amazing. Even now, he loved the remote isolation he felt from the large walls barricading their own little corner of the world from trespassers. The grounds were maintained by a gardener, who kept the main paths and gardens pristine and manicured, while the raw force of nature could be witnessed in every direction beyond their home.

The farmhouse mansion had come complete with wraparound porches and swinging seat to the rear. The two forward-facing gable windows were eye-catching features, rarely visible in the houses he had seen around the city. It offered a unique flair to the property, and the large windows allowed ample light to stream inside. He thrust his key into the lock, surprised to find his mother in the hallway, papers in hand.

"I didn't expect you home until—" His mother's face instantly morphed from concern into a welcoming smile. "Forgive me, where are my manners? I am Selene, Conrad's mother."

"This is Ashley, I've spoken to you about her." He hoped she would get the hint and keep at least part of their life private. "She needs your help."

"Of course, come in, come in. What can I do for you?"

Once the door was closed, he saw Ashley hanging back awkwardly. His hand slid into hers as if it were the most natural thing in the world, and he led her inside. Unsure exactly what to say, where to start, Conrad launched straight into an explanation.

"Mum, you know how you came here to study the statistical phenomenon relating to PB and unwanted transitions?"

"Well yes, dear, that and—"

"She's the reason—or was, before she was attacked." His nostrils flared as he tried to suppress his rage, drawing comfort from the pressure of her hand within his. "Ashley"—he turned to look at her, meeting her eyes as he spoke—"please, you can trust us. We would *never* let anyone uncover what we know. Let my mother examine you, she's a specialist in preternatural genealogy and has experience in... you know, trauma." He watched his mother's eyes mist as she understood what he was saying.

"Your father's working from home today, too. Conrad, go help him in the kitchen, tell him to set some extra places." Her gaze dropped briefly to his hand that was still intertwined with Ashley's. It was then he noticed he'd stepped before her, shielding her from the discomfort he felt radiating from her. "Go on." She waved him away as she placed her hand gently on the small of Ashley's back, encouraging her towards the door leading downstairs into her work space.

Conrad stood behind the door, his forehead resting against the wood separating them as he imagined her tearful eyes. Whoever had forced her to shed those tears would pay for each and every one in blood and pain. He froze, his hand raised to knock as another thought assailed him. He had seen the tears streaking her cheeks; why hadn't he thought to mention it? When someone became an Atelís, they lost the ability to cry. It was one of the first symptoms, not as recognisable as the altering shape of the tongue, but a symptom nonetheless.

Lowering his arm, he turned. His mother would have noticed. With an enraged growl, he stalked away, feeling the fury building within him. His kind were known for their righteous rage, the need to bring justice. He tried to focus his gaze upon the kitchen, to channel his attention elsewhere, but it was hopeless. The pressure building within him was unbearable, like no other need he had felt before. Pulling a stool from beneath the central island, he focused on his breathing, aware of the sheer heat being forced from his body. His gaze burned into the polished black granite counters, focusing on the smallest fleck. Breathe in, breathe out, an exercise he repeated for several minutes. When he felt more in control, he lifted his gaze to the outer parts of the enormous kitchen, where his father stood watching him, a look of concern deepening the wrinkles on his brow.

"What's happened? You smell wronged." He could tell from the way his father assessed him with a look of concern in his hazel eyes, that he had not yet managed the level of control he needed.

"I've brought a friend home," he muttered.

"Am I laying an extra place?"

Conrad nodded, watching as his father swept the dark brown hair from his eyes with the back of his wrist, clearly fighting back further questions. He wasn't sure what his father had seen, but it was unlike him to be so quiet.

"I didn't realise who she was quickly enough. She's been bitten." He saw his father stiffen, and whilst his revelation had not been the sum of his emotions, he hoped it would be enough justification for his father to explain his current temperament.

"And who is she?"

"The cure, the reason PB and unwanted transitions are so low."

His father placed the chopping knife down with a care that spoke volumes about the control he was mastering. As a Blue Coat, Conrad knew his father would have a barrage of questions, but clearly he had read his son well enough to know now was not the time.

"The cure's a person?"

"It was, until she was attacked," he growled.

"Grab a knife, help me cut up some more fillets." His father gestured towards the magnetic knife block on the wall. Grasping a handle Conrad saw his knuckles whiten and made a deliberate effort to slacken his grip, but he knew his father would have seen. He saw everything. "Get cutting. Let's get you looking a little less 'hell hath no fury like an if'—"

"Do *not* mention what we are!" He slammed the knife into the wooden chopping board, splintering the wood.

"I don't know why you're so ashamed. We're something incredible, pulled into existence by Solomon himself. Do you know how many other races can claim to be birthed by escaping from the sorcerer's cauldron? Our history is fascinating. Our very existence on this plane is noble. We hunt down murderers, answer the cries for vengeance from the deceased. How can you find shame in that?"

"I didn't use to. But you didn't see... you weren't there. Never again. We will not speak of it in her presence. I care for her, and even if we can never be together, I can't face her rejection."

∼

Selene listened intently as the young girl before her bared her heart, speaking in depth about things she had held so close for so long. She looked so pale against the redwood table. While her room was part laboratory, that section was sealed off by a wall-to-ceiling sliding partition, which allowed her to have this half of the basement room as more of a work space. Along with the table, where they currently sat, were several book cases containing rare and valuable research and data, along with a few of her own favourite books. Lined with carpet tiles, she liked to think the room had a homey feel, less sterile than had she not opted to divide the rooms. Ashley spoke to her not only of the attack, but of the gift she had awakened just before the age of fourteen. Hearing her talk was fascinating. Ashley was the very thing she had been searching for all these years, and now she had been stripped of her gift.

Selene wrapped an arm around her as she sniffled, speaking of all the things she had intended to do; how she would travel, finding a way to liberate those who had been claimed against their will. There were two things which were curious. The first was that her performing a single reversal of transition could place her on the border of unconsciousness. Someone who was intended to have this gift should have the facility to utilise it without such an extreme detriment. The second was the tears she shed. Ashley had said her saliva had lost its ability to cure, otherwise the tag would have faded, which meant there was no way to explain her tears.

"And they just fled without reason?" Selene continued asking her questions, committing every detail to memory. She watched intently as another tear fought its way through Ashley's damp eyelashes. With a quick movement, she caught it in a small tube, earning a curious look. "You're something special. Neither vampires nor Atelís can cry like this, partly because they develop a nictitating membrane from the moment of infection. It's something you lack." She answered the unasked question, studying her eyes again. "May I take some blood?" She pulled the metal trolley that had been near one of the bookcases closer, waiting for Ashley to nod before retrieving her supplies from the small drawers within. "Any family history of illness or preternatural bloodlines?"

"No. Well, I mean I don't know. I was adopted." Ashley played with the small tree of life pendant nervously, bringing it to Selene's attention.

"May I take a look?" The moment she lifted the pendant, the cool metal grew warm within her grasp as she sent a small amount of energy to probe it. Turning it towards the light, she saw a multitude of hidden etchings. She had not seen symbols of their like for a very long time. Any other being would overlook them, thinking the soft alterations were merely imperfections of the metal, but she could see the truth, the hidden disc within the pendant. Since their creation, her kind had been attuned to recognise the many works and seals of Solomon. Closing her eyes, she visualised the disc, gasping as the seals and binding works shone through. It was enchanted in levels, intended to increase in strength every seven years. That the person before her had unlocked any abilities at all was inexplicable.

"Do you wear it all the time?"

Ashley nodded as Selene released the pendant. She rubbed her thumb and fingers together, dispelling the intense heat that would have been agonising for any other being. "I think part of you knows this already, but you should never remove it, not unless your life is in jeopardy."

"Why?"

"Let me run my tests first, then I will answer your questions to the best of my ability. Now, with your consent, after we've eaten I'm going to give you an injection. It'll make you feel dreadful for a few days, but it's for your own safety."

"Will it suppress the cravings? I don't want to be one of them. I won't!"

"I'm not sure that's your biggest concern at the moment. As I said, we'll talk later when I know more. We have a guest room and I would feel better if you stayed for the night. I do have a few more questions about the night you were attacked. Did you know any of the people who attacked you? Did they feel in any way familiar?"

"No. I didn't get a good look at them, though. You don't think they'll come back, do you?" Hearing the fear in Ashley's voice, Selene reached forward, grasping her hand briefly and giving it a reassuring squeeze.

"I won't lie. If my suspicions are correct, you're in more danger than you could imagine, especially if whoever bit you that night knows where to find you." Selene flicked the test tubes containing the samples, her gaze fixated on the ruby fluid. Now it was away from Ashley, she could feel the power calling to her even from within the small, stoppered phials. She had a feeling she knew exactly what this girl was, and whoever had placed that necklace around her neck had saved her from a horrific life. But before she spoke with her about what the blood showed, she had to be certain. She had to run the tests.

"That's all for now. This'll take a while, so why don't you join Conrad. If you want to freshen up first, there's a bathroom just off the hall." Ashley nodded in response, whispering a quiet thank-you before leaving.

Selene turned her attention back towards the blood samples, a weighted expression lining her brow. She could not even consider keeping a record of what she was about to do. If this girl's blood fell into anyone's hands, her life would be over before it had begun.

Opening one of the small metal cabinets lining the far wall, she removed a tiny transmitter before plugging it in. When all the lights were aglow, she logged into her network, selecting her own personal decoy data mode.

One of the more convenient aspects of her role was the leeway she was given. Many of her groundbreaking discoveries had emerged from hypothetical work achieved by tricking the computers into believing something existed in order to see how things would react and interact. When first she had attempted this on a live system, she had created a building-wide panic resulting in a twelve-hour lockdown. Since then, she had been given a privacy tool, and a data mode which allowed her to utilise all the system's functions, while not broadcasting or storing the data unless instructed to do so.

The second benefit was, of course, this impressive laboratory, which had its own manner of preternatural-repelling Faraday cage specifically engineered to prevent detection and infiltration by magical forces. Anything that happened within here didn't exist as far as anyone outside the room was concerned, which was just as well, given what she was holding.

CHAPTER 6

Ashley stared at herself in the mirror. It had seemed like a good idea to wash her face, hoping to remove the tell-tale signs of her tears. The problem was, not only had it failed to soothe the redness of her puffy eyes, but now that she had washed away the make-up, the harsh tone of the purple bruise seemed to stand in stark, eye-drawing contrast against her pale skin.

Her stomach churned and she wished she could hide herself away in the bathroom until she could leave. Gritting her teeth, she forced her shoulders back and emerged from the safety of the locked room. This family now knew more about her than any of her closest friends. She had felt compelled to tell them the truth, to share her burdens. More than that, she had felt safe. She liked to think of herself as strong and independent, but the truth was, since the attack she had felt anything but. Steeling herself, she walked slowly through the entrance hall, hoping the hair falling across her face would hide the mark.

Following the sound of a hushed conversation, Ashley made her way towards a large room. It was a kitchen any chef would dream of.

Black granite work surfaces encompassed the room corner to corner, sitting atop of the ebony cupboards with their contrasting white outlines. In the centre of the grand room was an island, with a number of high stools surrounding it and a vase of brightly coloured flowers. The sizzling from the brushed steel hobs drew her curiosity as the fragrant aromas assailed her senses.

"Please tell me you were serious when you said I could stay for food." She tucked her hair behind her ear coyly. "It smells heavenly."

It had only taken Conrad turning to look at her, for her to regain her internal balance, to feel at ease. It was strange the effect he had upon her; one look from him seemed to set her world to rights. But his smile faltered as his eyes were drawn to the bruise. Before she could rearrange her hair, he closed the distance between them, his eyes smouldering with anger as he raised his hand, gently cupping her face. The touch sent small jolts of energy chasing through her and she felt herself leaning softly into the touch her, own hand finding its way on top of his, almost as if to hold him in place as their eyes met. She found herself frozen, losing herself in the powerful emotions in his gaze. The golden flecks seemed to intensify, growing brighter until gazing within his eyes was akin to staring at the golden hues of sunlight upon a turbulent ocean's surface. Dazzling. She felt herself being drawn closer, the heat from his body enveloping her in a strong aura of protection. Biting her bottom lip, she committed herself to this one final pleasure, bringing her lips closer to his. His warm breath upon her flesh caused her heart to quicken as she moved to close the remaining distance.

"Welcome, pull up a stool."

Ashley startled on hearing another voice in an existence that, for a moment, had only been herself and Conrad. She hadn't even noticed the other figure standing there. Heat flushed through her, her cheeks burning in embarrassment as she turned away, removing his hand from her cheek as she turned her back to Conrad and the other figure.

"I'll get you a drink," the older man said. She could hear the amusement in his tone, and dared a glance towards him, relieved to see his easy smile. With a nudge, he handed the spatula to Conrad, urging him towards the cooking food. "What's your poison?" She must have paled because he stammered over his next words. "W- what I mean is, we've a well stocked fridge. Orange juice, apple, lemonade, something stronger maybe?"

"Orange will be fine, thank you, Mr Mendel." She smiled.

"Reuben," he corrected, opening one of the cabinets to reveal an integrated fridge.

"You doing okay?" Conrad asked over his shoulder as he attended to the skillet.

"I'm sorry about earlier. That wasn't how I wanted to tell you." Ashley grasped the glass, turning her focus to the orange segments floating on the surface of the juice. She took a sip, seeing a flash of annoyance cross Conrad's features. It wasn't until he spoke again that she realised he'd misinterpreted her statement.

"And how did you want us to find out? When you suddenly had to deal with the blood-lust, or were you planning to go missing?" His eyes bore into her accusingly, reading something in her expression. "That's it, isn't it?"

Closing her eyes, Ashley promised herself that as soon as she could, she would have to work on guarding her expression, as Conrad read her too easily.

"What I don't get is why I can't smell their affliction on you. You'd been wronged, but why didn't I know?"

Ashley brought her hand to her nose, giving herself a tentative sniff. "I do shower, you know." She blushed, feeling strangely defensive.

"Yeah, but..."

"Haven't you noticed, Con?" His dad quirked an eyebrow, taking over the cooking. He wafted the rising steam towards him before reaching to the wooden spice rack to add something from one of the many tiny glass jars. "She doesn't carry a scent at all. Just laundry powder and soap."

"Scent? Wait, are you—"

"Shifters," Conrad interrupted, before his father could respond or offer a correction to whatever she may have been about to say. The realisation caused her mouth to hang slightly agape as she finally placed the feeling she had within his presence, although a second later she felt her brows furrow. That couldn't be right. What she felt when near him wasn't the same as she had felt in the presence of other shifters. There was something pure, earthy and natural about the sensation she normally had from them, but being near Conrad caused her temperature to spike and a pressure build within her chest. Being near him somehow seemed akin to a warm drink on a bitter day. Warm and comforting—*safe*—her mind added. Every preternatural species seemed to possess their own different sensation. The only time it seemed wrong, something other than natural, was when someone had been forced into a change against their will. That was when her saliva worked, or had. It didn't reverse preternatural alignment, it merely gave those who had been forced into the life a chance to be born anew.

"So you can't tell specifics then. How did you know when you're needed?" Conrad questioned, something akin to relief in his voice.

"It's hard to explain. Natural preternaturals have a certain feeling about them. I knew you weren't human, but I couldn't place you into any group I've encountered. I guess different shifters must have different presences, it's not something I've noticed, but then again, it's not like I go around asking people what they are. My talent wouldn't undo the natural or willing, only those exploited or forced into something they don't want. It's like their essence calls to me, telling me of the violation. Those in desperate need will seek me with their eyes, their souls calling to mine. The further into their transition, the more taxing it was to reverse."

"That's why you collapsed the other night. He was a vampire." Ashley saw something akin to relief flicker briefly across his stunning features, before his eyes rested on her with such intensity, she couldn't help but shiver.

"He was, but it looks like those days are behind me now." The sound of a plate being placed down caused her to startle.

"Just in time." Selene smiled as she saw the table being laid. "After we've eaten, we have something important to discuss. Ashley, I'm going to have to ask you to trust us. Do you think you can do that?"

Ashley raised her gaze to meet Conrad's and she knew the answer without any hesitation.

~

Ashley's cheeks burned from the easy smiles that had crept over her during the meal. It had been a long time since she had last sat around a table with a family. She had almost forgotten how it felt. Reuben had dominated the conversation, telling her about the area where they had lived before coming here. It wasn't until he started recounting some of his more grisly investigations that she realised who he was, but his tales were soon cut short by Selene warning him that the meal table was no place for such graphic stories. When Selene excused herself from the table at the end of the meal, Ashley stood, collecting the plates and taking them towards the large double-sink.

"Please sit," Conrad instructed. "Mum would not approve of a guest helping out."

"But you cooked, so surely I should clean?" she protested, clutching the plates close.

"Our house, our rules," he teased, echoing a phrase she had used during their movie night, when he had attempted to help her clean up the following morning.

Clicking her tongue, she placed the crockery down and returned to her place, sitting awkwardly as Reuben scrutinised her. After a few moments of silence, the sound of running water and dishes being loaded into the dishwasher gave him the perfect cover to ask the question that had clearly been preying on his mind.

"Did you file a report?" His intense gaze was overbearing, the weight of his stare causing her to shift uncomfortably in her seat. It was no wonder he was so renowned for his investigation work. Just being trapped in his gaze made her want to confess her every indiscretion.

"Pardon?" she questioned, adjusting her cardigan slightly. Her fingernail snagged in her hair, making her feel even more flustered than before.

"Sorry, I couldn't help noticing the bruise, and Con mentioned you'd been—"

"Dad!" The dishwasher door slammed closed, causing the crockery within to rattle. "You're not at work. Ashley's our guest."

"A good detective is never off duty," Reuben proclaimed, before passing a hand through his hair. "But he's right. Sorry, Ashley, I didn't mean to make you feel uncomfortable."

"'Interrogated' is the word you're after, dear." Selene placed her hand on Ashley's shoulder, causing her to flinch. "Honestly, this is why our son never brings anyone home." She shook her head slowly, her gaze fixed on her husband until he seemed to wilt before her unimpressed expression. "Speaking of privacy, I'd like to discuss what your blood has revealed but, given what I've learnt, I'd like for Reuben to be present. What I've uncovered is complicated, and I would value his input. However, the decision is yours."

Heat chased through her as she realised Conrad had moved to sit beside her, his hand on hers creating a comforting warmth that spread through her to combat the cold dread that had threatened to take hold.

"I know trusting us is a lot to ask, but I promise, my parents would never betray your confidence, that's why I brought you here in the first place." He squeezed her hand, his gesture reassuring her beyond any words he had spoken. She glanced between the faces of those present before her eyes fixed upon his, savouring the feather-light sensation of his thumb as it caressed the back of her hand.

"Will you stay, too?" she asked, glancing up at him, giving him the full benefit of her pleading eyes as she looked up at him through her heavy lashes. He gave a slight nod. "Okay, what did you discover?"

"Not here." Selene gestured towards the hall. "This conversation is one to be had in the protection of my room."

Her saying that seemed to spark a reaction from both Reuben and Conrad, and Ashley swore she felt the pressure in the air almost solidify. Rising from her seat, she followed, placing a hand to her stomach as it churned, making her wish she hadn't eaten quite so much.

When everyone but Selene was seated in the room, a heavy blanket of silence descended. Selene seemed anxious. Her finger tapped her chin as she paced, as if finding it difficult to decide on the best approach.

"The reason I suggested speaking here is because nothing leaves this room. Nor can it be overheard by any manner of technology or magic," she explained, her eyes fixed on Ashley. "Before I talk about the results, I believe Reuben may be able to offer some closure on one of the issues you're facing, but first, since Ashley has agreed to have you here, I'd like her to relay what happened the night she was attacked."

"Mother!" Conrad snapped, coming to her defence, clearly not wishing for her to relive the events of that night again.

"It's fine." Finding the same small imperfection she focused on last time she was in here, Ashley began to recount the events, her vision occasionally chancing a glance towards Conrad, who sat beside her, his fists balled but resting on the table. She saw his anger, his jaw clenching as she spoke about how they had restrained her, tearing into her flesh. When she spoke about them fleeing, his shoulders seemed to relax, his fists uncurling ever so slightly. It was a moment before she realised why. "Conrad, I'm sorry, I didn't think. You thought..."

"No, I assumed, given where the bite was and what you told me. It changes nothing, though. Those bastards attacked you and—I mean, just look at that scar, that's not intent to turn, it's intent to kill!" He gestured towards her leg where she had pulled her loose-fitting Lycra trousers up to show them her injury. It was a decision made in haste and embarrassment at being the centre of their intense stares, rather than something she'd intended to do. Fumbling with the trouser leg, she pulled it down again, shifting her vision.

"So the first question, before anything else, is why did they run?" Selene took control of the conversation much in the same way a professor would. "Well, the truth is, I don't believe they did. Reuben?" Selene prompted.

"Self-defence, pure and simple, but still—" he began.

"That is not self-defence," Conrad snapped and his palm slapped the table, punctuating his point.

"No, sorry, let me explain." Reuben held his hands up apologetically. "A few nights ago, I was called out to a suspected crime scene by a couple of rookie Blue Coats. One was a shifter, and you know how the saying goes, the nose knows. They were patrolling the park and came across some scorch marks, two, near the bandstand. Forensic data came back today to show the ash samples present contained vampire DNA. We are in the process of opening an investigation and appealing for witnesses, but no one saw anything. Which is just as well, I assume, based on my wife's expression." Ashley watched as a piece of paper exchanged hands. "Is that accurate?" His eyebrows raised as his gaze peered over the paper towards her.

"Afraid so. Was there any blood at the scene?" Conrad's hand slid across the table to rest lightly upon her arm as if he'd sensed the rising nausea that enveloped her. If she was correctly understanding what they were saying, her attackers hadn't dropped her that night to flee. They were dead. She recalled hearing the sound of a scream, a scream that, until now, she had honestly believed had been her own.

"I'll check the crime scene notes once we're finished here. I don't believe they found anything. There was a theory about it being suicide, given the thorough manner in which the bodies were destroyed." His vision dropped to the paperwork still held within his grasp. "I can't imagine any new evidence coming to light, so the case will go cold. Did you leave any traces of this?"

Ashley felt herself begin to tremble as Reuben inclined his head towards her while addressing his wife. She felt almost invisible, like a child being discussed between two very concerned adults, and she still didn't understand all of what was being said.

"Nothing. The samples I took were destroyed. You hold the only record of the results, and I've already initiated a full-scale system wipe."

"What is going on? Why would you need to wipe your systems? They're protected." It was as if Conrad had sensed her building fear. Perhaps it was the way she had shuffled closer to him, her hand now gripping his arm. Hearing his outburst, Ashley released her grip, realising her knuckles had turned white.

"I can't be too careful. Ashley, your blood shows you to be preternatural," Selene revealed.

"But that's because I was both bitten and ingested blood, though, right? I've seen the tag, it's full transition."

"Normally that would be the case, but you're creating cells to neutralise the vampire toxin."

"Like antibodies?" She frowned.

"No. Unlike antibodies, these cells aren't working with your body to destroy them, rather they're changing them into something different, but I can't ascertain what. That said, your blood itself is not like anything I've seen. You've got Elder bloodline markers, but there's another—"

"You mean she's a sovereign hybrid?" Conrad questioned. "How's that even possible? I thought cross-species procreation was impossible."

"Almost impossible. It can be achieved if the female was a breeder, and yet her DNA shows neither of the parents held any breeder markers. The reason she was conceived must have had something to do with her father's lineage, and whatever gifts he passed on to his child allowed her to survive."

"Can you tell who—what my father is?"

"No. I've not seen a genetic composition that even resembles what you have, and I have access to the most extensive catalogue ever compiled. Whatever line your father is from is so well hidden, even we don't know about it, and his genes not only allow you to maintain your genetic purity but would allow a foetus from any race to survive. That necklace you wear is the only reason you're safe. If anyone were to discover you could sire a child, not to mention pass on Elder blood..." Selene shook her head. The Elder bloodlines were powerful preternaturals thought to have initially been conceived with divinity, making them into something more. The blood was passed down to each genuine heir, but they were few in number due to the difficulties of procreation, which meant those who did exist were held in renown by all the clans. Their position being similar to the archaic monastery system for each species' faction.

"I don't understand. Do I hold the breeder gene or not?" Ashley wrapped her arms protectively around herself. She knew from her studies that those capable of bearing offspring to preternatural beings were identified at the age of fourteen. Breeders, being very few in number, possessed no rights and were destined for a life of servitude. However, a family who bore a breeder child was well compensated, but had no right to deny the sale of their offspring. A preternatural breeder was almost unheard of. Most hailed from the human race, but generally only one was located every few decades, making them a sought-after possession to be used and sold on after bearing the family a child.

"No, not in the traditional sense. You're a preternatural whose breed is capable of bearing children. Until today, I didn't even know such a race existed. Others will not only smell this on you, but taste it, too."

"But she doesn't have a scent," Conrad interjected, echoing the words his father had spoken just hours before.

"And now we're back to the necklace."

"Wait! Doesn't her chip contain historical data of her family's genealogy?" Reuben questioned, straightening slightly in the chair.

"I wasn't chipped—at least not until I was adopted. My adoptive parents arranged the chip, but not knowing my birth parents meant the information completed was limited."

"How old were you?" Selene questioned, finally pulling up a chair to join them sitting around the table.

"Six, almost seven."

"That's before children come into their gifts. Given you were also wearing the suppressor, you would have read as human. Only tests completed after this age would have shown your blood to be different and, because of the necklace's holistic suppression, your scent won't have triggered any mandatory examinations from peers. Very clever." Selene dipped her head slightly, lost in thought for a second.

"And it has never been updated because you always refuse to go to hospital," Conrad said, with a dawning realisation.

"I've never really been ill, not until I started collapsing, and my brother insisted a place full of preternaturals beings was not the best place for someone to go who can undo their nature. That's why Tess and Jack knew what to do at the cinema," she added, glancing at Conrad. "So what exactly do I do with this information?"

"For now, keep that on at all times." Selene gestured towards the necklace. "I assume from how it reacted to me earlier, that it is protected to ensure no one but you can remove it. I'd like to arrange some time together to study your abilities once your body has expelled the remaining virus. I'm curious to see what that necklace is suppressing. It may offer us answers as to your father's species, but we'll have to be careful. You've worn it since before you came into your magic, so if it's removed without some manner of buffer in place, the results could be disastrous. We'll have to proceed with caution. I can fashion some lower level seals and we can work on altering them accordingly. I'll have Conrad set something up that works for you."

～

Alex ducked as magical bombardment flashed and ricocheted overhead, illuminating the metal girders of the large warehouse. Tables lay strewn and broken while the shattered glass from the manufacturing lab sparkled in the explosive light of the crossfire. One of his arms protectively shielded the head of a young boy from the Aphrodisia Clan—the clan name given to beings whose presence induced feelings of lust and love—as the false ceiling rained down fibreglass.

A quick glance towards his partner, Bindu, who sheltered several feet away, confirmed the Anthousai—more commonly known as a flower nymph—had also been successfully retrieved. A resounding crack sent a shower of sparks from above, shorting out the remaining lights, plunging the warehouse into darkness for barely a second before his partner released her magic, sending several glowing orbs soaring above. They spiralled upwards towards the ceiling for a moment, before homing in on their attackers, providing Alex with the perfect markers. Ice left his fingertips in silent, deadly attack. The crumpling of the bodies crunching upon the shattered remains of the laboratory confirmed his aim had been true.

For the last twelve months, they had been setting up this sting operation, their operation slowly leading to the ringleader of the drug chain. It was one thing for humans to ingest things created by their means, but when preternaturals perverted their vice market, it led to trouble. Hard-hitting and highly addictive, this new drug—known on the streets as zeal—had taken the country by storm.

While this side of the barrier preternaturals still lived in the shadows, they had their own network in place, facilitated by the countries' leaders who—after being sworn into power—were shown the world's true history, ensuring their cooperation. Their knowledge was bound, ensuring that, even should they wish to, they were unable to even hint at this concealed community.

Alex's unit was one of many that ensured this hidden world stayed undiscovered and protected. His team had been assigned to investigate a string of abductions thought to be related to the manufacturing of zeal. After a year of undercover work and a fictitious relationship with the ringleader's sister, Katrina, their diligence had paid off.

Katrina had been the one to first seek help. As Madam of a brothel, she employed both humans, preternaturals from the Aphrodisia Clan, and nymphs. The flower nymphs, in particular, gained much interest. While few in number, they were able to reproduce any aspect of a plant's nature and were often craved for the drug-like effects they induced on exchanging fluids with their client, creating a natural, risk-free high. It wasn't until her third employee had vanished that she contacted the P.T.F., the Preternatural Task Force. She had been certain her brother had been involved, but at the time lacked any proof.

Alex had been impressed by her decision to turn informant in exchange for the promise of being taken to Mython, a place where she could choose whether to live in the shadows or flaunt her talents. For years, her brother had forced her to run his brothel, but when her employees started vanishing, and others confided to her that he was forcing them to act as mules and peddlers, her tolerance expired and her fear of him evaporated.

It was her Intel and cooperation that had brought the operation crashing down, and now it was clean-up time. Alex couldn't deny his relief that this mission would soon be over, he could shed his glamour. Not that it made any difference, his very nature meant very few people actually knew he was a natural blonde with eyes as blue as the ice he controlled. His aura held a constant glamour that altered from person to person, protecting his identity, which was why undercover work had always been his forte.

It was approaching Ashley's birthday, and this was an important one. It was time to tell her the truth about what she was, and how his father finding her and taking her in had been more than just good fortune. It should have been his parents' job, they had taken her in knowing full well the danger. But now it fell to him. At first he had resented the little intruder who inserted herself into his life disrupting their balance. She was monopolising time with his parents that belonged to him. But his dislike soon thawed and now he would do anything to protect her.

'That's the last of them, Lex,' came the telepathic communication from his team beta who had taken point on the other side of the warehouse. Just a few hours ago, they had brought down the kingpin, Katrina's brother. His execution sentence was completed instantly, which had meant targeting his distribution chains and warehouses had to be done quickly, before they destroyed any evidence along with the innocent lives of their captives. Alex glanced at the young boy. The makeshift bandage he had applied to the bleeding needle wounds was doing its job, but a mere bandage was nowhere near the level of help he needed. It would take more than that to heal him. Judging by his gaunt appearance, it had been months since food had passed his cracked lips. He had been kept alive by drips, chemicals, and feeding tubes while the rest of his body was coated in animal fat and scraped raw. He had never imagined enfleurage could be used in such a way as to harvest this clan's pheromones. The poor boy was days away from a deadly infection, which of course had only made him more potent, in a hope to lure a prey closer to save his life.

'Excellent. Great job, everyone. Call the cleanup and let's get the survivors passed to medical and regroup back at base.' Alex turned as his partner's hand patted his shoulder. She offered him a faint smile, her tired brown eyes matching her weary posture. The young girl she had recovered hung onto her leg, her tiny hands clutching Bindu's black combat trousers tightly as her frail legs trembled under the strain of her weight.

'Bet you'll be glad to get back to your sister,' she continued telepathically, but Alex knew it was a conversation shared just between

the two of them. Bindu was the reason this group could communicate across the distances telepathically. As a psychic vampire, she created a link between the task force; as long as the number in the task force was geometrically stable, it caused no detriment as the linking of minds created a web of joint energy-sharing which actually enhanced the team's overall powers. She worked best with five or six, but had been known to link as many as fifteen people. Her light affinity also gave her the ability to utilise the power of light in a similar way that normal vampires could manipulate darkness. Energy, after all, could become light.

'Honestly, I'm dreading what's to come more than this raid.' Alex blew out a breath as the now-opened roller shutters came into sight. Waiting outside were the cleanup crew, complete with ghouls to dispose of the bodies before the area would be purged. 'But at least I'll make it in time to tell her before her magic awakens. I was worried it was going to be a phone conversation.'

'You're going to talk to her about joining us, right after she's finished studying? Our unit would be unstoppable. Not to mention I heard tell they have rejuvenating abilities. Imagine what linking with a replenisher could do.' He could feel her excitement in her thoughts. Two medics approached, their reassuring smiles and soft tones instantly putting the two children at ease. They watched in silence as the medics escorted the children into the waiting ambulance, noticing another two vehicles pulling away, no doubt containing the adults who had been discreetly escorted to safety before the attack began. There had been no way to approach the children without being seen.

'Dad told me her species used to be known for their ability to replenish, purify and empower. Although he also told me he believed they had been hunted into extinction. Ashley could very well be the last of her kind, or there could be more, hiding.'

'I don't know how you've managed to keep her a secret.'

'Her mother took care of that. My father was lucky enough to recognise the sealing charm. But when she reaches her birthday, her nature will start to filter through, and being segregated from that part *of herself all her life is going to cause complications.'* Alex groaned internally. His father had already secured the Mython base C.O's blessing to take his sister in when she came of age. They had one of the only training areas that could withstand if she went berserk, which was a very real possibility given how such a large part of who she was had been repressed for so long. His father had ensured the measures were in place, and had even left instructions in case he was on a mission when the time came. As it turned out, his father's obsessive planning had been a blessing.

'You've got until May, right?'

'Yeah.'

'Good, that's a month or so to figure out how to break the news she's not only preternatural, but could sell her services to the highest bidder. Did they ever find her mother?'

'Yeah.' Alex gave what translated as a mental sigh. *'Dad's team found her discarded on some abandoned tracks a few stops away, drained. She was an Elder Witch. Apparently, there are still a few with that bloodline this side of the barrier.'*

Elder witches were few in number as the blood coursing through their veins traded fertility for power, leaving them barren. The only reason their line continued at all was because the witch, male or female, was given one opportunity when they turned twenty-eight to create a child. But in doing so, the child took all that made their parent Elder into themselves, leaving its mother or father powerless. The blood for this line was literally passed from parent to child, except, it seemed, in Ashley's case.

'Father?'

'Murdered. That's why they were fleeing. Her mother had reached out to my father through P.T.F., that's why he was on site and able to retrieve Ashley so quickly. If whoever got her mother had discovered there was a child, it would have been unthinkable for her. We had no idea what her father was until Dad saw the charm, and the only reason he knew it was because of what we are. In a way, she was already family, albeit very distant.'

'Well, try and have her come to our side. We could use a power boost.'

'At the moment, I'm just worried about getting her through this transition. Imagine if your abilities had been suppressed, then all of a sudden you found yourself with a limitless supply of power and no idea how to channel it. I've already made arrangements for her to stay with me at the base. We can arrange getting her registered, too.'

'Why hasn't she already been?'

'Because until she knows how to protect herself, registering her will be like painting a target on her back, especially since the Blue Coats are no closer to discovering how the abduction victims' chips are being disabled. Until that's resolved, she'll be in danger, and she's too young to sign up to P.T.F. until her birthday.'

'You think she will? What if you tell her what our logo really used to stand for?' The P.T.F. had been dubbed the Preternatural Task force, but when first their agency began, the initials had actually stood for Pathway To Freedom, because their objective was to ensure everyone could live in safety and freedom. But this secondary name had been the one to stick.

'I don't think she has even given it any thought. I know she wants to use what she has, but I don't think she has any thoughts on how. Besides, this gift she has now, it's a drop in the pond. I'm hoping if I talk to her about us, she may conclude she can do more good as part of our service. But first, I have to help her come to terms with a secret we've kept about her all her life. I don't think she'll thank me for that.'

Bindu placed a hand on his shoulder gently and he gave her a smile, opening the passenger's door to their vehicle.

"Oh no, it's my turn to drive," she scolded, plucking the keys from his grasp.

With a slight chuckle, Alex got in the car, prepared to clutch the seat for dear life. Combat and raids he could handle, but he was the worst passenger in the world.

Reuben sat with the crime scene data displayed upon the surface of his office desk, scowling as he rechecked all the information. He swiped a report away, replacing it with another before glancing towards the open fireplace. He watched the flames dance for a moment, bringing with them the cries of the wronged as they begged him to bring them justice.

These voices were one of the reasons they'd had to move to Overton. While they begged an ifrit to bring their killers to justice, they provided no insight into how they met their demise, or by whose hand. When Solomon had pulled their ancestor from the realm of the dead, they had maintained their connection to that plane and now, whenever an innocent life was taken, the person could cry out to an ifrit, seeking justice. This was the reason his kind found work in homicide. Often, they were drawn to the scene of a murder by the blood of the wronged, but whoever had killed these people had been careful. He could sense it had happened in this territory, and the only reason he would be unable to locate the scene of their death was if someone had driven an unused nail into the blood. They hadn't done it quickly enough in some cases, but Reuben was certain there were more deaths than there had been calls for justice, and the fact someone knew to take such action spoke of the murderer's age. Very few knew of this ancient lore.

Rubbing his temples, he turned his focus to the paper map lining the far wall. While technology was also used to track data, sometimes seeing the information this way helped him to interpret it better.

Small red pins marked the areas of abductions. Normally, the map would possess black pins too, but no bodies had been recovered. Those in the department were hopeful this meant the victims were still alive, but he had informed them at least some were deceased. Worse still, there appeared to be no correlation between the places people were abducted from. By now, normally some manner of pattern had emerged, but here, the only pattern was that there wasn't one. Nor was there a specific profile. The people being abducted didn't fall into any age bracket, nor did they all share a single interest or trait.

Leaning back, he turned his thoughts to the evening. Selene had been correct, it had been a long time since Conrad had brought anyone home to meet them, and he couldn't remember the last time his son had smiled so much. They had been sitting watching an evening movie together, as a family, when he had noticed that Ashley had closed her eyes and beads of sweat were forming on her forehead. As he examined her more closely, he could see she was shivering. Nudging Selene, he drew her attention towards her, noticing Conrad had already seen his friend's condition. She jerked almost fitfully, as if lost to a nightmare. When Conrad had lightly touched her arm, she had startled and, letting out an ear-piecing shriek, had struck out before realising what she had done. She froze, like a deer in headlights, her chest heaving. After a flustered apology and explanation about the night-time fever and hallucinations, Selene had given her something to help her rest, and Conrad had shown her to the guest room, deciding to turn in for the night himself.

Reuben had spent the time since checking and rechecking all the crime scene information. There had been a lot of foot traffic disturbing the gravel, but no signs of a struggle. The forensics came back with a lot of results, most of which had been ruled out as things expected to be found in such a public place. With no evidence of any foul play, it seemed likely this case would either be ruled a suicide, or go cold, as he predicted. It wasn't unheard of for two vampires, whose clans were at odds, to take their lives together in a grand romantic gesture; perhaps they would believe this is what had occurred in this instance. One thing was certain; from the evidence he had seen, Ashley was not at risk of being discovered.

"What's the verdict?" Selene questioned, moving to stand behind him and placing a gentle kiss on the crown of his head.

"She's clear. But we do have another problem. I witnessed something in the kitchen today. We're going to have to talk to Conrad. She turned his eyes gold." There was a heaviness in his voice that even he heard, and he regretted that it stole the smile from his wife's lips.

"Ashley?"

"Mmm, before dinner. I'm sure he must have felt it himself. Do you think she's the one he was talking about when he was asking if a human could survive courtship?" He moaned in delight as Selene's fingers began to work their magic on his shoulders, easing the building tension.

"I have no doubt. You'd have to be blind not to see the way the two of them look at one another. It reminds me of us," she said, kissing the crown of his head gently.

"Except you were never in any danger of been combusted if things got a little too heated."

"I don't know, you still make me burn," she said, chuckling as she moved her kisses to his cheek. He swivelled his chair, grasping her hips, pulling her to sit on his lap.

"Do you think the Elder blood will make a difference?" After what happened with his last girlfriend, Reuben had been certain his son would shun romance of any kind, such had been his vow, sworn in anger and heartbreak after her hateful reaction. It was something he couldn't understand, a reaction that had no explanation. The fact Ashley had managed to dissolve his resolve so quickly sung to the connection he felt. It pained him as it seemed this romance, too, was doomed to fail.

"I honestly don't know. That girl's a law unto herself. I imagine it's possible, depending on her affinity."

"I did discover something interesting, though." He teased another kiss from her. His thoughts of Conrad's emotional pain made him more appreciative of his own happiness.

"Oh? No, wait, don't tell me you've run a background check on our son's friend." Her brow creased in a scowl that warmed his heart. He would never dare tell her, but the way her nose wrinkled, combined with the skittering of freckles, made her appear more cute than menacing. Although she did have one look in her arsenal that never failed to make him wither, and she had used it today at the dinner table.

"Turns out her brother, Alex Ciele, is part of the P.T.F. Just like his father. His father brought Ashley back with him from the other side of the border and adopted her."

"They're preternatural?"

"With an ice alignment. They were frost birds."

"*Were?*"

"Ashley's adoptive parents were killed in a crash a few years ago, hit and run. A vehicle pushed their parked car over the edge of the road. The case went cold."

"Reuben, don't you think you should give the girl a chance to tell us about herself on her own terms?" she scolded, attempting to pull herself free from his lap, only to be pulled back down by his firm grasp.

"Maybe, but Selene, his eyes were gold."

"He loves her."

"It's beyond love. Both sides of his nature are agreed, she sings to his soul. What if it turns out her family adopted her because, even through the seal, they sensed a shared affinity?" Ice and fire, the two were mutually destructive, but when beings of that nature combined, only one would walk away, and an ifrit's fire was not just mortal flame, it was born of Phlegethon itself. Even a soul bond wouldn't protect a being of opposing affinity.

"Let's not worry about that now, the answers will come to us. The moment I can study her, we'll be able to tell what element she's aligned to."

"Do you think we should tell Conrad?"

"Have you not noticed he's already fighting his heart? Until he's willing to tell her the truth about what he is, he won't pursue her, and Rei damaged his confidence more than he's let on. I still can't believe she managed to turn the whole academy against him because another ifrit had served justice to her father. But I guess that's banshees for you, always screaming about something." Reuben laughed at his wife's attempt at humour, his face growing serious as he heard the notification. Lifting his wife from his lap, he grabbed his device.

"Another missing person, male, thirty-five, reported missing an hour ago when he didn't come home from work. His chip data vanished this afternoon."

"I'll better let you get to work then." She placed her forehead to his, and for a moment he closed his eyes, relishing how her touch set his skin aflame.

CHAPTER 7

Ashley slept like the dead, a phrase she thought would have been apt after her infection. After a night at Conrad's, she had returned home to change, relieved to witness the fading tag mark on her leg, although the pink scar remained as prominent as ever. When the mark vanished completely, she was to let Conrad know so she could arrange a day with Selene to discover what secrets her amulet hid. She had to admit, after discussing everything with Conrad and his family she felt as if a huge weight had been lifted from her shoulders, and after the restful night's sleep she was already feeling less exhausted.

Today, lectures had passed in a blur of excitement and, despite her exhaustion, her focus was returning. Looking in the mirror this morning, she had noticed her tongue was no longer doing that strange flickering thing Conrad had seen. Which she'd happily shown him when he made a sly comment about women taking too long to change, even though she knew she'd only been a few moments!

After her final lecture of the day, she had stayed behind in the cafeteria, helping to gather discarded dishes and wash pots while she waited for Tess. She had made Tess promise that, when the time came to make the final payment on her bike, she would be there, and so, with today being payday, she had waited for her friend to finish her lecturers. With her temperature still being elevated, she was still receiving notifications from work to advise her it was unsafe to attend, but a phone call to the home's administrator had eased her financial concerns after he agreed to take her sick days as holiday since she had so many outstanding. Holidays were earned based on days worked, so the more shifts she picked up, the more hours of holiday pay she incurred. They had been more than happy to comply with her request, especially since in all the years she had been working there she rarely took time off, instead preferring to have the company buy the days back rather than take the time away from work. This day had turned out better than she had imagined was possible; everything had simply fallen into place.

When Tess arrived, they began their short walk towards the busy town centre. After several discussions about their day, Tess grasped Ashley's arm gently, and she knew what was coming.

"Now, are you going to tell me what's been going on, what happened?" Tess asked, as they approached the dessert shop.

"Later," Ashley acknowledged, knowing all too well that the answer was less than satisfactory, especially since it was the same answer she had given earlier today. "In here."

Ashley led Tess into the dessert parlour, treating her friend to their favourite sharing ice-cream. The enormous glass bowl sparkled in the afternoon sun and as they shared its contents. Pretending to fight over who got the chocolate pieces, she steeled herself for the conversation. After a little while, Tess looked up at her, as if sensing she was ready, and Ashley told her everything she could as her friend listened in horror, unaware she was not being given all the information, just enough to explain the attack, the blood tag, and her unexpected immunity to the vampire toxin.

"So you weren't even going to tell us, you were just going to..." Tears sparkled in her friend's eyes, the hurt about Ashley's decision to keep something so important from her clearly evident. It stirred her shame. How she had wanted to confide in Tess when she saw the tag, but in order to disappear, it hadn't been an option. Even now, there were still things left unsaid. It was too dangerous to broach her other discoveries in this location, and continuing to keep secrets only gnawed at her shame more.

"Okay, I know that wasn't one of my best decisions—" she began.

"You're damn right it wasn't," Tess scolded. "Do you think we'd just let you disappear and not come looking for you?"

"Anyway, it doesn't matter now." Ashley reached over, grasping Tess's hand, stilling the gentle tinkling sound of Tess's spoon as it trembled in her hands against the glass. "Forgive me?"

"*Don't* do it again. No matter what you think you need to do, or protect us from, never cut us off like that. We're meant to be friends, to have each other's back, not turn and run when things get hard. Surely you know we would have stood by you, supported you? Thank goodness for Conrad. I mean, really Ashley, how could you?" Tess's manicured nail rose, wiping a tear from her cheek. Ashley lowered her gaze, unable to look any longer at the hurt clearly evident in her friend's expression.

"I *really* am sorry. I thought it would be easier for you if I just vanished. It was stupid, I know that, but I was scared and the thought of being consumed by blood lust and putting any of you in danger..." Ashley shook her head, before allowing her gaze to fall on her watch. "Hey, since we've finished in time, shall we go pick up my bike?" Her grief morphed to a smile as she heard Tess chuckle.

"Smooth! You may have well have shouted, hey look, a distraction!"

"But, my bike," she whined, pouting playfully before unleashing her best puppy dog eyes.

"Alright, but I'm still cross with you."

Leaving the dessert parlour with a quick thank-you to their server, Ashley and Tess made their way to the second-hand store. Ashley felt her grin broadening more with every step. By the time the antique bell rang above the door, she was beaming.

Hesitating for a moment as the door closed, she took time to once again soak in the unique atmosphere of this curio shop. Dark shelves filled with bric-a-brac towered over antique furniture. This store carried everything, from old vases and wooden chests, to much loved furniture and toys, not to mention the more unusual items—things which seemed to hold an air of magic or mystery. The entire store possessed its own heady aroma, a mixture of wood, dust and incense. The olde-worlde feel was further enhanced by the bespoke wall-mounted lamps, designed to resemble old-fashioned oil lamps in both look and lighting effect. The overcrowded stock in the store meant the tightly packed wares could sometimes cast an eerie shadow, or make someone think they could see movement where there was none.

"Today's the day then?" The elderly lady, recognising her visitor, hobbled from around the counter, using its sturdiness for balance as they approached through the only uncluttered pathway, which led from the door directly towards the old-fashioned cash register.

"Good afternoon, Mrs Huston," Ashley greeted, fishing in her purse before producing the remaining notes. "Thank you so much for holding it so long for me."

"Of course, dear, and like I've said before, do call me Ethel. My Mabel would never forgive me if I had let it go to someone else." Her trembling hand reached out, finding the silver bell on the counter top and gave it three soft taps to send its summons into the air. "Are you feeling better? She told me you've not been in work for the last week or so. Missing you something rotten, she is. She says having a youngster there keeps them young."

"I had a temperature so they wouldn't let me work," Ashley explained.

"Where is that boy?" Ethel chuntered, chiming the bell three more times. "Honestly, these last weeks, getting that grandson of mine to do anything has been like pulling teeth."

"What is it, Gran?"

Ashley, thinking she recognised the voice, turned to see Will near the door into the rear area. He gave her an energetic smile as he realised who the customers were. She couldn't believe he was here. She had known his gran owned a shop, but she hadn't even considered these two were related. They looked so different to one another.

"Fetch young Ashley her bike, would you?"

"Sure thing." He pushed his hand through his golden hair before disappearing through the bead curtain into the back, causing it to rattle.

"Oh goodness me, you're *that* Huston? I never realised," Tess blurted, before she could help herself.

"What do you mean, love?"

"The Holistic Hustons."

"Now, there's a name I've not heard for a turn or two. Seems like a long time ago now." The old lady's features seemed to mist over, a smile tickling her lips.

"My mother used to sing your praises. She wondered what happened to you. I never realised Will—"

"I became too old, love, and our son never took an interest in the family business, he was born without the gift, you see. It ended with me, I'm afraid. Besides, my boy was all into antiquities and curios." She gestured to her surroundings as if to make her point. "After he passed, we hung up our crystals, so to speak, to keep his dream alive."

"Sorry it took so long," called Will from the back. "You know, I heard you talk about paying off a bike, I just hadn't put two and two together." Ashley felt her heart begin to race as she set sight on the object of her desire. It was the most magnificent thing she had seen. Its midnight blue frame glistened, and its small engine shone, as if it had been recently polished.

"Yeah, thoughts of this guy have got me through many a tough week. Speaking of tough weeks, we've hardly seen you lately. Is everything okay?" she asked, her fingers tracing the frame affectionately, learning its every contour.

"You know me, I sometimes get busy. I got involved in a project group, it's consuming all my free time. I'll be sure to make it up to you soon, maybe a movie one night?"

"That would be great. You know we miss you. I can't believe I didn't realise Mrs Huston was your gran. How dense can I be?"

"It's a popular name. There are three others I know of in our academy alone." He gave her a charming smile, his gaze seeming a little too intense, as if he was waiting for something.

"Ashley!" Tess broke away from her conversation with Ethel, looking at her friend's purchase for the first time. "You never said it was a dynamo!" Tess gushed, with a girlish lilt to her voice. She dropped to her knees before the bike as Will fully released it into Ashley's possession. Tess ran her hands across its frame, studying the complex mechanisms that charged the in-built battery which allowed the rider to switch to assisted pedalling if they grew tired, so long as they had stored enough energy. "They don't even make these any more. Does it work?"

"Of course it works, love," Ethel chimed. "We changed one of the bulbs in the front light, but other than that it was in good condition."

"Now I see why you wanted it." Tess grinned, still running her hand appreciatively down the frame just like Ashley had done moments before. Ashley smiled back, her gaze straying to Will who stood watching them in mild amusement.

"Well, we should get going. I can't wait to try him."

"Don't tell me you've already picked out a name?" Will teased, leaning on the counter.

"Afterglow, because that's all you'll see of me," Ashley beamed. "Will you, Tess? Please."

"Alright, I'll get the stencils, my dad won't mind us using his paints."

"And tagging it?" she posed hopefully. "I've spent so long saving for this beauty, I'd hate him not to be registered."

"Hey, if you wait five minutes I can get it tagged for you."

Ashley turned to look at Will, wondering whether to accept his offer.

"We've got the kit in the back. We'll throw it in as a complimentary, right, Gran?"

"Thanks, but Tess's dad promised to check it over for me," Ashley replied hastily, before Ethel had the chance to reply.

Tess turned to her with a grimace. "I can't believe you kept it from me. When I asked him, I thought you meant a pedal bike."

"He won't mind, will he?" Will scooted around them, holding the door as Ashley began to wheel the bike forward

"Mind? It's all I'm likely to hear about for a week."

"Thank you, Mrs Huston," Ashley called back, before thanking Will for holding the door. "See you later, Will."

"Yes, thanks, see you tomorrow, Will," Tess said. "I'm glad he's looking a little better. I was getting quite worried," she whispered, once the door was closed and they were far from earshot.

"We've not seen him for a while now. I wonder what's going on? I know we don't have any classes together, but he always used to join us at lunch. I know he said he has a study project, but... I don't know, something about him seems off," Ashley said, realising exactly how long it had been since he last sat at their table.

"I'm not sure. He's been looking really burnt out, though. I spotted him coming out of one of his lectures the other week, but he wouldn't even talk to me. Something is going on with him, but at least he doesn't look like he's joined the ranks of the walking dead any more." Ashley felt herself blanch at the reference, earning herself a sympathetic look from Tess. "Sorry, bad choice of words. Now, let's get this bad boy back to my place."

∼

Ashley was fighting the urge to sleep, her head dropping as her eyelids refused to obey her will for them to remain open. After the second time her elbow had given beneath her as she leaned on the breakfast bar, dozing in and out of sleep, she surrendered, partially at least. If her eyes were going to betray her, then she would just have to complete the preparation another way. With a freshly-made strong coffee, she settled back on the sofa and, plugging her headphones into her device, she activated the text-to-speech function.

Allowing her heavy eyelids to rest, she leaned back, cradling the coffee protectively as the words washed over her. The soothing voice lulled her into further relaxation and the words became the bridge between wakefulness and sleep as she slowly transitioned between the two. Just as the words were fading into oblivion, a sharp knock at the door caused her tentative grip on the mug to slip. Gasping as the contents spilt, she jumped to her feet, now wide awake thanks to the dark fluid soaking through her pyjama top. Snatching several tissues from the wooden box on the table, she had just started patting herself down when the knock came again.

Tip-toeing across the living room towards the front door, she continued to dab at the stain, grimacing as the wet cloth peeled from her flesh with every step she took. Just as she was wondering who would call at this time in the evening, her vision wandered across to the antique clock that had been in the Ciele family for generations. Seeing it was 8pm, she gave a sigh. It felt much later

Cracking the door just an inch to allow her to see through, a wash of confusion enveloped her as she saw a dark-haired stranger standing on her stoop, looking nervous.

"Ashley Ciele?" he questioned, trying to peer through the door. She opened it a few more inches, instantly regretting the decision as his gaze turned to the almost transparent texture of her damp top. There was something in his expression she didn't like. Without thinking, her hand slid down the inside of the door jamb, her fingers grasping the handle of the metal baseball bat her brother had got her for protection, her thumb resting on the button which turned this weapon into a functioning torch.

"Yes?"

"Sign here, please." He thrust a device forward with a fingerprint signature request. Releasing a breath and the bat, she cracked the door a little further and reached through to touch her thumb to his screen before the young man produced an envelope. She met his brown eyes briefly, sensing something familiar in his presence that she couldn't quite place. She took the manila envelope, waiting for the dark-haired stranger to let himself out of the screeching gate before closing the door.

Turning the envelope over, she slid her finger across the fold, removing a small picture with a note attached by a paper-clip.

If you want me to keep your secret, you'll have to do something for me.

The back door, midnight.

Until then,

Liam.

Ashley focused on the picture, her heart quickening as she looked upon a still image of herself in the grasp of her attackers. Their faces were a mesh of anguish. The small time stamp on the bottom suggested it was a caption taken from moving footage, a recording. She felt her heart hammer, unaware the paper within her hand was aflame, being reduced to cinders. Swearing, she dropped it, stamping on the curling paper, but it was too late to salvage anything. Turning the envelope over, she looked for a post location, anything she could recognise, only to find the envelope was blank. Snatching the door open, she dashed down the overgrown path, cursing as her bare feet caught the loose stone chips as she hurried, hoping to catch sight of the delivery man. No address meant someone had handed it to him. She had to know who. Standing at her gate, she looked left and right, hoping to catch a flash of taillights or hear the roar of an engine being brought to life, but he was nowhere to be seen.

∼

Liam stood masked by the shadows cast by the overgrown back garden. The unpruned shrubs created the perfect cover for a slender man such as himself to fade into the background. He couldn't believe he was actually doing this, but her blood had saved him, brought him back from the brink and now it was all he could think about. He could still recall seeing her there, lying on the bandstand bleeding, fighting for life yet unable to prevent it from fading away. He had seen what she had done to survive and had lingered in the darkness, much as he did now, ensuring she was on the verge of unconsciousness before daring to approach.

It had been his intention to help her, nothing more, but he had been weakened and exhausted from the trials of the evening. But as he saw the injury, the enormous slice expanding from the upper part of her thigh to almost her knee, he knew to fail would be to let her die. As he had sat trying to staunch the flow of her blood and knit the wound together, he felt his remaining reserves wane and his instinct took over. It had been as if he had known her blood would rejuvenate him. Through a haze of exhaustion, he found himself latched onto her thigh, suckling in the same manner her attackers had. He had taken only a mouthful, maybe two, but he felt his strength returning and her wound sealing, reacting to the surge of energy which flooded through him. No longer caring for the intimacy of the location, he greedily devoured the remaining fluid, resisting the urge to bite her and draw more of the sweet ambrosia from the jagged scar he had left.

He had not felt that energised for a long time, but the high soon wore off, and now he needed more. It was the least she could do. After all, he *had* saved her life. Creeping forwards, he placed a small box on the back doorstep before once more retreating to the shadows. There was no chance she would recognise him; he had already confirmed as much when he delivered the doctored image. It hadn't been his best work, but it had needed to show very little, especially when her panicked mind would fill in the details. He had seen what she had done and mirrored it in the image as best he could. There was no reason she would doubt its authenticity.

He tensed as he heard the door handle rattle. Light spilt from inside, flooding the garden with the pale illumination, but he knew this place well. There were areas where shadows always remained dominant, especially since she had never gotten around to changing the bulb in the back security sensor.

"Hello?" He could hear the fear lining her voice, and for a brief moment felt guilty before assuring himself he was owed this. The fact that she stood there now and could call out like this, was because he had intervened. She was alive because of him.

"There's a box on the step. Pick it up." He watched as she stepped forward from the safety of the house, her rust-coloured hair reflecting the many red lowlights within as her eyes fixed upon the lock box. Glancing around again, as if to seek him out, she obeyed.

"What is it you want?"

"The contents are self-explanatory." He paused for a moment, thinking he should offer her a little more incentive to comply with his demands. "How is your injury?"

"Healed," came her snipped reply. "What am I meant to do with this?" she asked, a frown creasing her delicate features as she peered into the box at its contents. He suddenly realised his mistake. Anyone unfamiliar with Taphouses would have no idea what was inside.

"They left you to die." The coldness of his tone surprised him. He saw her shudder, the hand not holding the small box rubbing the chill from her arms.

"What is it you want?"

"I saw what you did to them. I had to wait until you were almost unconscious before I dared save you."

"*You?*" She straightened slightly, once more peering into the shadows as if they would somehow peel back and reveal him to her.

"Since that night, I've not been able to get you out of my mind." He stepped from the safety of darkness, hearing her gasp as he allowed the light to wash over him. Committing himself, he approached slowly, with what he imagined to be a sinister smile playing upon his lips as he thrust his shoulders back, advancing with confident steps that she mirrored in the opposite direction. Over the threshold, he continued his approach, his steps confident, driving her backwards as her fearful gaze remained fixed upon him. When she was but a few steps from being cornered, he spoke again. "I need more."

"More what?"

"Blood." He saw her back collide with the work surface, and a new fear cross her expression as she realised her retreat had granted him entry into her home. "It did something to me, something amazing. I need more." Ashley opened her mouth as if to respond, the crease of her brow showing a renewed resistance building within her, but the cold glare he fixed her with stole any words that would have come. "Before you refuse, bear in mind that I saw what you can do. I've tasted your blood, and I know people who will be *very* interested to learn of your existence. I'm not being unreasonable. I saved your life, so the least you can do is repay me."

"I..."

"You have a choice. You give me what I want, or I tell people, some *very* influential people, exactly what I saw and you'll find yourself a favourite among the Elite." He hadn't wanted to threaten her. He had hoped she would simply comply, pay him for his favour. But he could see nothing about this would be easy, not unless he played to her fears.

∼

Ashley only remembered feeling this helpless twice in her life. The first time had been as she heard the grinding boom of another car ploughing into her parents' vehicle, sending them tumbling off the road as passers-by restrained her attempts to run to them just seconds before their car erupted into flames. The second time had been the night she had been attacked. The night this man had apparently saved her from death. It was only as she felt the small of her back pressing into the corner of the kitchen unit that she realised she was still trying to retreat from his piercing stare. Even had her legs been able to move, owing to the way he had herded her she had nowhere to run. He stood before her, a boyish smirk on his lips as he studied her in the same way he had done when delivering that envelope to her door just hours ago. Back then, she had thought his gaze lecherous, but now she saw it for what it truly was; hungry.

A chill passed through her as she leaned against the counter, praying she could keep herself upright. The sickening realisation that he knew her secret burnt like acid through her veins, sending a hot flush of colour to her cheeks. This man had feasted upon her when she had been at her most vulnerable. She was alive because of him, she owed him a debt, and now he had come to collect.

Her eyes bore into him hatefully, committing his every feature to memory. His dark, tousled hair framed his pale face, making his brown eyes seem darker than the honey shade they were. In another place, at another time, she may have found the sharp contours of his jaw attractive, but now all she could see was images of him in her mind, latched upon her flesh, drawing her life from her, a life he thought belonged to him. Through her shuddering breathing she tried to look inward, to locate the feeling of heat that had flooded her before. If she could summon whatever had brought forth that vampire-slaying power, she could free herself of him, of the danger he posed. She could save herself. But where that heat had once burned, she now found only the icy tendrils of fear.

"I know what you're thinking. But if I don't return, the video is set on a timed release to my contacts."

Ashley felt herself trembling, willing the tears she felt forming to remain invisible. Tears only encouraged monsters like these. Selene had warned that if people knew about her blood, she would be in more danger than she could fathom. It left her with no choice. She either fed this monster or risked discovery, and something told her the creature before her wasn't bluffing. If he didn't get what he wanted from her, he would ensure she suffered.

With a resigned nod, she traced her hand across the work surface, using it for support as she crossed the kitchen to perch herself on the breakfast bar stool. She flinched as his firm hand grasped her shoulders and the tears she fought to restrain escaped. Pulling her hair aside, she tilted her head, exposing her neck and granting him the permission he sought.

"Don't mark me." Her demand came out as a strangled plea, and even with her eyes closed and her back to him, her mind conjured images of his twisted smile as he chuckled.

"I don't intend to." He grasped her hand, his fingers caressing her forearm tenderly, causing goose pimples to chase across her flesh before he removed the box she still clutched, from her vice-like grip, placing it on the counter. Within it, she once more caught sight of the unusual transparent creatures, questioning what purpose they had. "I'll not bite you. Not yet, anyway," he whispered, his breath tickling her ear as he fished one of the creatures from the box.

She flinched as its cold body made contact with the skin he had moments ago caressed. His hands returned to her shoulders, his fingers sliding across her bare shoulder as they weaved under the spaghetti-strapped pyjama top she had changed into after the earlier coffee incident. The touch was more restraint than he needed since she had already agreed to his demands. There was something about the way his thumbs rested at the base of her neck with a delicate yet controlling pressure that seemed almost familiar.

Focusing her attention to the creature on her arm, she watched with morbid fascination as its once-tiny form became swollen and its opaque texture turned red with the colour of her blood. Bile burnt the back of her throat at seeing it there, on her flesh. Despite feeling no real discomfort, she began to squirm, her eyes transfixed upon the creature.

"Hold still. It doesn't take long." She felt the pressure on her shoulders increase, a frown creasing her brow as she realised he was rubbing them gently. When the creature disengaged, he placed another in its exact location. She could feel the small resistance as it suckled, its small form swelling like her own nausea. "If anyone asks, you've been donating at the Taphouse for money, got it?" he whispered, placing the lid on his collection of blood-filled creatures. He placed one in his mouth and the sound of the fluid popping in his mouth turned her stomach almost as much as the sight of the bloodstained teeth he bore at her in a smile. For a moment, she dared another glance at him, at his smug expression.

"You have what you came for, now get out," she growled quietly, wiping her tear-stained cheeks.

"I'll see you again in a few days." He left the way he had entered, pulling the door behind him. Sinking to her knees, she looked at the wound before wrapping her arms around herself, hoping to still the tremors that assailed her.

~

Emily watched the hypnotic flickering of the lights that dotted the false ceiling of the new room. She believed she had been moved here just yesterday, but time had possessed no meaning for what felt like a lifetime now; for all she knew, it could have been a few days ago, she couldn't quite remember. Unlike her old concrete cell that had made her feel alone and isolated, there was nothing here but the wide open space between herself and the other Tabus who had earned the master's favour. The world seemed so large now, so full of light and luxury.

Master had said that since that she'd been a good girl, she should be afforded some small luxury, like being able to move about. Her shaking legs hadn't obeyed his desire, no matter how much she had attempted to please him. As a result, she heard she was to be given an increase in her nutritional feed, and had noticed her master looking on with approval at her latest blood results.

The single metal shackle around her ankle was weighted with a heavy chain. She often allowed her gaze to follow the winding path of the dull links to where they came to rest affixed to a metal plate within the wall. The chains sang softly with every movement she made, keeping her safe, and ensuring that when she was strong enough to stand without aid, she wouldn't accidentally stray beyond her space. Glancing towards the bandages on her wrist, she noticed the yellow staining from her sores no longer marred the clean dressings, although there was a tender swelling around the place her needle was inserted. She knew from this that it was almost time for them to change its site. The thought caused pimples to chase across her heated flesh at the thought of the long, shiny skewer they would thrust within her.

With a slight wriggle, Emily felt her skin peel from the plastic coating of the soft mattress that now supported her weight, easing the pressure on her sores. It was one of the things she liked most about being a good girl. The soft foam was heaven, and now she had a catheter inserted, the cold hosings were a thing of the past, replaced by soft, warm flannels and soap that smelt of perfume and antiseptic.

The most disconcerting thing had been to find she was not alone. There were two empty beds to her left, but just beyond them there was an older man. While she couldn't see anything specific, she could hear the occasional chime as his chains alerted her to movement and the slightest impression of a figure lying prone, but her tired, unfocused eyes could discern nothing more. When she had first been brought here he had tried to speak to her, his whisper too loud and abrasive against the silence that was expected. He told her Tabus who had graduated to this area were allowed to talk. But she had ignored him anyway, waiting until the master gave her permission to break one of the first rules he had given her.

She had tried to speak to him today, but since waking he been unusually silent. She wondered if he was dead, or if he had been moved during one of her dreams to the new households he was forever talking about.

Once a day, or so she imagined it to be, someone would come to her, lifting her moods and dismissing her into a world of bright and beautiful hallucinations. There was no pain in this magical place, just wondrous visions. She no longer felt the creatures being attached and removed from her like she had in the world of nightmares and horrors, where her mind had made them grow in size and each second was burning agony. She now knew only the bliss and euphoria of the dreams her master had seen fit to bestow upon her.

But she was awake now, trapped in her weakened body, awaiting the time she could once more fly. If she turned her head to the right, the haunting darkness from her old concrete cell could be seen, swallowing the room beyond its metal bars. Its darkness seemed all-consuming, like a gaping mouth open and awaiting for her to make a mistake so that it may devour her once more. She swore she would do whatever it took not to be returned to that cursed and lonely place.

Lifting her hand to her mouth weakly, she coughed, the sound far less abrasive than before, causing only mild discomfort through her chest as her breathing rattled. She lowered her hand, closing her eyes just moments before a loud noise startled her, reminding her again of her silent roommate. A man was being wheeled in, asleep. She hoped he was good so she could have some company soon.

CHAPTER 8

Ashley wiped her brow as she sat in the cafeteria picking at the peppers at the side of her jacket potato. She had really wanted it at the time, but now just the thought of eating caused her stomach to lurch. Blowing her hair from her eyes in an attempt to cool herself down, she shifted again, as a fresh wave of sickly heat enveloped her. She tugged at her cardigan, fighting against its stifling embrace before finally removing it.

"What is that?" Tess exclaimed, grasping Ashley's arm, her eyes fixed on the raw, swollen mark at the crook of her elbow. She had been doing her best to hide the mark, but the tail-end of her fever had caught her off guard. It was no longer isolated to night-time, but came on throughout the day. She imagined—she hoped—it meant it was finally coming to an end, especially since the tag mark had all but vanished. She looked at the angry-looking mark, rubbing it lightly. After the last letting she'd done for Liam, it was starting to itch.

"Oh, it's just..." She trailed off, glancing around, looking for the figure she despised. After his last visit, she had a growing suspicion that she had seen him somewhere on campus. Scanning the faces of the lunch crowd, she failed to see him, but when he came to her it felt almost as if he knew her, and while he waited for his latest fix of her blood, the small talk implied he knew more about her than should have been possible. It unnerved her to think he had been watching her so closely. Unable to see him, she leaned closer to Tess, finally hoping to confide in her friend and seek her advice.

"It's what?" Tess demanded, drawing Jack and Conrad's attention from their own conversation.

"It's—"

"Didn't she tell you?" Will questioned, placing his hands on Ashley's shoulders. As he approached behind her, she shied from his touch, discomfort welling as, despite her attempt to move away, he let his hands linger on her for a moment longer.

Seeing the mark, Conrad snatched her arm from Tess's grasp to study the inflammation. His piercing gaze lifted from the wound, demanding answers she couldn't give.

"She's been donating. I saw her the other night." Will moved around the table and shot an apologetic look in her direction before glancing over his shoulder.

"Shit, Ash, we talked about this," Tess interjected. "If you're strapped for cash..."

"Yeah, I know, but with having time off from work I needed to make up my shortfall." The lie spun easily from her tongue, but she knew Conrad wouldn't buy it. The question was, why had Will jumped in when he did? She glanced down at her arm, covering the wound with her hand in an attempt to prevent her friends from staring. "Look, I'm not proud of it, but it was essential."

"Yeah, you have to take care of yourself," Will interjected. He glanced over his shoulder again, an action which unnerved her, causing her gaze to stray in that direction, but she didn't see anything untoward. With a sigh, he leaned close, whispering so only she could hear, "Who knows what would happen if you don't."

"Did you need something, Will?" Tess questioned, no doubt

noticing the strange uneasiness of his posture and the way his words had caused Ashley to pale.

"Can I get a copy of today's notes from you or Conrad? My dictator crashed. I know we're not in the same lecture but I lost everything." His eyes flitted towards Ashley. "It's awful when things don't do what they're meant to. Now it'll have to be disposed of. Who knows where things like that turn up when they stop doing what they're supposed to?"

There was a darkness to his tone that caused the fine hairs on her arms to stand on end. Her burning fever was now replaced with a cold shiver. Now, more than ever, she was certain he wasn't here of his own volition. His warning was too on-point, too timely. Ashley searched the lunch crowd again as she pulled her cardigan back over her arms, still failing to find the dark-haired vampire who seemed intent on tormenting her.

"They get recycled into new parts," Tess volunteered, accessing her notes, swiping them across ready for transfer. "Connect?" He touched his device to hers and she transferred the necessary notes. "Everything okay with you, Will? We haven't seen you lately."

"I've been about." He shrugged. "I'm still tied up on that project. It's really eating into my time at the moment. We could always get together after classes. I've missed you guys, but"—he glanced over his shoulder again—"maybe we could do a stay-in film night." Just then Ashley tensed, feeling the looming presence of the vampires approaching. "Anyway, catch you later." Will raised a hand, turning from them to fall into stride with Devon's small group as they made their way towards their regular spot.

"Friends of yours?" Ashley heard him ask.

"Nah, just getting class notes."

"What was that about?" Conrad questioned, his vision still on Ashley who couldn't meet his gaze.

"I think Will's in trouble. Remember last year when his gran's shop started getting vandalised?" Tess began, her gaze drifting over to the vampires.

"You don't think?" Ashley questioned.

"Yeah, I think he paid them protection money."

"There's no way he could afford that."

"Did you notice the scarring on his arms? What he said about bloodletting, I think he knows because he does it. Speaking of which, are you insane?" Conrad grasped her arm again having brought the conversation full circle. For a moment, she was glad to have the extra layer of protection her cardigan provided. The heat from his touch soothed her, yet the manner in which he set his jaw spoke volumes about the anger he was restraining.

"I *needed* the money," she whispered through gritted teeth, trying to free herself from his grasp. She could have, if she'd have tried harder, but a weak tug was all she managed.

"We will talk about this later." He matched her volume, allowing both his concern and disappointment to hang in the air.

∼

Tess's fingers snapping before his gaze drew Jack back to the present as she questioned if he was okay. He realised he was still staring, but Ashley had long since moved her arm.

"Sorry, I zoned out there for a moment. Hey, where'd Will go?"

Ashley inclined her head towards the vampires, but it seemed their friend was no longer amongst them. He let his gaze fall back to Ashley's arm, relieved when the covered flesh caused no more images to assail him. Lately he had been daydreaming a lot, and it was the strangest things that triggered him to zone out in the way he had just moments ago. As he had stared at her arm, he had felt the familiar pressure building in the centre of his forehead, pulling him away to a reality where his daydream overlapped reality.

It was difficult to always remember what he had been dreaming, but this time he recalled at least a few of the jumbled images. Pulling out his sketch pad, Jack spread his art supplies across the table and started to draw what he'd seen.

"I should get to class." Tess rose, followed by Ashley and Conrad. "You got a free period?" Jack nodded, his pencil working its way feverishly across the page. "Alright, we'll catch you later then."

"Alright, oh hey, are we still on for tonight?" He lifted his gaze towards his friends to see their confirmatory nods. All except for Ashley, who shifted uncomfortably, her hand rubbing over her elbow self-consciously.

"Actually, I can't make it tonight," Ashley whispered, lowering her head to avoid his gaze. "I'm finally back at work, although I am only doing a few shifts for the next few weeks. Next time, okay?"

"Sure, but I can't promise not to spoil the movie for you." Jack smiled, finalising their meet-up arrangements before they left. Turning his page back towards his first sketch, he frowned as he realised he had moved on from the drawing of a bike resting on the pavement, to a picture of a dark figure standing in the doorway. He might not have recognised it as Ashley's kitchen if it hadn't been for the sheer number of times he, Tess, and even William had dined there, sitting on one of the distinctive barstools that was just visible at the edge of his drawing. The entire image had been sketched in black charcoal, except for the mouth of the figure, where a few red lines created the impression of blood-red lips. With a shudder, he turned the page, unable to recall what other images he had seen.

He leafed through his earlier drawings, stopping when he saw one of his grandmother seated on a bench overlooking a beautiful flower garden. His mother had told him for years to ignore her ramblings about psychics and gifts and understand they were nothing more than an extension of the fantasy she had created for herself, but Jack was sure he could remember her talking of such things even before his grandpa died. After his death several years ago, his nana had slowly started to slip away from them.

His mother said she couldn't face any world without him and had created her own reality in her mind where they were still together, as a way to keep going. His nana, however, told him she was journeying to a different existence, one where they would sit hand in hand on the bench of a beautiful garden and talk. When he showed her the picture he had drawn, she'd nodded, placing her weathered and wrinkled hand upon his with a smile that creased the corners of her wrinkled eyes. It wasn't long after this that his mother had made arrangements for her to be moved to the nursing home where Ashley worked, unable to keep up with her care needs as she deteriorated. She spent more and more time in her make-believe world, and it took a toll on her physical body. Now, she spent her days sitting in her rocking chair, gazing out of the window with a faraway expression, only pulling herself back from time to time to talk with Jack.

On one of the occasions he had visited, it had been almost as if she had awoken from her dream to the sound of his voice. She said his grandpa had told her to return to prepare him for what was to come. She had spoken of their family history, and how their tree could be traced back to one of the well-known oracles of ancient times. She told him stories of how their family tree had once been filled with Seers, and she could see that gift in him trying to awaken. It had been around that time he had felt the first tingle in the centre of his forehead, and a few days later when he saw his first nonsensical daydream. They hardly ever came at an opportune time, and so he committed what he could to memory, sketching them when time allowed.

Flipping through the pages, he saw as many vague and bizarre images as he did ones he could identify. He stared at the tombs and gasoline for a moment, before flicking forward to a moonlight sketch of the bandstand, with a figure lying on the steps. This he now recognised as a scene from Ashley's attack. If he had realised sooner what it was trying to tell him, perhaps he could have warned her... changed the future. He flicked through the many images, returning to the sketch of the kitchen, his finger tapping on the page as he wondered exactly what he could say to Ashley. She knew better than to open her door to strangers, so perhaps he was seeing it wrong, perhaps it was showing him a friend coming to visit. But if that were the case, he was unsure why looking at it made him feel so uneasy. Next time he saw her, he would speak with her, although he had no idea exactly what to say.

∼

Will sat in the small waiting room at the Taphouse. Tonight was unusually busy. There were two others who had arrived before him, and a few younger teens, smelling of alcohol, had stumbled in after he had taken his seat. He would never dream of coming here without his faculties in check, but apparently they had special codes for donors whose blood contained additional substances. He eyed the people before him, wondering if he had seen them here before, nodding his head politely when they looked in his direction.

"Liam7, we're ready for your screening," called Whitney's familiar voice from the door. As her gaze fell upon him, her smile seemed to brighten and she raised her hand, beckoning him through. "Take a seat. You know the drill, I have to make sure you're healthy."

Pushing a hand through his tousled hair, he took a seat in the cushioned leather chair inside the booth and produced his index finger, flinching when the small pin pieced his flesh.

"Let's see." A drop of blood pooled from the pinprick on his finger before being absorbed into the tab attached to the handheld device. "Hmm, count's good," She glanced up at him with an unusual expression. "I didn't think you'd be donor-ready for a few weeks yet. Okay, let me just remove the Tapped-out status." She glanced up again. "You know, your recovery skills are remark—" She stopped abruptly, looking at the device in her hand. Removing the tab, she placed a clean one in, repeating the drop test. "Huh."

"What is it?" Will stiffened as her eyebrows furrowed.

"MA+MI74. I don't know what your new regime is but I've not seen a blood purity this high for a long time."

Will looked up, his own expression mirroring her disbelief. Since he had first started letting here, he had been a consistent sixty, so to have a reading of seventy-four seemed unbelievable. It was no wonder she had rerun the test.

"If you want to continue with the donation, you'll be in a different banding than normal." She checked her device again, reading the information from her screen. "Let's see. For this, you are entitled to a twenty-five percent share of sales, but the banding is premium. If I list you, you're likely to be tapped-out by the night's finish unless you set a limit. Payment will have to be made via a transfer."

"Really? I thought you only did transfers for amounts exceeding—"

"That's correct." She nodded. Her hand traced down his arm as his mouth hung open for a minute while he tried to find the right words.

"I think I need to sit down," he gasped.

"You *are* sitting." Whitney's laughter was like the chiming of a fine bell, delicate and musical. Its harmonious sound seemed to return him to his senses and he straightened in his seat. "So, shall I list you? If you get Tapped-out in a single night, you're going to feel rotten. I could still put a limit on, you know, to make sure you stop before you get the shakes."

He watched the young woman's finger trace across the small spot of blood from his finger, her own eyes igniting as it touched her tongue. He knew she was a preternatural; after all, it had been Whitney herself who had first suggested the sampling of other preternatural blood in order to gain a temporary stat boon. She had worked here for a while now, and since she always found time to talk to him, she knew exactly why he was doing this, and her advice had helped to raise his figures from fifty-eight into the next banding bracket, meaning he took home a slightly higher percentage of sales.

"Not tonight, I really need the money."

"Is Devon's clan still hassling you for protection money?"

Whitney stroked his arm gently before giving his shoulder a reassuring squeeze.

"I couldn't let things carry on. It would have destroyed Gran to lose the shop. She thinks of it as the last piece of my dad."

"I'm pretty sure she'd be more hurt to lose you. Just be careful, okay?" She held his gaze for a moment, almost as if she wanted to say something more but then thought better of it. Her vision returned to the device in her hand. "You're about to go live, you may want to get comfortable. Have you linked to our system?" she questioned, pulling on her gloves and breaking open a container filled with syphons. He nodded. "Great. Lean back, enjoy some movies or whatever takes your fancy. Tonight, all entertainment is on the house."

"Seriously?" he questioned incredulously, straightening as the first syphon was placed on his skin. "Everything is free for purity of seventy and above. It's an incentive to come back."

By the time she was finished, five of the little creatures lined his left arm and were already swelling with his blood. Each one would consume 7.5 mls—the measure of a tablespoon—then disengage to fall into the tray that slotted just underneath the cushioned area of the specially designed armrest. As the bite wound was still open, a designated server would be on hand to attach another to the same position. This way, the donors would only suffer minor markings, which healed into small silver scars that eventually faded with time.

Whitney had been serious when she had advised he would garner a lot of interest. No sooner had a syphon disengaged than it was served to the next customer. Looking at the projected display from his device, he could see the back order. It seemed he had, as predicted, caused quite a stir of excitement. Within the hour, he was attached to more syphons than he had ever seen, and for the first time was donating with both arms, which had long gone numb. Whitney applied a cold compress to the bruising that occurred from prolonged exposure to the syphons, but he was past the point of feeling its relief. He offered her a smile, pleased it was she who had been assigned to him. Given the demand and his willingness to give until he was Tapped-out, management had insisted he had someone with him at all times to keep a constant vigil on his blood count and state of mind. He would have been lying if he said he wasn't enjoying her company. She was so easy to like.

"That makes a pint," Whitney stated, updating the record as the seventy-fifth syphon disengaged. A server entered, retrieving the deposited creatures with a quick smile. Normally, when he donated, Will opted for a twenty syphon limit, which would allow him to return on other nights and in the long run ensure he was able to give more donations per month and, when every penny mattered, even four extra syphons made a difference. "Your count's still good. Do you want to carry on, or call it a night?" He glanced at his tally, a cold sweat breaking out on his forehead as he saw the figure of his sales.

"How many more can I do?"

"Another twenty-five would take you to our maximum donation level," she advised, refreshing the compress. It was so cold his skin had turned red, and yet to him, he still felt the heavy numbness of his limbs.

"Do that then." He smiled at his earnings, knowing he could not only pay off the rest of the year's loan, but be in good standing for next year. He didn't even feel a wave of guilt as he planned his next visit to Ashley's house. If one syphon of her blood could boost his purity and count this much, he could earn a living on letting alone. Especially since he had been expended before partaking. The fact she thought Liam to be a vampire would only serve to ensure she didn't get too close to realising who he was. Although he swore he had seen recognition in her eyes. On some level, especially given her reaction to his touch earlier, he was certain she knew it was him.

"That's it for tonight, Will," Whitney announced, wrapping his arms in the cool, healing salve compress that encouraged the wounds to close, before bringing him a sugary drink. "You know the drill—drink, eat, rest. Before that though, can you sign the transfer consent?"

With great difficulty, Will raised his arm, pressing his thumb to her device and an instant alert from his own notified him of his inflated bank balance. He leaned back with a satisfied smile, allowing his head to rest upon the cushioned support, all his former feelings of guilt now but a speck on the distant horizon.

∽

Ashley felt the tears burning her eyes as she heard the familiar rapping on her back door. Each gentle tap felt like a physical blow. Liam had made a habit of calling on her in the evening, somehow seeming to know the instant she had finished her shower. Grabbing her housecoat, she slipped it on. He had already made it clear he didn't like to be kept waiting.

She felt his eyes rake over her, causing her to tighten her gown subconsciously. Stepping inside, he walked past as if he owned the place, and pulled the stool out in a gesture that, in any other circumstances, may have seemed gentlemanly. With a flourish of his arms, he motioned for her to take the regular seat at the breakfast bar. But as she approached and her gaze cast toward the tiled floor, he grasped her wrist, pulling her body toward him, his lips pressing against hers reminding her, once again, that *he* was in control. She stepped back, wiping her mouth with the back of her hand as she turned away.

"I prefer you without the gown," he whispered, licking his lips. Ashley felt his words echo around her ears, aware her hands were moving of her own accord to unfasten the cord. He stepped closer to her and a look resembling surprise flashed briefly in his eyes, almost unnoticeable before his hands seized hers as he took over. "Tonight, I want something a little different."

Moving behind her, she stiffened as his hands traced up her body to the neckline, pulling the silk robe down until the soft rustle of fabric against the floor could be heard. "Never forget I own you. You're mine," he whispered, pulling her close, brushing his lips across her neck as his fingers traced the lace pattern of her bra. He seemed to hesitate before removing his hands.

Ashley felt herself shudder, fearing what he had in mind. He had never used his thrall on her before, and the fact he did so tonight terrified her. She didn't want this to be how she remembered her first time, trapped in the clutches of a blood-thirsty monster.

"Sit," he whispered, his eyes once more surveying her as she moved without hesitation to obey his command. She felt the silk of her gown wrap around her shoulders, accompanied by a series of feather-light kisses across her neck. Her thoughts were flooded with new images, of his fangs tearing into her before he latched on, suckling directly from her. She had heard tales that it was a sought-after experience, that a bite was like an aphrodisiac, robbing its victim of all senses, but that was not how she remembered feeling in the park, and she very much doubted this would be any more pleasant. A sensual moan vibrated on his lips against her flesh, causing her to flinch. She felt his soft hand grasp her neck, pulling her back, exerting his control.

"Don't," she whispered breathlessly, feeling his other hand begin to trace up the jagged scar on her leg. She never thought it would be possible to relax when a syphon was placed upon her; not until she felt its damp presence on her thigh and his hand withdrew. Pulling her arms back through the gown, she tugged it closed, breathing a shaky sigh of relief. His hands returned to her shoulders, and she was thankful his unwelcome affections did not resume.

When the painstaking ordeal was over, he placed his lips to the free-flowing blood at her thigh, licking softly while his eyes looked up at her longingly. As he pulled away, she saw the wound had, as it had done before, healed.

"Kiss me," he whispered in her ear as she stood. "Kiss me like you would if I were Conrad."

Despite her attempt to resist, she saw his need as he looked down on her with fire and passion in his eyes. Her hands reluctantly lifted, tangling within his tousled hair as she pulled him close. She could feel the smile on his lips as they met hers with hunger, his hands moving over her greedily as he crushed their lips together.

He pulled back as if to savour the moment. "Until next time." He smirked, his gaze once more tracing her every contour. She looked down, fumbling to fasten the nightgown's cord. By the time she looked up again, he was nowhere to be seen.

CHAPTER 9

An unease had settled over her since Liam had left. Her trembling fingers checked the locks on the back door for what was easily the tenth time. Still locked, she assured herself. Yelping, she turned her gaze to the window as it rattled, relieved to see the overgrown privet scraping its branches across the pane. Her fingers went back to the lock, berating herself. She needed to be stronger than this but home no longer felt safe. He had sullied it, invaded her space and bent her to his whim. She knew vampires possessed a hypnotic thrall, but she had never expected it to be so dominating. She had tried to resist, to command her body to obey her own demands, but it had betrayed her. She was at his mercy, and with each visit he became a little more brazen, a little more possessive.

He had never used his thrall before, nor had he touched her the way he had tonight. Her mind circled, replaying the evening, recapturing the paralysis, the control, her weakness. Tonight he had been brazen, proving she was his to command. Clenching her fist, she glared to the darkness beyond the rain-streaked windows before focusing on her own reflection, determination setting her jaw. Just because they had an arrangement didn't mean she should let him hold power over the rest of her life. She'd be damned if she let that monster suck all the joy from her. Her agreement with him was one of necessity, but she was determined to file it away in the back of her mind and continue on, dealing with him only when necessary.

Ashley had been staring out into the jungle of a garden, wondering if she was still being watched, when a tickle of electricity charged the air around her just seconds before Conrad's sharp rapping sounded on her front door. She knew instantly who it would be. His presence always sung to her even before he came into sight. It was almost as though just being near him energised her, and burnt away all her problems. She thought back to that hateful kiss. Liam had seemed to savour it, but the only thing it had stirred within her had been the realisation of how much she longed to be held in Conrad's embrace, to feel his lips, the only ones she would welcome, upon her.

"Ashley, I know you're home." She shivered slightly. Nothing could rob her of the appreciation of how her name sounded as it rolled from his tongue. "Open up."

Flicking the kettle on, she shuffled towards the door. Rain hammered down outside, pouring from the blocked drain, sending a torrent of water drumming on the darkened paving.

There, in the dark, leaning breathlessly against the door frame, stood Conrad. Relief and fear mingled within her as she saw his intense gaze staring up at her through his dripping wet hair. His chest heaved, sending small billows of condensation from his lips into the rain. Rivulets of rain streaked his every inch, causing his t-shirt to cling to him. How she envied the t-shirt, wishing she could be that close.

He stepped inside, his faded jeans so tight that, now they were wet, they would need to be peeled off. She licked her lips, caught up in her relief at seeing him, allowing herself just one brief moment of indulgence as she imagined she would be the one to remove them. That was how a first time should be, wrapped in the embrace of someone you loved, someone who you could almost not breathe without. Not at the whim of a stranger who thought she was his property to play with as he saw fit. She had seen it in Liam's eyes tonight, the desire, and it scared her more than she could ever hope to express. She had seen Conrad looked at her with the same intensity, but when their gaze met, all she ever wanted to do was melt into his embrace and leave the world behind.

He pushed the door closed, and she braced herself for what was to come, but instead of harsh words she felt herself being pulled forwards, his arms wrapping around her with such firm pressure it stole her breath. Closing her eyes, she melted into his embrace, the sound of his heart, the warmth of his embrace, almost too much to bear. She pressed herself closer, seeking more of his heat, more of the protection his presence seemed to wrap around her. The cold wind howled through the house, its chill lost in the warmth of his arms, but then another thought surfaced. What if Liam was still outside, watching? What if he had witnessed her clinging onto this man with such desperate need?

A shiver ran through her as she recalled his words, *'Kiss me like you would if I were Conrad.'* He knew about Conrad! Fear stole her breath, her throat swelling with terror. He knew too much, far too much about her, about everything she held dear. He had already threatened Tess if she didn't cooperate, saying she would be found in possession of the exam papers from the tests she had aced. She would be shamed to the extent no one would think her sudden disappearance was unexpected. He was leveraging her friends against her, and even without his thrall she knew she would do whatever he asked. She would not risk them. But now he was showing her just how little control she really had. What would he do to Conrad, to her, if he understood how much she needed him, how he was her strength? If anything happened to him because of her—

"Hey, shh," she heard Conrad whisper into her hair. "It's okay, I've got you." It was only then she realised she was sobbing. Not just crying, but wailing in his arms.

Conrad placed the warm drink before Ashley as she sat on the sofa. Her racking sobs had become nothing more than small hiccups. He had intended to speak to her about today's events as they were too important to ignore. One look at that injury at lunchtime had exposed her lie. If she had been letting, there would have been more than one mark. The crook of the elbow was generally only used if someone wanted to disguise what they were doing, since the small silver scars left were often unnoticeable against the fold of the elbow. He had known something was wrong, and her reaction on seeing him only served to confirm his suspicions.

He wished he could have come earlier, but he hadn't known then what he did now. He had thought she'd be at work. Another lie. He, Tess, and Jack had watched a movie as planned. They had enjoyed a relaxing evening together and, with them parting ways so close to the time Ashley was due to finish, he had decided to surprise her and walk her home. It would have given them plenty of opportunity to discuss what was really going on.

He had stood under the nursing home's eaves for half an hour, sheltering from the rain, when the matron had stepped outside, asking if he was in need of assistance. It was only then he discovered Ashley had still not been cleared for work. With his stomach churning and heart pounding, he sprinted to her home. He needed answers and he didn't care if he had to drag her out of bed to get them. That mark had been distinctive. There was no denying the Y-shaped wound tied in with bloodletting, and yet Will's story sat uneasily, because he knew Ashley would never risk doing something so stupid. Not after what his mother had told them.

When she had opened the door, his heart had stopped. Her eyes were red from tears, their almost black shade of grey stirring his own sorrow. All his fear, all his concerns and questions, were pushed aside the moment he saw her, and the only thing that had mattered, the most important thing in the world, became holding her and making her feel safe. He didn't know how long he had stood there, grasping her firmly, enveloping her in his protection while his soaked clothes left a pool of water on the floor. He would have stood there all night, clinging to her as desperately as she did to him, but as her sobs calmed he lifted her in his arms, carrying her to the sofa before wrapping the blanket that hung across the back of the beaten leather chair around her. When she calmed, he lifted his arm from around her shoulders, hunting his way around the kitchen in order to make her a warm drink.

"I'm sorry," she whispered between sniffles. As he placed the cup down he felt her trembling hand grasp his wrist, almost as if she was worried he would leave. The welling tears in her eyes caused his chest to ache to the point where he found himself subconsciously rubbing it. When he found out who had caused her to shed these tears, there wouldn't be enough left of them to identify. He would tear them apart. It was a few moments before he trusted himself to talk.

"Does this have anything to do with what we saw at lunch?" he ventured. She nodded, her rust-coloured locks falling to hide her profile from his view. Stooping, he tucked her hair behind her ears, his hand cradling her cheeks as his thumbs wiped away the escaping tears. "Can you tell me about it?" She shook her head, her eyes shifting to look anywhere but upon him. "If I took you home, would you feel safe enough to tell me about it then?"

Her nod spurred a flurry of action. Pulling out his device he requested a cab, his vision panning the room until it fell upon the backpack she had left abandoned just inside the door. With a reassuring smile—he internally prayed it did not look like the snarl it felt like—he rushed upstairs to pack whatever she might need for an overnight stay. He stared at her laundry basket, filled with clean clothes next to her bedroom drawers and grabbed a few items before throwing in anything else he thought she might need. If he forgot something, he was sure his mother would be more than happy to lend it to her. His sole focus became getting her out of this house as quickly as possible and uncovering where he needed to direct his building rage.

～

Conrad cradled her arm tenderly. Now that he'd applied some anti-inflammatory ointment and cleaned the wound at her elbow, he could see many criss-crossing silver scars. When she'd lifted her nightdress to reveal the latest one, she flinched as he growled, his hands trembling so much it took him three attempts to remove the ointment lid.

"Why the hell didn't you say something sooner?" Conrad seethed, his finger examining the wound on her leg, noticing how it had sealed. He heard the protesting groan of wood as he realised his other hand gripped the chair's leg, and he attempted to slacken his grasp. What he didn't understand was why this monster was toying with her. The wounds had been healed, and yet the irritation on her arm confused him.

Vampires used saliva to seal their victims' injuries. Often the regenerative power meant no scars or marks were left. Yet this man—who had apparently saved her in the park as well—always left scars. He couldn't tell if it was his way of marking her, ensuring she remembered him in some twisted form of torture, or if there was something else going on that he wasn't quite seeing. There was no reason she should be scarred so badly, or have any reaction to the use of siphons, if he was sealing the wounds afterwards. Another question that bothered him was why this vampire was using this method to extract her blood when he obviously craved the intimacy.

The chair cracked again, a reminder for him to take a deep breath. "People like him never stop, not once they know you'll give in to them. He'll just take more and more liberties. Ashley, you should have said something."

"Why? It's not like it would make a difference. He knows about me, he knows everything."

"I could protect you."

Grasping her hand, he searched her eyes, wondering if she even realised there was not a risk he wouldn't take or a sacrifice he wouldn't make for her. He would protect her with every ounce of his being, every gram of his power. If she would let him, he would make sure no one ever hurt her again. He would make her strong, teach her all he knew. She would be able to stand alone, and yet he would always protect her; not because she was weak, but because without her he would be nothing.

He dropped his gaze to the floor, feeling his desire building. He could lie to himself no longer, he loved her, he wanted her for his own, but fate was cruel, it mocked him. He loved her so much, yet he knew anything beyond friendship would be impossible as he would not be able to suppress his need, his desire, enough to keep her safe. She was everything to him, and he could never forgive anyone who brought her harm, especially if that someone ended up being him.

"From a vampire that's who knows how old, who has measures in place to ensure my cooperation? I can't even fend off his thrall."

"Thrall? What did he..."

"Nothing. He wanted to make sure I knew he owned me."

"*He* does not own you." She flinched at the venom in his voice. He could feel the molten fury of his other-self begging for release. She had been wronged and, as an ifrit, he was not only aware of it, but was duty-bound to execute justice.

"He does. It's not just the thrall, or him knowing what I did. He knows about my friends. He said if I don't give him what he wants..." she shook her head, "and he knows about you, how I..." She trailed off but it was impossible not to notice the flushing of her cheeks.

"I won't deny he has us at an advantage," Conrad mused. "That doesn't mean we can't track him down. You said he uses syphons instead of biting. That means he has access to a Taphouse, or a supplier, and he knows about your personal life, so he probably attends or maybe teaches at the academy. Is there anything else you can tell me? Anything that stood out?"

She began to shake her head, pausing as a frown creased her brow. "It sounds silly, but I keep thinking I should know him. It's hard to explain, but when I look in his eyes I feel like I've done it before, and he has this way of putting his hands on my shoulder... it's hard to explain."

"I'm going to start looking into it. Why don't you take the guest room, get some sleep. You know you'll be safe here, right?"

She gave a small nod. "Conrad, this is bad, isn't it?" she whispered, accepting the hand he had offered to help her stand. He was reluctant to release her, his fingers disobeying his wish to pull away for longer than they should have.

"I think if he were going to tell someone he would have done so by now." He led her to the guest room, pausing at the solid oak door awkwardly as he bid her goodnight. As he turned to leave, she reached out and the way her fingers caressed his arm stirred a shudder from his core. She was making this impossible.

"Will you stay with me, please? I don't want to be alone." Her witch eyes held him under her spell, rekindling the desire he fought so hard to dispel. She stepped closer, erasing what little distance there had been between them. The floorboards creaked as she lifted herself onto her tiptoes, her hands sliding behind his neck, setting his skin aflame. It would have been so easy to steal the kiss he so desperately craved. All he needed to do was to stay still. But he wasn't going to do that. He wanted to protect her, not destroy her.

Her presence was like a drug, and he knew if he surrendered, if he allowed her soft lips to rest upon his own for even a moment, he would be ruined. It took all of his resolve to resist her, to turn his head aside and step away. Hurt and confusion flickered through her eyes as she looked at him questioningly. He saw the pain his rejection caused and closed his eyes. She would never understand. She was his world and to kiss her now would be to one day watch her burn. Few other beings could truly withstand the true power and passion of an ifrit, and there was one thing he knew for certain, regardless of her new preternatural status, and that was the fact that she was neither an ifrīt, or incorporeal. Anything between them would be disastrous. The way her heavy lashes dropped her gaze towards the floor ensured he regretted his refusal. The way his heart and mind fought caused him to seek a compromise.

"We could always watch a film until you're ready to sleep."

∼

Emily could hear the struggle, the loud scraping of the metal-framed bed against the concrete floor, and knew the newest Tabu was awake. One of the dream-weavers—as she called them—had left him just moments ago, leaving them alone again. She tried to call to him, to tell him that if he was still, if he was good, they would treat him well, and remove him from the darkened prison to a place filled with light where he would be looked after. Since she knew better than to raise her voice above a soft whisper, she doubted he could hear her. She wondered if anyone had tried to tell her the same when she had been in his position.

A thunderous crash reverberated in her ears, the deafening sound causing her heart to hammer in her chest. Pushing herself up slightly, she peered towards her old cell, watching in horror as a form crawled from the darkness. She raised her arm, trying to gesture him back.

The way the light glistened on his dark, matted hair as he crawled spoke of his fever. She cringed as she heard another noise, the grating of a broken chain scraping across the floor, getting louder the closer he came. She whispered a warning, telling him to return to his room, to be good, but he kept coming, the noise getting louder, closer, until she could smell the offensive odour of his perspiration and turned her head away, hoping his actions wouldn't cause the master to be angry with her.

"H-H-Hold still, I'll have y-y-you out soon," rasped the voice through chattering teeth. His movements were uncoordinated, as if his limbs were too heavy to be properly controlled. Closing her eyes, she lay still, hoping if she ignored him he would go away, but the tugging at her ankle, accompanied by the damp grasp of his trembling, clammy hand, betrayed his continued presence.

Opening one of her eyes, she peeked towards him, watching beads of sweat dripping from his jaw while his hand jerked during his uncoordinated attempts to push a needle into the manacle around her ankle. She hadn't given her bindings much thought, but had watched them being removed enough times to understand what he was attempting. She could see the crimson fluids on the needle's tip as it jolted from side to side with each of his attempts to push it into the place where the magnetic pin sealed her restraint in place. The trail of blood from his arm began to stain her bed, spreading out across the soft sheet she had recently been given. She gathered it protectively around her before casting a glance to her arm and confirming her own needle was still safely inserted.

His frown deepened as he tried again to drive it into the shackle. This time, despite the unsteadiness of his limbs, he was rewarded with true aim. When she heard the pin drop, she realised the familiar weight on her leg was gone. "C-C-C-Come on," he stuttered breathlessly.

Emily stared at him in dismay before turning away, not daring to look in his eyes for a moment longer. His dilated pupils made him look possessed, like a demon in the flesh. He was trying to tempt her, to make her disobey the master. But she knew better.

He grasped her arm, audibly swallowing back whatever fluids had given his breath the sour, acidic stench of decay. "C-C-C-Come on." He tugged at her, yet she refused to budge, refused to be part of his rebellion. The master was good to her, he looked after her, helped her get well, and saw she had wondrous dreams instead of haunting nightmares from which there was no escape. She would not jeopardise what she had.

Emily heard her sigh of relief as he finally gave up. Using her bed to pull himself to his feet, he staggered over towards the solid wall. Orange vomit sprayed from his mouth as he rested, panting as his tremors become visibly worse. She watched as he staggered a few more steps in the direction of the exit holding a distant staircase. He had made it only a few more steps when his eyes rolled backwards into his skull and he struck the floor, his body racked with spasms as vomit bubbled from his mouth. After a few moments he was still. Turning over, Emily tried to put him from her mind, pulling her blanket back around herself as she curled up and attempted to sleep.

"That's the second OD this week." Emily startled as she heard Devon's annoyed voice. She turned over to see him and another figure hunched over the body.

"You know not everyone is cut out to be a Tabu. They can't all be like our little Lightning Flash here." The figure saw her watching them and winked, his compliment bringing a smile to her lips.

"Take him to the ghouls. They always enjoy a good O.D." Devon's vision turned towards her, noticing the loose chains on the floor.

"I'm sorry, I didn't want him to, Mister Devon, I promise," she whispered, fear turning her skin cold at the thought he would blame her.

"Don't you worry, the master sees all. He was so proud of you. He says you're ready for a new home, a place with your own room, and a comfortable bed. He's making arrangements as we speak."

"The master doesn't want me any more? Did I do something wrong?" She felt the tears track down her cheek. "I've been good. I didn't want him to come near me. Please, I can be better."

"It's not a punishment, the master is rewarding you," Devon responded. He stooped down, lifting the shackle, giving her a smile as she presented her foot without being asked.

CHAPTER 10

Will entered the cafeteria, his gaze searching each crowd for Ashley. He had lingered outside her Cryptobiology class, keeping just out of sight, waiting for her, but she had been nowhere to be seen. Neither had Conrad, which had annoyed him no end. He knew it would have been impossible to overlook her, she was like a beacon to him, more so now than ever before. He licked his lips, his thoughts lingering on the kiss. The warmth of her lips on his was everything he had ever imagined it would be. In time, he was certain he could divert her affections and, if not, he could use the healer's voice on her again.

It was only since partaking of her blood that he had discovered this new ability. His grandmother's handwritten texts said it was common for a healer to possess a thrall-like quality in order to better calm and aid those in need, and to encourage people out of a dangerous situation. It had many applications, including a hypnotic effect. He hadn't meant to use it on her last night. He still remembered his own surprise as her hand went to her gown, unfastening it. At first, he had eagerly misinterpreted it as an invitation. Despite what he was doing, he thought his kindness, his easy conversation had won her over. After all, she seemed to like a bad boy if her history was anything to go by. It was only when she tensed at his touch that he realised what had happened. He had masked his disappointment well. If she wouldn't warm to him of her own accord, then he could use his new-found talent to possess her in other ways.

Since last night, he had been experimenting. It seemed his healer's voice only worked for short times, and outside his aura of influence the effect was rendered useless. He wondered if he could find a means to extend it, to plant a thought within her mind that would grow each time he nurtured it.

"Well, if it isn't Liam7." A heavy hand fell on his shoulder. It belonged to a voice he would never forget. Devon. "I must say you surprised us last night." The wicked grin turning the corners of Devon's lips made him falter and, shrugging from the vampire's touch, he took a moment to compose himself, passing his hand through his golden hair. He would have tried his influence again, but he and Devon had matters to attend to.

"New diet." He shrugged, dipping his hand into his jacket pocket to remove his device. "I was looking for you. I want to settle the loan."

"I guess business was profitable last night." Devon's arm snaked around his shoulders as he inhaled. "You still smell delicious. Tell me, does this new diet have a name?"

Will once more shrugged free of his touch, lifting his device, hoping to return to the business at hand. "I-I told you. It's a new diet, detox."

He hoped the heat coursing through him wasn't betraying his lie. His heart sped as a consequence he hadn't even considered reared its ugly head. The Taphouses issued their own aliases for privacy reason, to ensure things such as this didn't happen, but Devon knew him, he'd been the one to introduce him to the establishment as a way of making payments in the first place. All at once he was relieved Ashley wasn't here. If Devon could still smell the effects of her blood on him, surely he'd have no problem tracking it back to the source.

"Oh, now you wouldn't want to be holding out on me." The way

Devon was playing with his device caused his stomach to churn, wondering what outlandish early settlement fee was about to be added. He was surprised when Devon placed the device before him, displaying the outstanding figure with no interest or additional charges added. Placing his finger to the device, he confirmed the transfer. "The buzz from last night got everyone talking. Come on, we're friends, you can tell me."

"I really can't. Maybe whatever buzz you felt was from the purity level or something."

"Hmm, maybe." He gently slapped Will's face, causing him to flinch. "I don't suppose you've given any more thought to my offer?"

"Sorry, no. I like the Taphouse, it feels... safe."

"Your loss. Well, that's our business tied up. That is, until next year. It's been a real pleasure."

~

Devon watched as William made the worst casual, hasty retreat he had seen for a long time, a smile twitching at the corner of his lips as he idly turned his device over.

"So, is he the next target?" whispered one of the small group he chose to associate with.

At first, he had really detested being assigned to the campus by his clan's leader, Vincent. He thought, after his previous indiscretions, it had been a way of showing him he was still a child in his eyes. It was only as things began to evolve that he understood his placement here. The Academy was the only tertiary learning institute in this territory, and not only did students travel a long way to attend, but some stayed on campus and many chose to get jobs to help cover living expenses. Being here gave Devon unfettered access into the lives of the students, their connections and friends. Having eyes and ears around the campus was a way to learn about people. Someone was always talking about that prude at work, the person who enjoyed to party, or the person no one would miss. Students gossiped, and he and his group listened, marking targets from idle gossip to become their next Tabu. That was where the real money was made. The Black Card Menu was mostly Tabus, which was the name given to people dragged from their pitiful life only to be infused with whatever poison their selective members sought. Those who showed high tolerance and the possibility of extended production were later sold off in silent auction. With stock usually rotating every month or so, everyone was happy. Especially Devon. His reputation had blossomed in his clan, many thinking of him as a favourite amongst their leader.

"No, it wouldn't do to have him vanish. He's too high profile at the moment. Besides, what would it look like if someone who had just paid off our protection were to vanish? No, Liam7 is fine just the way he is."

Leaning his chair back against the wall, he surveyed the room, keeping his attention divided between the idle gossip of those near and his device. They were in need of some more Tabus. After the latest disaster they were down to just fifteen, of which six would soon be auctioned to a new home, usually for use in whatever prestigious event they needed catering.

He had left William's information open. The corner of his mouth twitched smugly as he opened the location data. He had hoped William would have been willing to give up the source of his boost, but when he spun his first lie he knew there was no point pushing him too hard, not when he could obtain the information easily himself. Studying the device, he saw there was only one place he had frequented recently that didn't tally with his previous activity.

Whispering into his second's ear, he excused himself, his anticipation rising. He had some duties to attend to, but first, a little daytime reconnaissance was needed. If William could produce such pure quality product by taking a boost from whoever lived at that address, taking it from the source directly was bound to hold no comparison.

Today had been the first day Ashley had been cleared for work and, with a shift request pending, she intended to take advantage of it. Her work had always been more than a job to her. She loved spending time with the elderly residents, listening to their stories, helping with their needs. She always thought of them as extended family and found she missed their company. Besides, the awkwardness about what happened—or rather didn't happen—with Conrad yesterday refused to give her peace. Her mind ran in circles, questioning if she had misread the signs, misinterpreted the gestures.

She had been waiting, ready to transition their friendship into something they both seemed to want. Even now, as she replayed her moment of humiliation, she swore there was no mistake. She saw the same desire burning in his eyes as she felt rise within herself, his gaze often so intense it caused her breath to hitch. After everything that had happened, she decided she was done waiting and that she would make the first move.

Somehow, she had been mistaken, clearly overlooking something people who dated knew to look for. The moment she had discovered her gift all courting had stopped and when her parents died, boys were the furthest thing from her mind. Until Conrad, she had simply possessed no interest in a relationship beyond friendship, even though she had noticed the way Will sometimes looked at her. Although maybe that was something she misinterpreted, too.

Last night, they had fallen asleep on the sofa watching a string of terrible movies, laughing at the poor acting or the terrible special effects while sharing ice-cream and popcorn. His arms around her shoulder had brought her more warmth than any blanket. She had fought to stay awake, fought to savour every second until she drifted asleep in his arms. When she had woken with her head on his chest, listening to the soothing sound of his heart, she hadn't wanted to move. She had wanted to stay there in his embrace forever, or at least for just a moment longer. There had been nothing but the two of them and she dared to dream that one day, she could raise her chin and wake him with kisses... kisses he would return.

She would have stayed like that until he stirred, just relishing their closeness, but her morning needs saw her slipping from his grasp and when she returned he was making breakfast. Part of her wondered if he had been awake, savouring the moment as she had. Then she recalled his rejection and everything became awkward, a strained silence neither seemed to be able to fill.

She had agreed to skip lectures in order to inform his mother of what had been happening. She had just finished taking a new round of blood to see if the virus had been completely destroyed when the notification had come through from work, asking if she was available to come in early now her temperature had abated. It had been the perfect excuse to leave.

Conrad had taken her home on his bike so she could change. After last night, the thought of being so close to him unsettled her, and while he had offered to take her to work and pick her up, she had insisted on taking her own bike. Of course, that hadn't stopped him riding with her, even though it meant slowing his motorbike to a crawl to keep pace as she pedalled.

As she dismounted, a notification had come through from Liam telling her he would be visiting this evening. Conrad had taken her hand in his, promising she wouldn't be alone and arranging to meet her from work. He said they needed to talk about what happened last night, and his words had left an empty pit in her stomach. This agreement seemed so long ago now, and her shift had passed all too quickly.

Pulling on her jacket, she grabbed her helmet from behind the reception area, hardly able to believe she was going home already. Her shift had passed without incident, although when it came time to unchain her bike she felt the nervous flutter of butterflies in her stomach. Glancing at her watch, she gave an approving nod. It had been a long time since they had let her leave at seven. They were short-staffed, but after a quick phone call from the administrator, the matron had insisted she take off early. Strange, but not unheard of if the night was expected to be a quiet one.

Her device flashed as she sent the notification to Conrad; nothing complicated, just a quick message to say was starting for home and would meet him there. If nothing else, she knew she could spend the next fifteen minutes preparing herself. Her gaze probed the dim lighting as she unchained her bike, her attention focusing on Whiskers, the nursing home's adopted stray, as he foraged in the undergrowth, no doubt waiting for his supper.

The moment she found herself on the road, her concerns drifted away. There was nothing else in her world, just her and her bike. She pushed her fears and doubts through her legs, using their power to propel herself forward, faster, harder, as she climbed the hill leading to the park. Closing her eyes for a brief moment as gravity began to take over, she sailed downhill, relishing the feel of the cold wind upon her face, the freedom of her hair billowing behind her. For just a moment, all her worries had been left behind and she felt at peace.

As the downhill road turned into a level run and the park gates made their appearance to her left, her legs began to pump the pedals, her breath quickening from exertion. The crunching of tyres alerted her to a vehicle behind her. Tucking into the curb, she made sure they had plenty of space to pass. The headlights bathed the road before her in their cool glow, and for a moment, as they pulled past her slowly, her stomach churned with tension. Once they had passed, the driver sped up, his tail lights disappearing into the distance, but the uneasy feeling remained, reminding her of what was to come this evening, wondering what exactly Conrad had in mind. It wasn't as if he could reveal himself to Liam.

When she reached the park entrance, the shadowed silhouettes of a small group of loiterers wolf-whistled. Their darkly clad figures almost blocked the entire entrance, instantly putting her off cycling past them in order to cut through. She decided to stick to the road skirting around the park instead. She found herself pedalling more slowly, unease mounting in her stomach as she reached the halfway point, closer to home. The once-dispelled fears began to rekindle, memories of Liam's touch, the thought of Conrad's rejection, all causing her pace to slow. Tonight, she would have to face them both, a prospect she wasn't looking forward to.

Her bike wobbled slightly, warning her to increase her speed just moments before headlights once more flooded the road before her. The roaring engine showed no signs of slowing as the car rushed past, far too close. She cursed as her handlebars jerked, her balancing faltering as she wrestled to regain control. Unable to recover, she braced herself for the fall. The impact of her body slamming against the pavement knocked her sick. She had been so focused on the horrors awaiting her at home, she hadn't even noticed the streetlights here were out until the world around her suddenly became bathed in red as the car's brake lights illuminated the dark street and the passenger jumped out.

"I'm so sorry, I didn't see you in this darkness, your back light must be out. Are you hurt?" the male apologised. He crouched down, offering his hand. Pulling her to her feet, he patted her arm firmly, before stepping back, checking her over.

Confusion washed over her as she saw the strange fletching left in her arm where his hand had struck. He moved quickly, hooking his arm under her as her legs gave beneath her. "Steady."

Pins and needles began to spread throughout her body as her eyelids became heavy. She knew then that his words were only meant to satisfy the curiosity of any passers-by. She glanced around for help, but no one, not even the group who had been obstructing the park entrance, was anywhere to be seen. Even the lights had extinguished on the car, bathing everything in a stifling blanket of obscurity. Her bike, abandoned upon the pavement, was the last thing she saw as the figure lifted her into his arms, carrying her towards the car. His voice echoed as she felt herself succumbing to the darkness. "We'll circle back and deal with the bike once we've taken her to Devon."

Conrad checked the time on his notification against the current time and resumed pacing. Ashley should have been here fifteen minutes ago. He looked at the time again as another minute ticked by. Pushing his helmet on, he hopped onto his bike. She should have been here. His engine purred as he brought his bike around. It would only take him a few minutes to check she was okay, to find her on the route home. He knew he was being paranoid. She had probably had to nip back into work for something, but he would feel safer knowing and, for the last fifteen minutes he had felt a steady chill creeping over him, starting deep in his core, the same place that her presence sang to.

This had gone on long enough. Once she was safe at home, he was going to tell her all about himself, what he was, reveal the horrific visage of his other-self, the form that sent people screaming, the form his ex-girlfriend Rei had called horrific and unlovable. If she could still bear to be near him after she had witnessed the monster within, maybe he could also make her understand why he could not claim the kiss he so desperately craved. It wasn't that he didn't want her, he wanted her more than he could ever hope to express, but it was impossible. She deserved the truth. She deserved more than him sitting awake on the sofa holding her, praying she wouldn't wake for a little longer so he could savour the closeness, the comfort that being near to her brought him. If she couldn't accept him for what he was, if she reacted the same way as his last girlfriend, then at least he wouldn't have to concern himself with being unable to resist the temptation of her advances.

The street near the park was bathed in darkness, reminding him of the recent outbreak of vandalism. Flicking his lights onto main beam, a reflection of light blinked into existence. Dazzling at first, the chrome beckoned his attention as he recognised the discarded frame. Touching his brakes too hard, his bike skidded to a halt, falling against the road with a loud crunch as he jumped from it, running to the abandoned bicycle. The name Afterglow stencilled upon its frame struck him like a solid blow. Removing his helmet, he pushed his hand through his hair, turning full circle as his gaze desperately panned the surroundings, hoping to spot her. He called her name, and when she didn't answer he did the only thing he could think of. He called his father.

A car slowed as it drove around his abandoned bike, the passenger asking if he needed help before continuing on their way. Unable to think, he removed his device just as it started to chime.

"Tess, I was about to call you." He could hear the tremor in his voice giving away barely a tip of the torrent of emotions he was feeling.

"Are you with Ashley?"

"That's why I was going to call. She was meant to meet me at her house, but when she didn't show I went looking for her. I don't know where she is. I've found her bike, but..." He trailed off, his vision once more desperately searching the surroundings, hoping to find her, to find answers. The more he spoke, the more he felt his panic rise. This could not be happening.

"I'll be with you in five." The call disconnected, leaving him to wonder exactly how she knew where to find him, but his time for reflection was soon interrupted as the flashing lights appeared at the end of the street.

He watched helplessly as his father's car pulled up, followed by another black vehicle with three other Blue Coats inside. He sent them to question the nearby residents while he cordoned off the scene, his vision continually flitting to his son with a look of obvious concern.

"Give me a hand moving your bike, Con." As he lifted it up, his father swept up the plastic shards from the broken indicators. It was busy work, but Conrad was glad of the distraction as he wheeled the bike further away, resting it on the kickstand. His father watched him, opening the passenger door of his car as he returned. "Come sit, tell me what happened."

"Has her chip been disabled?" Conrad questioned, the moment he pulled the door closed.

"First things first, tell me what happened." As Conrad relayed the events of the evening, he noticed his father open the windows, dispelling the building heat that had misted the glass, creating a blur of flashing lights and shadows. As he brought his account to a finish, Conrad turned, holding his father's gaze.

"Has her chip been disabled?" he questioned again.

"You know I can't tell you that."

"Dad, this is Ashley we're talking about. After what's been going on, there is no way this can be random." Pushing himself back, he heard the seat protest against his sudden and violent shifting of weight.

"Right. Now it's time to let me do my job. You go home, there's nothing more you can do here." A slight rapping on the back window alerted him that one of the Blue Coats was seeking his attention. After a hushed exchange, a small zip bag containing something was passed through the window. "Do you recognise this?"

Conrad studied the smashed contents, the sight of them rekindling memories of all the times he had placed his hand upon Ashley's. "That's Ashley's watch," he confirmed. "Why would someone remove something so valuable?"

"It's the latest model," his father said, turning the bag over in his hands as he scrutinised the contents. "It has a tracking feature inbuilt in case someone got into trouble or broke down. If so, the watch can be used to send an instant SOS without the need to go through the chip identification process."

He heard what his father hadn't said, that the feature had been added in case someone was abducted and their chip disabled. It was an extra measure of security included due to the growing concerns.

"Okay, Con, you've done all you can. Try to get some rest. I know I promised not to say anything about what we uncovered, but I think at this point I need to let the precinct C.O. in on what we know about Ashley. That way, he can start looking into known trading rings. I'll open a line of communication with P.T.F. and see if they can locate her brother. He needs to know what's going on, and maybe he knows something about her origin that will help."

"Dad." Conrad's hands were grasping the legs of his jeans so tightly that his fingers cramped. His gaze remained unfocused, with the threat of unshed tears forged from anger and fear. He couldn't bring himself to say what he wanted to.

"I known, son." Reuben patted his hand gently. "I'll do everything I can. In the meantime, don't do anything rash. Head home and fill your mother in on the details."

"*Rash?* You think I can just sit around and do nothing when Ashley's been taken who know where, for we can only imagine what purpose? If you think I'm going to sit around and do nothing—"

"That's precisely what you're going to do. We already have people looking into the disappearances."

"And how's that working out?" he snapped. "Last I heard, you're running into dead end after dead end."

"But we have something we didn't have before, a crime scene. We don't even know if it's the same people. They're been careful before, but leaving her bike was careless. You getting here when you did could be the only reason we have what we do. But there's nothing more you can do here. Let me do my job." Conrad couldn't help but notice that, despite the assurances that they would do all they could, his father never once said they'd get her back, and he saw a shadow in his father's eyes he'd never seen before.

When Conrad stepped out of the car, he saw Tess and Jack straighten, their pale faces looking washed out against the glow of the emergency lights. Someone must have told them he was being interviewed, because they had been waiting for him, their hurried footsteps closing the gap at speed. Their expressions of concern and fear were no doubt a mirror of his own.

"Conrad, thank goodness! No one would tell us what happened." Tess pulled him into a quick embrace, her gaze drifting towards the bike currently being examined. "What's going on?"

"Not here, there's too many ears. But just answer me one thing.

You knew she was in trouble, didn't you? That's why you called." Tess nodded. "You've been tracking her using her watch."

"Yes. I knew something was wrong. The notification came on that she'd left work. When it didn't dismiss, I checked her data. I was hoping she'd just lost it. I gave it her so I could check on her, especially with everything that's been going on and the insane hours she was working."

"Tess, you have a spare key to Ashley's. Can we head over to her place? There's still a chance to get a lead." Conrad glanced around, ensuring no one was close enough to overhear. "If Liam is how they discovered her, then our best hope is that he doesn't know what's happened and we get answers."

"Who's Liam?" questioned Jack and Tess almost in unison.

"I'll explain everything on the way."

∼

Ashley's small house stood bathed in an oppressive blanket of darkness. While it still looked like the same place where they had shared movies and created fond memories, it somehow seemed darker. It was a place no longer filled with laughter and friendship. Devoid of their friend's presence, the charming, ramshackle property in need of a few touch-ups had morphed into a broken shell, cold, rundown and abandoned.

When Tess had opened the door, he had stood for a moment upon the threshold, savouring the lingering scent of her clothes and hair. The drink he had brought her just last night still sat abandoned on the small coffee table, awaiting her return. He stepped inside, plucking it from its place and swilling it in the kitchen sink. He had decided it no longer mattered who knew what Ashley was, what she was capable of. She was already in the worst imaginable danger and so, as he pottered around, returning things to their places, tidying her home just a little for when she returned—because she would be coming home—he told them everything. Every single detail. Including about Liam.

"I can't believe all that has been happening under our noses, but I knew something was off." Jack sighed as Tess dropped heavily onto Ashley's sofa.

"What do you mean?" Tess questioned, shifting slightly to remove the headphones she had managed to sit on.

She tossed them on the table, where Conrad scooped them up, wrapping them tidily. He sat for a moment, before finding something else that needed his attention. The fragrances he associated with her were everywhere, reminding him of how he had failed to protect her. If only he had ridden to meet her like he wanted to; but he had been grateful for the extra few minutes to decide exactly what he was going to say, and now he may never get the chance.

"That day Will said he saw her come out of a Taphouse, it didn't sit right, and I drew this." Jack tossed his open sketch book onto the table.

"What's that?" Conrad lifted the book, his gaze lingering on the black charcoal figure before being drawn to the adjoining page, which showed a discarded bike on the pavement. He stood in silence for a moment, flicking through the sketches, a frown creasing his brow. "What are these?"

"Pictures, images I've seen. I can link most of them to things that have happened," Jack confessed. He glanced to Tess. "I told you my nana said we're from a family of Seers. I think that's what these are. I've been seeing." He raised his fingers, drawing air quotes around the final word.

"You drew these?"

Jack nodded as Conrad flicked to the beginning of the book. "Tombs and gasoline?"

"That's one of the few I can't figure out."

"I think this was about Ashley. After she was bitten, she was going to seal herself in a tomb and incinerate it, rather than live as a vampire," Conrad disclosed, his grip tightening on the book as he turned the page to the picture of the bandstand. "She told me the night she stayed at mine, but when my mum uncovered what she did about her, the plan changed." He flicked to another image, a carving of Medusa, her neck being pierced by Perseus's swor, bordered on one side by shadow.

"I think we have other problems too," Tess warned, glancing up from her device. "I just checked Ashley's historical location data. Given everything you told us, it seems obvious, but I wanted to make sure, she's never been near a Taphouse. So why would Will say she had?"

"He had to know more than he let on. We should get him here. Maybe he knows who this Liam guy is. After all, he has been cosying up to the vamps lately."

CHAPTER 11

Darkness enveloped Ashley, her eyelids refusing her demands to open despite the rising dread that surged through her. Her mouth felt dry, lacking the saliva needed to ease the unpleasant taste in the back of her throat. Mind racing, she tried to reconstruct her last few hours. She had been on her bike, that much she remembered, but everything else was a little hazy. She probed her memories for answers, wondering if she's been in an accident, but then, when she heard the voice, a cold dread sped through her and everything came flooding back in a nauseating realisation.

"Assign her designation FAB-EB98V." The voice seemed to echo in her ears, the sound bringing some awareness to her body. She could feel a cold breeze upon her and her finger finally twitched in response to her attempts to move. She tried again, relieved when this time her finger obeyed with only minimal delay.

"What's her poison?" asked someone to her left. A strange heat swelled within her. The room, even through closed eyes, felt as if it were in motion. Moving her head to the side she vomited, flinching as a cool cloth wiped the mouthful of bile from her skin.

"With a purity like that, none. We'll get her listed on the Black

Card Menu tonight. When Devon told the master he had something special, I never expected this. I don't think I've ever seen figures this high. It must have something to do with the Elder blood."

On hearing this, panic consumed her and her arm jerked, hoping to connect with her kidnapper, except, for all her effort, it didn't move far. The movement caused pressure around her midriff to increase, returning the waves of nausea. She jerked again, still gaining no leverage, this time feeling the sharp bite of tight leather around her wrists and elbow, pinning her arms to her side. "Looks like she's coming round. I thought you said she'd be out for hours," scolded the voice.

"She should have been."

"Not to worry, she's not going anywhere. Those bindings have held shifters far larger than her." Ashley heard herself whimper as a firm hand grasped her face, turning her head from side to side as if studying her. "The Elites will be fighting over themselves for this one. We'll exhaust her tonight, that's for sure. I don't think she'll cause us much trouble after that."

"What do you think he'll want to do with her?"

"Could go either way. If we treat this one right, we could keep her on tap for years before we see any degradation of quality. We'd have to cycle the houses, of course. But there's always the chance he'll sell her on. Depends on how tonight goes."

The voices began to fade, as if whoever was in the room with her was leaving. She tried to pry open her eyes, once more finding them unresponsive.

"You think there's something worth bidding on, aside from the purity?" At his words, she felt herself stiffen, knowing, for the moment at least, they had not uncovered all her secrets. She had to make sure that remained true. She needed a plan, an escape. But first, she needed to regain something more than just the sporadic control of her arms.

"I can't tell. But that charm she's wearing nearly turned my hand to cinders, and the only reason someone would wear something like that is if they needed to hide."

Finally finding her voice, Ashley screamed, crying out for help, hoping someone, somewhere would hear her. It was a short-lived sound, countered by the paralysing charge that ripped through her body and plunged her back into the dark abyss.

∼

Will pounded on Ashley's front door, each strike seeming more urgent than the last. When he had received the emergency notification from Tess asking him to come to Ashley's house immediately, he knew something was wrong. After being let inside, Tess filled him in on her disappearance and all of a sudden the room felt suffocating.

"What do you mean, Ash was abducted?" Will paced, pushing his hand through his honey-coloured hair in distress. This was his fault, it had to be. Or maybe someone had been watching her, waiting for an opportunity to strike. But if that had been the case, then he would have noticed. After all, he had spent many a night lurking in her garden, waiting for his visit.

"They only found her bike, her chip has been disabled. The Blue Coats say it matches the MO of the other abductions." Tess's voice was filled with panic, and the way she sat huddled close to Jack, his arm around her, showed the extent of her distress. "They even had the sense to remove the watch I gave her." She sniffed, barely holding herself together.

"What can I do?" Will sat for a second before rising once more and pacing. "Shit, this is all my fault." His hand passed through his hair again.

"What do you mean, your fault?" Conrad demanded. Turning towards him, Will was overcome by the intense glare being levelled at him. Tugging his collar, he turned away before removing his light jacket. It was really getting hot, and he was certain he wasn't the only one to notice.

"I had to take out a loan for protection for my gran. I was struggling to make the payments so I started going to the Taphouse more often," he began, knowing there was nothing for this situation but the truth, no matter how shameful. It could be their only chance of finding Ashley. "I was working my way back through the park. I was exhausted. My final letting put me back to Tapped-out but I'd barely reached their threshold, anyway. I remembered what one of the servers said about getting a boost if I ingested some blood." It was a partial lie, but Will was about to confess his greatest sin. They didn't need to know everything.

"Everyone knows that only works for other preternaturals," Jack interjected.

"But technically he is one, he's a healer," Tess deduced. "It just never manifested in your dad."

Will nodded, tugging his t-shirt as sweat began to prickle his upper lip. "What's that got to do with—"

Will felt his head snap back and Jack's voice sounded muted as a fist connected with his jaw just seconds before another strike followed, driving him into the wall, where the only thing he could do was raise his arms to shield himself while Conrad lashed out verbally, each word punctuated with another crippling blow that stole the breath from his lungs and sent swarms of darkness across his vision. Blood poured from his nose, each twisted expression of pain causing his swollen lip to split further. The devastating blows kept coming, pummelling his torso and the arms he barely managed to raise to shield himself. The agony of every strike jolted through his body and he continued to scream even when the pressure abated. With his legs too weak to hold him, he slid down the wall as the pressure pinning him there abated and, through his defensively raised arms, he saw Tess and Jack wrestling Conrad away, his eyes maddened with vicious hatred, the like of which he had never seen before.

"Conrad, what the hell?" demanded Tess, the strain in her voice revealing the effort it was taking to restrain him. Will knew the only reason they were succeeding was because he didn't want to hurt them. With punches that powerful, the two of them would have no chance of restraining him, not unless part of him let them. Perhaps he was even finding a measure of control through their touch.

"He's Liam. William healed her in the park," Conrad spat, his eyes narrowing. "That's why the scars are so prominent, why he's never bitten her. So what, you were Tapped-out, your energy waning, and you thought you'd just have a taste?" Conrad growled, shrugging himself free of Tess and Jack as they stood staring at him in disbelief.

"Yes," he admitted, cradling his midriff. "But if I hadn't, she would not have survived. Luckily, her blood gave me a boost, enough to finish healing her."

"That's why there was no blood when I found her," Tess commented, her disgust clearly evident. From the weight of their repulsed looks, he had to wonder just how much they knew, how much Ashley had dared to tell them. He tried to move, pain splintering through him despite his own energy already working to repair the damage.

"The thing was, I'd been so exhausted, and then her blood... it rejuvenated me and I never remember feeling so powerful."

"So you went back for more." The fire in Conrad's eyes scared him and sweat—or perhaps it was blood—trickled down his face as waves of heat washed over him. There was no doubt in his mind, the only reason he was still alive was because Tess had positioned herself between them, her dainty hand and manicured nails pressed firmly against Conrad's chest. "You used your friendship to manipulate her, some kind of glamour to make sure she didn't know who the hell you were. You terrorised her in her own home, threatened her friends, and—"

"I'm not proud of it. I was desperate. You don't understand. Devon said if I fell short again, Gran would have an accident, just to remind me how seriously I should be taking my debt. He'd already had me steal data from the faculty office to make up a minor shortfall. I couldn't take the chance. I used a glamour charm, my letting name, and implied I was a vampire. I knew her blood would help me get my count back up and I could let again."

Conrad, whose expression had turned smouldering, clenched his fists, clearly using every ounce of restraint to control himself.

"Who did you tell?" Conrad growled. His fist connected with the kitchen door frame with a splintering crack. Tess jumped, retreating backwards a step. For a second, Will was just relieved he hadn't been its target.

"No one, I swear."

"So how did someone find out about her?" Tess pressed, as Conrad turned his back to them. Will could see his shoulders heaving, hear the slow, deep breaths. He was furious, and the subtle change in his aura suggested he was fighting hard not to shift. It was at that exact moment that Will realised exactly how much Conrad had been holding back. He was on the verge of change, his anger and distress so extreme that whatever lived inside him was clawing for release, hungry for the blood of the one causing such internal disharmony. He released a shaky breath, wondering if any of his friends knew Conrad's secret. He was preternatural. What exactly, he couldn't be sure, but given what he was seeing, a shifter of some kind seemed likely. No, not a shifter, some manner of fire elemental.

"I went to the Taphouse a few nights back. My purity was seventy-four, I'm normally a sixty, turns out that caught a few people's attention," Will explained, his voice lacking any strength, as he stared at Conrad's back.

"Her blood made yours purer?" Jack questioned stiffly. "She made you feel more powerful, rejuvenated you, and we know she can also reverse unwanted transitions, which was maybe what protected her from being changed after the attack... Oh shit." Jack snatched his bag from the sofa, his hand grabbing something Will couldn't quite see from within. "Shit, shit, shit," Jack repeated before he dared to interrupt him.

"What?"

In response, Jack opened his sketch book, flicking through the pages before throwing it on the coffee table. Trying to see what was so important, he pushed himself upwards a whole few inches before collapsing back down.

"Isn't it obvious? She's a Phoenix, a Perennial."

Will bit back through the pain, pulling himself to his knees, crawling to the chair to drag himself up high enough to see the drawing on the table of a woman engulfed in flames with what looked to be flaming wings expanding behind her.

"Impossible. They were hunted to extinction," Tess interjected.

"Apparently not." Jack gestured again towards the drawing.

"There's a bigger issue," Conrad announced, finally turning back towards them. "They won't just want her for her blood. As I told you, my mum ran her blood, and it showed she had Elder blood and an unknown lineage. What I didn't mention was, if the wrong people get hold of her, her life is over, they'll think she's a breeder."

"What?" Will questioned, sending a fresh dribble of blood from his split lip as a looming feeling of dread built in the pit of his stomach. "No, that's impossible. Breeders aren't preternatural, and she incinerated those guys at the park. I mean instant ashes."

"Because her life was in danger. If she's really a Phoenix, she's not just Elder blood, she's part Perennial and trust me when I say if you have two parts, one doesn't like it when it's locked away. My mother said her necklace had layers of seals. Each new septennial, a preternatural's power increases. She was almost seven when she was given the necklace, then when she hit puberty she discovered she could remove an unwanted transition with a kiss. My mother thought this septennial would see the seal's power fail."

"Wait! So that's why she kissed all those people?" Will asked incredulously. Suddenly, her actions made more sense. The manner in which she would single someone out of a crowd, how no one ever spoke about what she did, and the way her friends, instead of stopping her, made ridiculous bets.

"We used to call it Salvation's Kiss, because before becoming a Ciele she said her name was Ashley Salvation," Jack answered.

"Salvation?" Conrad echoed. "As in one of the seven Perennial families believed to have been involved in the creation of the barrier?"

"What have I done?" Will despaired, clutching his side. He was grateful for the support of the wall at his back. Conrad's punches had hurt like hell, but there was no doubt in his mind he had been pulling them, holding back.

"Sold your friend to into a nightmare where she'll be drained and passed between blacklisted Elites to swell their ranks with sovereigns, that's what," Conrad snarled.

"So what do we do about it?" Will asked, consciously moving his energy towards the worst pains, despite knowing he deserved to feel every agonising throb.

"We rescue her, hopefully before someone realises exactly what they have." Jack snatched his notebook from the table, bringing his attention to Will for the first time. There was no question about it, not one person could stand being in the same room as him. Not that he blamed them. He didn't like himself at this moment, either.

"But where have the abductees been taken?"

"My father was working on a theory that it was being done by one of the Taphouses. The earlier abductees had *all* visited the same chain, but it only allowed them to get a warrant to search the property and check their records. Everything came back clean. They couldn't apply any further pressure since all the victims also all went to our academy, and had other connections, but it was after this the MO changed and became more random. Since nobody has ever been recovered, there's no evidence of their fate, and no clues as to where they were held."

"So they could still be alive," Will muttered softly.

"Don't be naïve. If we're going to act, we need to do so now, and discreetly. Chances are the Taphouse is already under surveillance by someone in my father's team"—his eyes met Will's, causing him to shrink back—"which is the only reason your friend here is still breathing. He's a familiar face there, we need him."

CHAPTER 12

*D*evon straightened his tie, smoothing out the wrinkles from his black, form-fitting suit. Even after only two years as Vincent Master's head of acquisitions, he still appreciated the feel and look of this rich material, and if he was being honest with himself, he knew how amazing he looked. The clothes had been tailor-made and, whilst he wore the casual trimmings of a student while in the academy, here he was required to dress to his position.

The Taphouse, like many things in society, was divided by class. The commoners would dine, drink, and partake in their vices in the tavern-like area below. Whereas those of standing would reserve one of the many suites. Not all within the grand luxury of the Elite world were subject to all the benefits of this status. Tonight, there were but a few whom his sire, Vincent Masters, had approved for their special Black Card Menu.

This Elite menu was nothing more than a business card with the name of the establishment beautifully penned in golden ink upon the high quality card. Except its surface held a secret. When exposed to a low dosage of ultraviolet light, it would reveal the categories along with the abbreviation of the opiates in use with their Tabus. Within one minute of exposure the writing would fade, leaving no evidence of its existence except in the mind of its recipient. Such methods were but one way they ensured their illegal dealings remained unseen.

Entering the suite belonging to his sire and clan leader, Vincent Masters, Devon placed the card before him. His heart was aflutter with excitement, knowing his most recent addition to the Black Card Menu would be certain to please. Bending slightly, he placed his mouth to Vincent's ear, whispering softly the identity of the woman brought in tonight, FAB-EB98V. His sire's approval embraced him and, with a smile, Devon took his seat, sinking down into the luxurious armchair. Vincent owned this establishment and many of the local franchises, and had only a few years ago pulled Devon through the ranks into his most trusted circle, leaving him in charge of Tabu acquisitions. This recent morsel, however, had been his crowning glory.

Vincent raised the card to the small lamp, its specialised light illuminating the menu, critically studying the list of available Tabus.

"This appears to be a good selection. Any difficulties?"

"The new recruit was a little loud, but a good jolt from the collar soon brought her into line. I doubt she'll repeat that mistake again. It worked a treat, just as you predicted." Devon smiled. The most frustrating thing about breaking a new Tabu was the noise they made, the screams and cries for help. This new collar would ensure a peaceful transition, maybe even a speedier one. Although they had been warned not to use it during any Tabu's opiate-induced delirium.

"That would be the near pure one? I think tonight, myself and my esteemed guests will partake of your latest acquisition. If these predictions are correct, we'll discuss a plan to extend"—his eyes cast to the almost faded ink on the card to confirm the sex—"her longevity."

Devon never normally partook in the merchandise, but it was Vincent's insistence that tonight they all sampled the treat before them. The syphons were served upon a golden platter, their outer membranes allowed a few moment to become crisp. With a nod, they each took one, waiting for their sire's permission before placing the creature into their mouth.

Devon felt his eyes widen as a uniform silence followed the initial popping sound created by the breaking of the syphon's shell. The rich fluids pooled in his mouth, creating a cacophony of sensations. Teasing the fluid with his tongue, he closed his eyes, lost to the rapture of its unique bouquet. He could taste the power, the raw and primal energy, and it was more than he had ever imagined could be possible. As the first moan of delight escaped him, he couldn't even bring himself to feel self-conscious, unaware that others around him mirrored his euphoric elation. For one long minute the world around him ceased to exist, and his existence was but himself and the overwhelming sensations that engulfed him in their rapture.

"Pray tell, where did you find an unprotected Elder?" Vincent questioned, sucking the remnants from between his teeth as Devon's eyes opened. Looking around, he saw the sated expressions of his fellow clan members before his gaze turned to his sire, surprise marring his features as he beheld something unfamiliar in his gaze.

"She's a local, would you believe?"

"How is it conceivable that not one of our clan scented her? With blood this potent, she should have been brought into our fold long before now." There it was again, that look, hunger, desire, and still there was something else, an unanswered question.

"That's just it, she's veiled somehow. Her chip, before we deactivated it, showed she tested human."

"Refuse any cina-cu offers and ensure a fifty syphon limit. When business closes, I intend to examine this female myself."

Devon nodded, wondering what had got his clan leader so intrigued. He couldn't remember the last time Vincent had shown any interest in their Tabus, but there was something in his eyes that was positively aglow, and the fact he was dismissing any cina-cu offers spoke of his intention to feed from her directly himself.

"As you wish." Devon excused himself to notify their guests

accordingly. Cina-cu was available for each one of their Tabus. For the right price, the selected party would be relocated to an isolated feeding room just outside the basement area, where they were permitted time with the Tabu alone and allowed to partake directly from the source in almost any scenario they desired. While the syphons were delicious, when it came to good quality blood there was nothing quite like it being drawn fresh and warm from the body, and the qualities which made this female so desirable to the Elites would only be enhanced in her presence. Many liked to hear their victims beg, or feel their warmth as they fed and, for those special few, for the right price anything was possible.

∽

Conrad's foot was tapping uncomfortably as he sat in the back seat next to William, his fists clenching and releasing. It was taking every ounce of control he had not to reach across and crush the breath from his body. As soon as William had mentioned about the boost, everything had fallen into place. Until then, he had never known what it meant to see red. He wasn't sure exactly what had happened. He remembered fighting off a crushing rage and then Tess and Jack had been pulling him back, away from William's bloody figure. He wished he remembered the satisfying feeling of striking him.

He didn't feel remorse. He wanted more, to do it again, and the fact he'd had the nerve to heal his injuries made him want to keep hurting him until even his body wouldn't know how to repair the damage he'd done. Even in his mind, he showed restraint with this fantasy, because the only thing he truly wanted was to destroy him, body and soul. He wanted to drive his fist through his face and not stop until there was nothing left but an unidentifiable pulp and shattered bones. He was alive now for one reason, and one reason alone. He was needed.

In front of him, he saw Tess jump as her device erupted into a siren-like wail. Answering it quickly, she turned to face the passenger window as if it would afford her some privacy. But the small confines of the car were unforgiving, and while he couldn't hear who she was speaking to, her own whispers were perfectly clear.

"Lex," she whispered, cupping her hand over the microphone. "I'm so glad you called...Yes, how did you?" She was silent for a few moments, nodding her head as if he could see. "Yes, of course, as soon as we know anything," she reassured the caller, lowering her device with a pained sigh.

"Who's Lex?" Conrad questioned. He leant forward, making an effort to unclench his fists.

"Ashley's brother." She raised her hand, stopping further questions. "I've been keeping him updated on how she's doing while he's away," she explained. "He's part of the task force on the other side of the barrier. Your father managed to get a message to him, he's heading back." She glanced outside, but before Conrad could ask anything more she spoke again. "Okay, Will, we're almost in position. Are you ready?"

"Drop me here," he muttered. "I'll walk the rest of the way. I'm sure the Blue Coats will know your car since you've been told to stay away." Conrad hated that something logical had come from his offensive mouth. But he had a point. His father would have alerted whoever would be watching the Taphouse, and he knew Conrad would not be able to sit idly by. Which was why he was sporting the ridiculous-looking cap, for when he had to do his part.

"Don't screw this up, you've already caused enough trouble." Conrad glared at him as he stepped from the car. When this was over, when Ashley was safe in his arms, Will had better watch his back.

∼

The Taphouse waiting room was packed. While normally quiet this early, it was the start of a weekend and everyone wanted some extra drinking money, a way to continue the party beyond their budget.

The overwhelming scent of alcohol drifted from a group of teenagers in the corner, the heavy odour tainting the air as the girls busted out the latest provocative dance moves to the music blaring from their device, making them seem more like private lap dancers to their male counterparts. Not that they were complaining.

"You, out! I've told you before, no underage drinkers. This is your last warning. You come here again and it'll be the Blue Coats escorting you out, not me." Whitney clicked her fingers twice towards the group, before pointing towards the door, left ajar in the hope of clearing the drunken stench they carried with them. One of the young men jerked aggressively towards Whitney as he passed, uttering curses and threats. Instead of the intended startle he expected, his effort was rewarded with a clip across the back of the head that shocked him into silence.

Whitney scanned the waiting room, her expression brightening as her gaze fell on Will. "Liam7," she called, gesturing him inside. He glanced towards the waiting patrons, knowing he was skipping the queue. Linking her arm through his, she escorted him towards the only empty booth. "Okay, you know the drill."

He produced his finger, noticing her usually friendly smile was bearing the weight of an unpleasant evening. He extended his finger, flinching as the sharp needle pricked his flesh. His reaction brought a genuine smile to her face as her musical laughter filled the air.

"I don't get you," Whitney said. "You'll sit for hours with those the syphons and don't even blink, but one little prick and you jump out of your skin." The small tab affixed to her device chimed, letting them know the reading was ready. "So today you're MA+MI72," she advised. "To be honest, I didn't think you'd make the count so soon, but you're looking good. Do you have a limit, or do you want to run like last time?" There was something about the way she looked at him that made him feel exposed. A light frown creased her brow, but it was dispelled within a moment.

"Can we see how it goes?"

"Sure."

"Who's in today? Any new faces?" Will pried, glancing between the booths.

"You know we don't discuss..."

"I don't mean names. I was just wondering what my competition was like," he hastened to add, knowing if Ashley was here somewhere, even unseen, her ranking would give her away in a heartbeat.

"Ah, well, you can rest assured, no one here has anything on you." She winked.

"Historically, or tonight?"

"Need an ego boost, do we?" she teased. "You're the highest for about a decade. We had one guy, years back, around your range. Real fitness nut, big muscles and an ego to match. But why don't you just ask me what you want to?"

"What do you mean?"

"I am part of the screening process for a reason." She tapped her temple.

"You're a telepath?" Will felt the heat flush across his face, now understanding the strange expression he had seen just moments ago.

"Of sorts."

"Then, can you answer my question?" Not wanting to voice anything so incriminating aloud, he put extra effort into projecting his thought.

Whitney winced, the same way someone did when someone had shouted in their ear. He watched her eyes study their surroundings as if to ensure they had complete privacy. "There's no one I know of higher than you, but the Elite seemed excited about something. Not that I have access, but I can feel something even from here." Catching his next thought, she continued to answer. "I'm not sure about the missing people, but a number of them were in our systems." She glanced around again. "I can't say any more, except perhaps that I have heard rumours of a Black Card Menu. Although I've never been able to prove anything."

"What's that?"

"Rumour has it the Elite get their own menu as well," she whispered, attaching the first of the syphons. "I can't be certain, because people in there know how to shield their thoughts, mostly. I did hear rumour of Tabus—you know, people who have other less kosher substances in their blood. Of course, that practise is illegal and I've found no evidence of it happening here, after all, you can't really call the stray thoughts of blood-drunk Elites evidence."

"So, if they have a source beyond us common folk, where would their donors be? Are they on site, or is it shipped in?"

"That's just it, I don't know." She squeezed his hand gently. "I hope you find your friend," she whispered, before excusing herself.

He wondered if she knew what he needed to do and was deliberately turning a blind eye. On her way past with another donor, Whitney gave him another one of her million-watt smiles.

CHAPTER 13

While Will investigated the donor area, Conrad, pulling his cap down as far as possible to avoid recognition, entered the main Taphouse, cosying up to the bar.

"Credentials," demanded the young man behind the counter. Rolling his eyes, Conrad lifted his wrist, giving the best bored expression he could muster. "A pleasure, Mr Mendel." He dipped his head, clearly recognising the name. "We have a few items in this evening that one such as yourself may enjoy, if you're looking for a boost." The young man passed him a menu, which went blank for a second, before the display altered, updating with the latest donor and removing the one whose services were no longer available.

His device buzzed, revealing a message from Will. He read it quickly, bristling. Did Will really think he needed *his* help? Of course he knew places like this had their own selective menu; his father was in law-enforcement, after all. His annoyance must have been apparent as the barkeeper stepped back half a pace, tugging his collar. An odd reaction, given how many troublesome customers he must deal with on a daily basis.

Turning his focus back to the server, he returned the menu,

noticing the vibrancy of his eyes as the golden flecks burnt with the fury he felt, a sign his other-self was restless. He blinked, trying to dispel his tumultuous emotions, but his thoughts were lingering on Ashley, on how William had betrayed her. "I was informed you may have something more... upmarket."

"Can I draw your attention to Liam7?" The opaque menu changed before his gaze, revealing the premium list. "He is a regular, our clients have been very satisfied."

Conrad let out a slow breath. "I'll confess his stats are good, but when I partake, I find males have something of an unrefined, bitter taste. They don't agree with my palate at all." He tapped his finger on the bar for a moment as if in thought. "My mother's considered amongst the Elite. I have certain expectations and a taste I became partial to in my old haunts. I came here because I heard that you were one of a few places in this backwater city that had something of a Black Card Menu."

He played the entitled brat role well. He had known so many of them, and had even moved in their circles for a time during his mother's prestigious events. His mother was a woman of means, and his father had been the recipient of a number of medals and honours in his own line of work, so their success raised his status. He leaned lazily forward on the bar, winking mischievously at the young man who was becoming more flustered.

"I see. Unfortunately, I'm afraid our establishment doesn't offer such services."

"Really? I seem to remember being here recently." He produced a midnight black card from his pocket, twisting it idly within his grasp, hoping he had selected the right shade. There were only certain shades of black which could hold temporary menus. His father had retrieved a few before now, but being blank except for the tavern name, any evidence that had once been upon them had been lost, and no trace of chemicals suggested that whatever had been upon its surface eroded quickly and without a trace. The server eyed the blank card with confusion, the genuineness of the reaction a clear indication that if something like this was occurring in these walls, only certain people were privileged to the details.

"Very well." Conrad gave a sigh. "Are there at least some Elite areas vacant?" He placed his fingers to his temple. "I can't be expected to sit amongst the rabble."

"I'm sorry, sir, Elite areas must be reserved in advance. We have an opening next Friday, if you're interested."

Pulling up his calendar on his device, he shook his head. "No good." He allowed his frustration to edge his voice as he mentally vowed to hunt down anyone who so much as hurt a hair on Ashley's head. Without another word, he turned to leave, his device subtly snapping a few more photographs, ensuring to get one of the mechanism separating the Elite area from the commoners.

～

Vincent's eyes travelled the contours of the female before him. By human standards she was attractive. Her rust-coloured hair framed her face in a tangled mess that betrayed the desperation of her struggles. The eyes that glared at him with a mixture of fear and hatred sent a tickle of amusement through him. He could see the power of her Elder blood in her glare. If she was older, trained, she would have been a formidable trophy, but she was something better, she was vulnerable. Never before had it been possible to restrain any member of the Elder bloodlines. Not only were they too well protected given their sovereign status, but they were too well trained, too powerful. He had managed to get a number of them to agree to lettings in exchange for services. Their power was formidable and whatever force restrained this female's gift didn't dilute her blood, it just made her easy to control since no power would answer her struggles.

Leaning close, he inhaled, noting the lingering odours of lavender, honey, and—he lifted her hands, bringing her fingers to his nostrils—antibacterial hand wash. Her skin glistened with perspiration, but she seemed to have no scent. Bringing his finger to her clavicle, he traced his finger slowly along the bone before wiping the escaping tear from her eye and bringing it to his lips. He wanted to confirm what he believed he had tasted before, and the moment his taste-buds registered the ambrosia of her pheromones, he was certain.

Placing an arm around her shoulders to lift her from the bed slightly, he touched her face again. The whimper she gave as he traced her jaw with his fingers sent a shiver of delight through him. He had long dreamt of this pleasure, of having one of such powerful blood helpless before him. He felt his base desires stir as he lowered his lips to her throat, his tongue savouring her taste. His breathing quickened, desperation enveloping him. He would wait no longer before succumbing to his desire. His fangs unfolded like a snake's as what appeared to be his canines hinged forwards to uncurl the hidden remainder of his predatory teeth. At the same time, his tongue pressed upon the gland at the roof of his mouth holding the anticoagulant agent, avoiding the secondary one; he wanted his prey to feel every last sensation. As the fluid coated his fangs, he took another long, slow breath before sinking them deep into her flesh. He felt her tense as she cried out beneath him. His hand braced against the side of her head, keeping her still as he drew the first mouthful of fluid with a shuddering breath. He could feel her struggling, her legs attempting to kick as she flung her body first one way, then another.

Screams pierced the air as he suckled greedily, her distress sending a tingle of electricity jolting through him. She was so much more than the syphons had revealed. With every mouthful of her life-fluid, he felt himself strengthening as a vitality he hadn't known for years filled him. He felt invincible, unstoppable. He noticed the moment she became limp within his arm, when the fight faded from her and her screams became muted whimpers. He knew he should release her, allow her time to recover, and yet he was reluctant to end this feast. His tongue traced her flesh, greedily devouring the ruby fluids that had mingled with her sweat. Pulling away, he saw Devon watching him from the cell door.

"She has breeder potential. Move the silent auction forward. We cannot keep this female here, she's too high profile. The way her abilities have been sealed, her scent disguised, all suggest she's been hidden by some powerful beings. We need to unload her quickly. Attend to the notifications, mark her as an Elder blood breeder. She'll fetch a good price, especially for those banned from acquiring breeder services. How many other Tabus do we have ready for re-homing?" Vincent wiped his mouth. Her blood had left him thrumming with power and he intended to utilise this feeling while it lasted.

"Seven including her, but she's not broken."

"Not our problem. That's what restraints were made for, after all. Get her cleaned up and into something presentable." He caressed her face once more, suckling the tears from his fingers. Any other time, he would have kept her for his own, but it was too risky. Especially since he knew the Blue Coats still held him as a person of interest regarding the abductions.

～

"What now?" Jack questioned as they regrouped. He had made it obvious to Tess that he hated how everyone seemed to have a part to play but him. Will had got to scout out the donor area, Conrad the lounge, and now she was studying the pictures the two had managed to take. Just moments ago, they had detached the small plug from the port of their device, placing them in a small petri-dish style container, while Tess copied the images across.

"Well, thanks to Tess's gizmos we were able to bypass their privacy security measures, but I'm not sure how much good allowing the camera to stay active actually did." Will transferred the data to Tess's device. She held a finger up as several pieces of software sprang to life, running a program she had created on the fly while waiting for the two to return from reconnaissance.

"Okay, good news, none of the active donors are on the missing person's alerts," she said finally, her brow furrowing.

"Bad news?"

"I can't see any way to bypass the locks to the Elite area without access to their system. It requires fingerprints as well as access credentials. It's updated nightly, so there's no chance we're getting in there without getting past their firewalls."

"So it was a waste of time?" Will chimed in.

"Not really." Tess zoomed in on the system screen where the orders were displayed. "I can't hack the security systems without direct access, but the menu system—now, that's a different matter. But I can't do it from here, we'd be too easy to track."

"Where to?" Jack questioned, the engine roaring to life. Tess glanced at her watch. It was a little after half nine. It seemed impossible that only two and a half hours had passed since her friend had been abducted. This last hour felt like a lifetime.

"Drive to the city," she commanded, programming a route into his navigation system before reaching under his seat to remove an old slimline laptop, complete with integrated keyboard. It was an ancient treasure, just what she needed for something like this.

"How long has that been stashed there?"

"Since forever," she answered, as he started to drive. The route she planned would offer enough varying signals, tethers, and networks to ensure no one could track them. Removing one of the—as Will had called them—'gizmos' from the container, she affixed it to the book-sized laptop. "This'll let me hop between each establishment's connection. Even if they figure out what's going on, they won't be able to pinpoint us. It'll look like I've bounced the signal."

"I have no idea what you just said. You do it, I'll drive."

"How are you still at the academy with those skills?" Conrad asked.

The smile that spread across her face sung of a hidden secret. "I probably should have come clean when we were sharing, but I'm not actually a student. I work there. I'm the new engineering and programming mathematics lecturer."

The silence was punctuated only by the sound of her fingers

rapidly clacking upon the keys. She gave an internal sigh. She had been waiting so long to tell everyone, and now the person she wanted to know most, the person she wanted to celebrate with, might never be found. She wiped a tear from her eye before blinking away more. She needed to focus. If Ashley was here, she *would* find her.

"Wait! You what?" Jack glanced towards her briefly before returning his focus to the road.

"No! But you have a class with me!" Conrad interjected.

"To refresh the basics. I've been working as a lecturer since my last exams."

"Basics? *That* is not basics," he announced incredulously.

"It is when you grew up in a house where such topics were considered playtime." Tess fell silent, diverting her focus back to the task at hand.

"What about Cryptobiology?" Conrad queried.

"I thought it would be fun, plus it was a good excuse to spend time with Jack and Ashley." Tess paused for a moment before her fingers once more became a blur across the keyboard. "Right, I'm in."

"That seemed easy," Will commented.

"I used the menu as a back door to the system. Now..." Her eyes scanned fervently down the screen as the files copied. "Nothing about a Black Card Menu, but there's a separate account for the Elites, but only some of them. So..." she trailed into a series of mumbles before disconnecting the laptop from any network connections and taking time to study the captured files. "These are too big, their profiles are ten times larger than the others. So if I... and then... got it."

"What've you found?"

"I'm not sure yet." Several long moments passed, the only sound that of the engine humming almost silently as she studied the data before her. "It's some kind of separate account. We're talking big money. LFFB+NM64, EFB-MI68, SMMB-NM64V, there's a whole lot of these numbers. I'm just not sure what they mean."

"I'm not sure about the first two letters, but everything after is blood rankings. I'm MA+, male A-positive, NM means non magical, MI means Magic Innate. If we're looking for Ashley, you're going to want some high number values. Do you know her blood type?" Will offered.

"She's AB negative," Conrad advised.

"So look for FAB-MI and a high number."

"There's only one AB, FAB-EB98V."

"What's EB?"

"Elder blood, perhaps?" Conrad volunteered.

"There's no way Ash is a virgin." Will frowned. "Is she?"

"Actually, she is," Tess announced sternly. "She's not really had time for relationships, with trying to pay the bills and study. It's hard enough to grab a few hours with her friends, or hadn't you noticed?"

She saw Will close his eyes as an expression of regret crossed his brow. It was clear that until recently, he'd thought she played fast and loose. Tess imagined it was an easy assumption for him to make, given how many times he had seen her kissing a complete stranger. He had probably assumed her sex life was the same.

"I'm a real bastard," he muttered, covering his eyes with his hand.

"No arguments here," growled Conrad, before turning to Tess. "Any sign of where she's being held?"

"I told Lex about the Taphouse theory and he sent over blueprints. Cross-checking them against the photos you took, all the areas are accounted for, but I seem to remember about four years ago it was closed for renovations after a fire,"

"I remember. We were going to watch the new superhero movie from beyond the barrier, but the whole block was cordoned off," Jack added, checking his blind spot before filtering into traffic.

"What if the fire had been an excuse? What if instead of just interior repairs, they added a basement?"

"So what are we going to do?" Will questioned, flinching as a car sped past them too quickly on the inside lane.

"I'm not sure, but we're going to have to do it quickly. One of the hidden files is a bidding invitation. They're going to sell her off."

"We need to call my dad," Conrad insisted.

"I'll send the data now, but by the time they mobilise it could already be too late." Tess typed quickly, attaching the documents, sending them through to the Blue Coats while including Conrad's father on the message personally. She hoped they would see it in time, but even if they did, with the length of time it would take to get the necessary paperwork, it was unlikely they could mobilise quickly enough, especially since it seemed they were planning to move Ashley along with six of the other captives tonight.

"If you can find a way to her, I'll get her out," Conrad asserted. "I just need a way in."

"Sure, the all-powerful Conrad," snapped Will. "You've not been doing a very good job of protecting her so far."

"She wouldn't even be in this situation if it wasn't for you."

"Enough!" Tess's voice commanded the car. "That's enough. So here's what's going to happen. Will, go back and blood-let, say you've found yourself with some extra time so you thought you'd give more. Once inside, place this on any of their monitors. It will allow me direct access to their interface and thus their security system. Jack, I need you on standby outside. Keep the engine running and keep your eyes open for the authorities. I'll be loitering close enough to piggy-back on their system and use the access without drawing suspicion. Conrad, you're the only one of us who can walk about in there. With Will's chip in place, I can trick any door into opening for you, but you'll have to be near it so I can find its location on the security network. Find the basement, get her out. I won't have visual, so I will be relying on your verbal cues." She gestured for his hand, placing an earring in it, while putting its partner into her own ear.

"You're a shifter. I assume you have some skills at your disposal. What kind are you, anyway?" Tess held his gaze. While he had disclosed he was preternatural earlier tonight, claiming himself to be a shifter, he hadn't actually told them what he was. She was certain the only reason he had shared this information was because he knew they would need someone to scope out the other part of the

Taphouse. She hadn't told him they'd already had their suspicions. Ashley had looked at him in a very distinctive manner when they had first met, so there had been no question of him being human.

"I've got it covered. If you can open the doors, I can get her out."

"Cocky, much?"

"Not cocky, just unwilling to compromise." Tess saw Conrad look at the earring in his hand. Gritting his teeth, he pushed it through his unpierced earlobe, wiping away the small trickle of blood. "Testing, one, two, three," he whispered, receiving a thumbs-up from Tess.

∞

Making his way past the crowded tables, Conrad threw his shoulders back, adding inches to his height and an air of confidence to his gait. Knowing the layout of this Taphouse from his earlier visit helped, as it allowed him to saunter straight past the booths to the segregation door. In the guise of scratching his earlobe, he tapped his earring three times, the agreed signal, before bringing his thumb to hover over the sensor, aware that the young lady behind the bar was watching him closely. When Tess's voice echoed in his ear confirming it was ready, he reached out, pushing the door, his heart pounding.

It opened with an almost silent click, and the server smiled as he glanced back, giving a polite nod. To his left, a grandiose staircase served to escalate the Elite above the land of the common-folk. He knew that to follow the ivory marble stairs would be to look upon unparalleled luxury and privacy. It was not the place to locate a sordid den of inequity. The Elite enjoyed their taboo luxuries and their thrills outside the law, just so long as they could plead ignorance. The kind of establishment that offered Tabus always protected the money-bringers, thus they would house their victims separately.

Skirting down the corridor that ran parallel to the staircase, he briefly acknowledged the carved statue artwork of the solid handrail which would, hopefully, obscure him from the view of anyone who descended. He could hear Tess speaking in his ear, telling him what to look for, signs of a third door, one not present on the blueprints. Each step caused the pounding in his chest to quicken as he hoped, prayed, that he could find her. He had just passed the first doorway when something he'd spotted from the corner of his eye caused him to freeze.

On the staircase was a mural. He had been aware of it, but he hadn't realised exactly what it was. The figures he had seen carved into stone were meant to be just that, statues. Where he stood now was Medusa. Perseus stood behind her, his sword raised into the air as if to deliver a fatal blow. He had seen this before, in Jack's sketchbook. But then it had been different. Then—he reached up, his fingers tracing the sword, to find that it moved slightly beneath his touch. Pulling it down, the blade appeared to sink into Medusa's neck and as it latched into place, the marble panel opened with a click. He released a breath. This was it! If they were going to hide her somewhere, it would be here. Why else go through all the trouble of having a secret door? *I'm coming, Ashley*, he thought, grasping for the familiar tug of their tether, convincing himself its absence had no meaning.

"I found it, behind Medusa," he whispered, taking a quick picture. The door opened, creating the same black border he had seen on the drawing. Opening it wider, he ducked inside, his stomach churning as the cogs on the rear of the door turned, resetting the mural and sealing him inside the brightly lit area. The stone staircase had two thin, equally spaced grip ramps on either side, making it easier to transport things down. The button on the side of the wall suggested it was electric, conjuring images of Ashley being dragged down there, fighting, screaming, afraid, while hands grabbed at her, keeping her still as the ramps whirled, easing whatever she was secured to down the steps. He heard his teeth grind through the set of his jaw, reminding him to breathe. His every muscle bristled with energy, the need to tear this place to shreds as he sought her, but that would help nothing.

At the base of the stairs there were three large openings, one on each wall, and a smaller room just behind him to the left, which he could see was empty but which held all manner of restraints, from wall-mounted shackles and suspension cables, to Saint Andrew's crosses and shackled benches. Somewhere to the right he could hear the sound of screaming—the kind of screams that set every primal nerve aflame. Edging forward, he saw the first room was divided into sections. Small concrete walls created a line of cells in the rear, while empty beds were secured at intervals in the light. The entire area was paved like a wet room, with large drains at intervals. The undertones of bodily fluids assailed his senses, growing stronger as he approached the first cell.

The door wasn't locked, merely pulled closed. The concrete enclosure was nothing more than a room with a metal-framed bed secured above a large drain. Looking inside, he could see the spasming body of a man. Froth from his mouth stained his matted beard. Stepping inside, Conrad unfastened the restraints, feeling the man's paper-thin flesh tear beneath his grasp as he turned him on his side while the foaming vomit continued to flow. There was no time for this. No time for anyone but Ashley. He had to find her.

"Tess, we need medics here now. They're definitely Tabus, I'm going to check the other cells," he informed her.

Conrad moved from cell to cell, room to room, seeing gaunt and emaciated figures, hearing their pleas and screams. At each turn his desperation rose. His senses fought through the offensive odours, trying to catch even the faintest hint of Ashley, of lavender and honey mingled within the stenches. But all he found were more strangers, imprisoned in the same manner as the first. He was about to enter the final collection of rooms when the sound of hurried footsteps caused him to falter. A booming voice froze him into place and he cursed beneath his breath, his vision straying to the final room. She had to be in there. His muscles tensed, ready to run, ready to push him to the final room. She had to be there. She just had to be.

"Hands where we can see them. On your knees, now," commanded the voice from behind him. Conrad obeyed instinctively, dropping to the floor, his hands upon his head. He felt his arm being pulled behind him and the sharp cut of cuffs being fixed into place. He knew better than to speak, than to agitate the Blue Coats who flooded the area, moving from room to room relaying orders. "All clear, Detective Mendel."

Conrad heard his father descending the stairs and hung his head. Despite his gaze being fixed upon the floor, he noticed the medical stretcher being wheeled from the right as other medics—identifiable by the Rod of Asclepius clearly displayed on the front and back of their body armour—continued to weave in and out of the rooms.

"What did you think you were playing at, boy?" His father was enraged, he could feel the heat radiating from him. "Coming down here on your own, disobeying my orders? Of all the—"

"Did they find Ashley?" he whispered, fearing he already knew the answer. He had watched the medics wheel two sealed bags from the only room he had yet to enter. His father's hand fell heavily on his shoulder before he felt the restraints on his hands slacken. He rubbed the ache from his wrists. The metal used by the Blue Coats had been specially crafted to ensure no preternatural being could utilise their abilities while in custody.

"There's no way of knowing yet." His father's voice held a soft compassion, a tone usually unheard during a scolding. His vision strayed towards the staircase. She couldn't have been there

"Please, I checked all the rooms but that one." He gestured towards the departing gurneys, who froze as his father raised his hand. "Please, I need to know."

He could feel the dampness on his cheeks as his mind reeled in turmoil. Should he hope to gaze upon the dead and find her, or pray she had been sold into a life of abuse and suffering? Which fate should he wish upon her? Life! He had to hope she was out there somewhere, because if she was, he *would* find her, no matter how long it took. He felt his shoulders sag as the medics resealed the bags. He would find her.

CHAPTER 14

When Conrad was escorted from the premises, the noise on the streets was almost overwhelming. Sirens blared, vehicle doors slammed, instructions were relayed, all amongst the uneasy chatter of the confused crowd and growing number of spectators. His head hung low as he wondered where they could have moved Ashley to, and when. His gaze sought Will, wondering if he had betrayed them, alerted them of their plan, but as he gave a statement to a Blue Coat, he seemed distressed. *Good*, he thought.

His fists clenched. He wished they could have arrived sooner, that he had met her from work like he'd intended to. If he had, then none of this would have happened. He should have made her stay, made her wait. No one would have laid a hand on her with him there. He winced as his nails caught his scalp as he passed a hand through his hair, while images of all the horror awaiting her assaulted his every sense. Nausea rose and rage followed. His other-self was becoming harder to restrain. It cried out for him to find her and destroy anything that got in his way. He knew a rampage would help no one, achieve nothing, but holding back the tide building within him was becoming impossible. She was his.

He had wasted too much time—time spent fretting that he would hurt her, ignoring the fact she felt like home, like a missing part of himself. He should have known better, he should have trusted himself and because he hadn't, she could be lost forever. Tess had mentioned an auction, so perhaps there was still time. If she was sold, the chances were they would never see her again, and if they did, it was doubtful she'd be the same. He drove back the despair, the sadness. He needed his anger, and he had plenty of it. It would be his crutch, it would keep him going, drive him onward until she was safe.

Two arms were suddenly embracing him. He became aware of Tess talking, pulling him back from his thoughts as she told him how the Blue Coats had appeared without warning with a seek-and-recover missive, and that the call about the located Tabus had not come from them, but from an undercover P.T.F. agent who had been assigned there due to telepathic abilities. Apparently this person had heard Conrad's thoughts before Tess had even had a chance to take action.

Glancing through the crowd, Conrad saw Jack sitting on the bonnet of his car, talking with one of the agents. His dark combat gear had the P.T.F.'s distinctive emblem on the back. The figure turned as Conrad emerged, fixing him with a stare that demanded answers whilst also possessing another quality—hope.

"She wasn't there." He glowered as he approached Jack and the agent.

"Now what do we do?" Tess questioned, jumping when Detective Reuben's voice spoke from his position directly behind her.

"You leave this to the professionals. Don't make me lock you up. What you did was brave, but it was also downright foolish," Reuben scolded. "What the hell were you thinking, going in there half-cocked? What if things had gone south? What if the basement hadn't been deserted? Do you even realise what you could have walked into? I know you're worried about your friend, but that's no excuse to put yourselves in danger. I expected better from you."

"I'll keep an eye on them, sir," the stranger said. "Alex Ciele, P.T.F. squad alpha."

Conrad suddenly realised who this person was. He was Ashley's brother. As he watched him, he noticed Alex tap a decoration on his left arm that showed he was in command of his own unit. Reuben eyed him warily before nodding.

"Come on, I'll take you back to my sister's place. We'll come back for your car in the morning, grab any personal items you've left there." Escorting them into his large vehicle, Alex saluted respectfully towards Reuben before departing.

"You can't seriously be keeping us under house arrest? Not now," Conrad heard himself growl. "Ashley's out there somewhere. We can't just leave her. If you're not going to help us, let us out here, we'll find her somehow. I have to. She can't, we can't—" His fist connected with the soft leather of the seat as words failed him.

"Conrad, I assume. Ashley is my little sister. I know better than anyone that there is a time when you have to let the professionals do their thing. But this isn't one of them. Your father has my respect, but he's not up to point on this one. His hands are tied by bureaucracy, treaties and red tape. He may as well be fighting with both hands tied behind his back, deaf, and blindfolded." Alex glanced in his rear view mirror at Conrad. "Thanks for what you did back there. Not a lot of people would have the courage to go it alone."

"I wasn't alone." He glanced towards his friends appreciatively but, as his gaze fixed on Will, he found it hard to muster any gratitude for the person responsible.

"Now we're far enough away, here's the plan. I'm going to turn off in a moment, and Jack, you're going to get that sketch pad of yours out and get drawing."

"It doesn't work like that. I wish it did."

"Tonight it does. We'll make it. But it won't be pleasant."

The car wheels crunched beneath the forest debris as Alex turned off onto an old dirt track. Conrad sat in silence, watching, his vision constantly flicking towards the mirrors. He couldn't quite tell if

Alex was looking at him, or trying to make sure no one was following. When the vehicle rolled to a halt, Alex unclipped his belt, the noise loud against the hopeless silence that had descended. "Come on, we're here."

∼

Jack looked through the car window at the blanket of darkness above that was occasionally punctuated by a star, making itself seen beyond the swaying branches of the surrounding trees.

"Come on, Jack," Tess called, alerting him to the fact everyone was out of the car now except for him.

Shaking his head, he unclipped his belt, hurrying toward them. The bare trees whispered eerily, their noise as the wind raced past drowning out their footsteps in the thick mud. Keeping his mind clear, Jack tried to recreate the feeling of tension behind his third eye, to call a vision to him. But it was to no avail. Before, he had complained about not being able to do anything, but now there was a task that fell to him he feared his ability would fall short. After several minutes of hiking and more failed attempts than he could count, they encountered a barrier of luscious green pine trees. Their shed needles created a thick, cushioned blanket on the floor in such a way that it almost seemed artificial.

"What are we doing here?" Jack questioned, as Alex continued to lead them. Suddenly, they emerged into a clearing and found themselves staring at a henge. The first thing Jack noticed was the enormous purple gemstones buried within the earth, tracking their path. He saw them spiral inward, their colours mirroring that of a rainbow, until they finished at a large quartz circle in its very centre, overlooked by a huge altar stone. This large, flat crystal was surrounded by a horse-shoe shape of raised stones. But by far the most amazing feature was the three circles of standing stones. The whole area surrounding the stone monoliths had clearly been maintained, possessing a distinctive manicured appearance. Wild flowers grew sporadically, yet there seemed to be a pattern to their locations, a meaning Jack couldn't quite decipher.

"This henge was used by the Perennials when erecting the barrier. It is a place of power that joins with others of the same nature across our land. Sitting at its centre allows a person to fully tap into their abilities. It is a place utilised by the P.T.F. to ensure its members are fully aware of their capabilities. Its boost is only short-lived, but it allows the assessors to catalogue the full range of a person's capabilities, so they know how hard to push them."

"So, what are we doing here?" Jack asked again.

"You're going to utilise it to help us find Ashley. But you're going to need help. This location provides a boost to dual-nature preternaturals, those of us with two aspects to our self. Human preternaturals, those with magic, are often too inexperienced and delicate to survive the surge of energy. That's where your friend Will comes in. As a healer, he will be able to divert his energy to you so you don't burn out, while making sure you suffer no lasting damage," Alex explained.

"You up to that, William?" Conrad spat bitterly.

Jack knew what he was thinking; he was thinking the same thing. His life was in the hands of the person responsible for this situation in the first place.

"He will be." Alex turned a cold glare towards William. "My little sister saw to that, didn't she?" There was a menace in his voice that caused even Jack's hairs to stand erect. "Let's do this quickly. Every moment wasted increases the chance we won't find her." There was the weight of something left unsaid to the sentence, and Jack knew each one of them heard the unspoken concern.

Jack nodded, his feet moving of their own accord, guiding him through the stone circles until he stood upon the quartz stone, his sketchpad clutched in his trembling grasp. Alex motioned that he should sit, while positioning William just outside the stone horseshoe. He leaned in close, his deep voice an inaudible mumble as he whispered something into William's ear that made him visibly pale as his posture deflated.

"Okay, Jack, now all you need to do is ring the bell, close your eyes, and focus on Ashley. I'll guide you," Alex promised.

Jack glanced around and spotted a rope trailing across the floor to the stones. As he pulled it, he felt the smooth movements of pulleys before a bell, somewhere behind him, chimed.

Closing his eyes, Jack allowed Alex's voice to wash over him, following his every instruction. He thought of Ashley, bringing her image into his mind. His body grew both light and heavy, and it was then that the pain started. It was subtle at first, a building heat, starting at the crown of his head and progressing to his root chakra. With each passing second, the heat became more intense, burning, smouldering until all he could feel was the pain. Alex's voice had been lost as the pressure intensified. He felt as if his forehead were spitting open. Agony enveloped him, dragging him into a world where it was the only thing in existence. He saw the odd flicker of an image trying to appear, but the shredding sensation radiating from within was too great for any clarity.

Just as he felt he could take no more, as the need to withdraw away from the barrier of pain he tried to force himself through became too great, and he felt his body screaming in surrender while the protective light he had imagined surrounding him turned into darkness, his body turned ice cold and everything stopped. Light as air, free from the burden of pain, he found himself looking down upon an unfamiliar building. He had the sensation of being drawn through its walls into a room forged from mirrors, yet he cast no reflection.

Shackled to the far wall, her arms above her head, was Ashley. Her rust-coloured hair had been styled to perfection, drawing attention to both her pale complexion and her delicate facial features. She was wearing a burlesque dress that fitted her form like a second skin, with long slits up the sides that exposed the jagged scar of her injury. The heaving of her bosom beneath the corset brought him comfort, revealing there was still breath within her body, that she still lived. He tried to call out to her, to stir her from slumber and let her know help was coming, but his voice never came.

A sharp tug yanked him away with nauseating speed. Light exploded around his eyes, replaced by darkness as his arms flailed, fending off someone's restraining grasp as he spilt the contents of his stomach. His body shivered and the cold sensation upon his skin began to burn. He moved, feeling the icy layer crack slightly, its white texture melting away to water just moments before he realised the strange shimmering had been from a film of frost. His muscles screamed in agony as pain pierced his temples. He felt someone's hands moving upon him, their motion leaving some manner of warm fluid smeared upon his skin and, for a few moments, a fraction of the pain eased. Turning his head, he saw Will, with blood tracking from his ears and nose. His complexion was so pale that the ruby fluid appeared black. He heard Will cough and noticed the spray of blood left in the cough's wake. He wanted to say thank you, realising Will had put himself within the circle, at the mercy of the same energy, to ensure he survived, but his arms gave beneath him as his body grew weak.

"No, you don't," Alex scolded, dragging the two figures to the outside of the henge.

Jack felt someone slapping his face gently. He tried to fend it off, his hands weakly batting away the unwanted touch. He needed to sleep, to descend into the pain-free bliss of the darkness that beckoned. It took a few moments to realise his assailant was Alex, who stood over him, pushing a pencil and his sketch pad into his hand, ordering, "Don't rest yet. Draw first."

Jack blinked, trying to focus his gaze, reminding himself what was at stake should his limbs fail to obey. He saw William lying on his back just a few feet away, bloody, exhausted, and choking weakly on his own blood. He watched as Conrad approached and, with a sharp kick, shoved William onto his side, allowing the blood to spill from his lips. It was a cold gesture, but the fact he had done it ensured Jack understood how much William must have risked for him.

His limbs felt like lead but, as Alex stood over him, a flashlight illuminating the area with its pain-inducing illumination, he drew everything he recalled. They were sketches created from unsteady lines, an aerial view, a picture of the house, Ashley. He only hoped it would be enough. Shadows swam before his gaze and he heard the tip of his pencil crack as darkness finally devoured him.

～

Vincent smiled as he led the selected bidders upstairs where his Tabus were awaiting, nicely packaged, like china dolls in their oversized boxes. This location was his pride and joy. It was one of the many discreet houses belonging to his clan, but this was the one he favoured. Its interior had been specifically designed for these events. The ground floor held a large foyer greeting area, where the papers for the silent auction could be found. A grand double doorway at its rear opened into a magnificent banquet hall, where, after the biddings had closed, he would take his guests to feast on both the best of the clan's enslaved donors and decadent foods. But upstairs was where the real magic happened. Upstairs, instead of bedrooms, was what he liked to call his maze of mirrors.

The corridors snaked around, but, in place of bedrooms, he had outfitted the entire floor with winding corridors of mirrors, where, at staggered intervals, boxes created by two-way mirrors placed the available Tabus on display. His clan trimmed and dressed them, selecting their attire carefully to ensure they looked their best. After all, trappings made all the difference, and he presented them beautifully with all their information displayed on the outside of each holding cell.

The cells themselves were forged from the strongest substance he could acquire. While inside appeared to be a prison created solely from mirrors, his patrons enjoyed the anonymity of exploring his wares from every angle. Often, Tabus were purchased not only on the strength of their unique ability to withstand the opiates forced into them, but because they were appealing to the eye. The bidders were buying a servant to satisfy all their vices, which is why he ensured they were broken, ready to serve. All except for one. Not that it mattered; those who would have the means to acquire her would be able to handle an unbroken breeder.

Breeders were identified easily at the age of fourteen, their scent becoming compelling to any preternatural. It was at this age that they would be purchased by the council and sent to a training facility. Two years later, they would be ready to serve their purpose. Finding a breeder this old, and with Elder blood, was unprecedented. He expected great things from her, and cooperation and subservience were not necessary for the role she would play.

"Now, if you could make your way back, you will find the bidding cards with the appropriate reference numbers in place. The auction closes in one hour. For those of you who were issued the platinum badges, if you could wait with me for a moment, there is one more product."

When everyone but the three carefully selected Elites had disappeared, he smiled, speaking again. "Before we continue, there are some terms and conditions attached to the sale of this magnificent creature. Mainly that the victor allows resale to the other bidders once the duty is complete. My fee is twenty-five percent of all sales, as well as certain... 'special privileges', shall we say?"

As he spoke, he led them through the winding corridor of mirrors to the isolated cell where his Elder blood breeder was displayed.

"Is this for real?" questioned Thaddeus, his eyes examining the digital statistics displayed, while his fingers traced the large scar across his left cheek.

"I have confirmed it myself. Now, it was brought to my attention that the council ruled that none of your clans be allowed access to any known breeders, due to your various indiscretions. What you see before you is an unregistered preternatural and, as you can see, she has very interesting chemistry." Vincent gestured towards a secondary sheet. "Even should she be caught in your possession, she lacks the breeder markers, meaning you can feign ignorance."

"Are you certain this creature can provide offspring?" Thaddeus questioned, moistening his lips eagerly. Vincent could tell by his longing gaze that, even if she couldn't, she was still of interest to him. She was just his type; pretty.

"I would place my entire power and fortune on it." He watched with satisfaction as they studied her figure, taking in everything her feminine form had to offer. "Of course, there is one drawback, which I am certain you gentlemen will be bound to enjoy. She isn't broken. Now, if you're ready to adjourn, you'll find her bidding card along with the others." He chuckled as they made a hasty retreat back toward the main lobby.

He lingered a moment longer, enjoying watching her struggle against her bindings just as the lucky winner would, and felt a pang of envy towards the one who would become her owner.

CHAPTER 15

Alex drew his car to a halt on one of the back roads leading to the mansion. William and Jack had been secured carefully in the back of his vehicle, neither showing signs of waking. Although, from what he had observed, he would be surprised if William would ever find the strength to wake without aid. He had expended himself beyond his tolerance even before throwing himself to the mercy of the henge. It had been a brave but foolish thing to do. The henge gave power, but it also exacted a cost.

If not for William's actions, it was doubtful Jack would have survived. He had never witnessed such an intense and violent reaction to a Perennial henge before. He had believed the healer would have been sufficient to create a balance, especially given what he had been doing to his sister. He had been wrong. William had been expended, on the brink of unconsciousness barely a moment after Jack had entered trance. Such energy-burning suggested there was some manner of warding protecting wherever his sister was being held. Jack had been trapped, suffering in a realm of perpetual pain as his mind tried to break through, and his refusal to fail saw the energy begin to shred him from the inside out. If it hadn't been for William throwing himself into the centre and taking his friend within his arms while he, too, pulled upon this ancient source of power, Jack would have died. But his actions had come with a cost. The healer's body had been injured, perhaps irreparably.

As he had sat there, embracing his friend, channelling the henge's power to push Jack through the barrier of pain and repair the shredding damage of the raw energy, their skin had started to heat, leaving Alex with no choice but to use his own abilities to cool their flesh. When Jack had finally broken through, William had been hanging on by a thread, his very pores bleeding as he refused to surrender until his friend was safe. This alone earned him a small measure of respect. But only a small one.

If not for William, Jack would no longer be with them, and any hope of finding his sister in time would be lost. Alex turned his vision from the rear view mirror, bringing his focus back to the here and now.

"Are we close enough for you to do your thing?" he asked, looking towards Tess, who nodded, pulling her laptop out. "Back-up is still an hour away. I'm sure I don't need to tell you that waiting is not an option. Even my own squad have a thirty minute ETA. I don't like this."

He tuned his focus to Conrad. "You're still green, but I know your kind pack a hell of a punch. Given the type of auction, I'm expecting vampires, so that's nothing your withering light can't handle if things go south. If you didn't have that in your arsenal we'd have to rethink. But, for the most part, our intention is solely retrieval. My team will handle the rest when they arrive. For now, we focus on Ashley, on bringing her home."

"Withering light?" Tess questioned. "What type of shifter did you say you were?"

Alex felt himself frown at her question. Surely she knew her friend was an ifrit, the most powerful fire elemental in existence?

One such as himself would surely not allow that misconception to stand. They were a proud race, after all.

"I'm ready," Conrad confirmed, clearly skirting the topic.

∽

When the silent auction closed, Thaddeus waited eagerly for the good news. He knew no one could have beaten his offer. He had wanted an offspring, a real heir, for centuries, but his clan's actions, both before and after the treaties, saw they suffered the harshest punishment. His direct line was cursed with infertility and forbidden from ever acquiring a breeder, along with all the other families who rebelled against the united council.

Preternaturals had difficulty naturally reproducing outside a soul bond relationship and, while their lifespan was extended, often only a single heir could be sired. To be rendered infertile was the second harshest sentence as it robbed the entire bloodline of the chance to parent a child. While a breeder could conceive even with such a curse in place, the blacklist meant their line was fated to be extinguished. Even vampires had a lifespan. They were not immortal like old legends suggested; their time was just prolonged greatly compared to many other races.

It didn't help that his clan was constantly being caught in breach of the laws. It wasn't his fault humans were so weak that they needed to be treated with a delicate touch he didn't possess. He enjoyed the sound of their pain, their screams. It wasn't his fault they had to fight, that he broke them. This opportunity had been too good to refuse. That breeder would pass on her Elder blood, and, combined with his own patriarchy genes, they would create an unstoppable hybrid and a sovereign from his own line, and thus any curse bestowed upon them would have to be rescinded since their clan contained a Elder blood scion.

He couldn't help but think Vincent had something else in mind as well. The other two family heads were in the same situation. He glanced down the list, hardly able to believe his luck. Assuming he was the winner, the agreement stipulated that after the first child was produced, following testing to confirm if the Elder blood remained, he had to sell her on to one of the approved families. All of which had stances opposing the council.

As everyone filed into the banquet hall to celebrate their acquisitions, there was one auction not announced for all to hear. Wondering if he had somehow been outbid, he was about to join the small gathering when he felt Vincent's hand on his arm, pulling him aside.

"It appears congratulations are in order," Vincent announced, presenting the contract on his device.

Thaddeus was certain the smile upon his lips had been answer enough as he pressed the appropriate place, leaving his mark, and confirmed the necessary transfers. When the transaction was complete, Vincent handed him a large iron key with a knowing wink. "It was a pleasure doing business with you, my good man. Now, if you'll excuse me, I have other guests to attend to and, from your expression, it appears you are eager to become acquainted with your newest acquisition. Can you find your way?"

"I can indeed." Thaddeus smiled his predatory smile and slipped away. He had waited too long for a day like this, and he wasn't going to waste another moment.

∼

Ashley startled awake, certain she was being watched. Her arms ached and her shoulders and wrists burnt from supporting her weight while she had been unconscious. Forcing her legs beneath her, she felt the pain explode as her arms moved, causing her knees to weaken.

The last thing she remembered was being dragged in chains from the room and showered down. At one point during this humiliating ritual another dart had found its way into her skin. Now she was here. But she had no idea where 'here' was. No matter where she looked, only her reflection stared back. The dark circles she knew were present had been expertly disguised by smouldering make-up. She stared at her reflection for a moment, wondering if it was truly herself who looked back. The hair, the make-up, the clothes, everything was such a contrast to her normal self. It was then she realised why she had been dressed so sensually. The words returned to her. The one who had fed on her and held her close as she fought weakly, had discovered what she could do. She was being auctioned.

The restraints were a single chain attached to the metal shackles on her wrist and secured into a locking wall plate above her head. Yanking the chains, she tried to twist, to pull herself free, but it was to no avail. Panic welled and fear churned, adding to the nausea. She had to get out of here. Turning, she placed her feet to the wall, using all her weight as she pushed and strained, hoping to break something. But no matter what she did, no matter what she tried, she was trapped. The only thing she achieved was to cause the throbbing in her head to intensify due to the abrasive sounds of her chains as she fought against them. Exhausted, she allowed herself to rest for a moment.

That was when she heard it, the sound of the mirror before her sliding open. Her pulse quickened as a darkened corridor briefly flashed into sight before someone stepped inside, leaving the door to slide shut behind them. Her panicked gaze absorbed his every detail at once. The smart-casual clothes had clearly been tailored to fit his hulking frame, his collar remaining unbuttoned so the cords of his thick neck muscles were visible. His dark hair was the colour of pine cones and mirrored the shade of his eyes. He lifted his hand to stroke the short stubble that didn't quite conceal the large scar across his cheek. But the most threatening thing about this imposing figure was the way he advanced, his hungry gaze greedily examining her every curve as the sound of his hurried hands unfastening his belt echoed through the silence.

Her breathing erupted into panicked sobs, the heaving of her bosom through the corset eliciting an appreciative growl from her captor. Turning her panicked gaze towards the chains, she tried to find a way out, a weak point, something she could break. She fought and struggled, using her entire weight to once more pull down on the shackles, but her attempts only amused him and she could hear his breathing quickening as he stood appreciating the display for just a moment, before closing the remaining distance between them.

"You're certainly easy on the eyes. Our child will be glorious," he whispered in her ear, pressing his body against her.

Without thinking, she turned her head, her teeth sinking deep into his throat, latching on, refusing to let go. He howled in agony as her jaw locked. His blood trickled down her chin and she tried to tear the flesh from between her teeth. Her breathing froze as he drove his fist into her stomach, forcing her to release him. Her body trembled until finally, she pulled in an agonising breath through a pain that had made the world around her dim.

He staggered backwards, his hand pressed to his throat, cursing her, but it was the amusement in his eyes that scared her most. She knew she couldn't stop now. Bringing her knees up, she used the chains to support her weight as she thrust her legs forward to connect with his stomach, forcing him back, away from her.

"I'll enjoy making you pay for that." He spat, causing his blood to stain the mirrored tile floor.

His hands fastened around her throat before she could even plan her next move, pushing her up the wall. Choking, she gasped for breath, using every inch of the space she had to twist and push, to try to manoeuvre away, to gain enough space to lash out again. But his grasp was suffocating her and she knew that if he didn't release her soon, she would fade into unconsciousness.

"You're mine now, understand?" He released her, pressing his lips to hers aggressively as he reached up to release the chain from the locking plate above her head. With a sharp tug, he sent her tumbling to the floor, allowing the restraint to fall from his grasp. Pushing to her knees, she gasped for breath and tried to crawl away towards the place where she had seen the door. The loose chain dragged across the floor between her hands, the sweat on her skin causing her to slip and slide upon the smooth surface. She screamed as she felt his hand clasp her ankle, dragging her back towards him.

Kicking and screaming, she tried to free herself as he flipped her over, positioning himself above her, his weight pinning her down. Her fingers brushed the cold metal of her necklace as she fought against him. Far from deterring him, her blows seemed to be encouragin, but she knew that to stop fighting was to surrender to this brute's will.

He was bigger, stronger. She cried out as her left wrist was pushed to the floor above her head, lashing out with her other arm, trying to swing the chain between the two restraints around his neck. But he was quicker. Her muscles burned as she strained against him, her fingers finding the cool chain of her necklace just as he thrust her hand above her head. He secured both her wrists in a single grasp, pinning her helplessly, his other hand now tugging at her clothes with a look of sheer elation on his face. He was enjoying every moment of her fearful struggle, unaware of her necklace breaking.

The sound was inaudible, the breaking of a single link. The heat she had been trying to call up engulfed her with force as he tore open her corset. She screamed as she saw the fire envelop the room, but hers was not the only cry. He wouldn't scream for long. He wouldn't run. Her fire engulfed him as her body pulsed with fire, melting the flesh of her attacker. He backed away, howling in agony, but he was trapped with her now, and the fire wouldn't still, it was hungry, enraged, and something inside her would not rest until everyone felt its fury.

Something inside her pushed through her core, taking control, relishing its freedom with a gleeful wail as the screaming figure before her turned to ash and still the power kept coming. The flames burnt hotter, leaving her body in an endless stream, melting and shattering the mirrors, destroying the ceiling, until an explosion shook the very foundations of the building. Everything her fire touched fell to its power, and everything that burned only seemed to provide more fuel. She knew then that she couldn't control it. She couldn't seize this primal force and thrust it back within herself. The fire poured from her endlessly. She could feel its hunger, its need to burn fiercely after being contained for so long.

CHAPTER 16

It was clear to see why this location had been chosen for such dealings. Eclipsed by trees, unmarked upon any map, and with no registered blueprints, it was the perfect place in which to disappear. Alex led Conrad through the dense forest, pausing as they reached the boundary to look up at the two-storey mansion. The white bricks stood in contrast to the dark embrace of night's shroud, while the warm glow from the Georgian-style sash windows spilt out onto the stone staircase leading to the front door. Above, as part of the second floor, stood a large, circular balcony supported by pillars and therein lay their entrance.

Motioning for Conrad to follow, Alex crept across the open grounds, his footfalls silent upon the manicured grass lawn. The lack of security seemed suspicious, but given what they were trading here, the fewer people involved, the better. It was not as if those inside were helpless; fifteen powerful clan representatives were not something to be underestimated. Tess had hacked into the dormant security system, using the installed biometric scanners to detect and confirm the number of people inside. It was far fewer than he had imagined, but still more than he was comfortable with, especially given that Conrad had zero combat experience.

Keeping low, they approached the windows, finding the immediate area deserted. Clasping his hands together, he motioned for Conrad to approach, boosting him up so his fingers scraped the overhanging balcony. He heard the white stone being clawed as he fumbled an ascent, before Alex used the pillars to follow. He had hoped to peer inside the many windows, but had already noticed the way they reflected the surroundings on their approach. He glanced at Conrad, relieved to have someone beside him, searching for the words to show his gratitude, but when nothing surfaced he simply offered him a nod.

They knew the Tabus would be located here. Tess had isolated seven signatures, six to the right of this entrance, close together, and one segregated alone to the left. Their plan was simple. Locate Ashley, and extract her, along with any Tabus they could free as they made their escape. His team were due any time in the next fifteen minutes and knew their role.

The door leading inside from the balcony to the first floor was a naïvely simple design. Clearly, the owner had never expected anyone to attempt what they were about to. With careful precision, Alex channelled his ice energy into the lock, manipulating the tumblers within until it opened with a satisfying click. To anyone looking on, it usually appeared as if he had simply placed his hand upon the lock to release it.

Suddenly, a deafening roar shook the very foundations of the house, blasting the door from his grasp before he could open it fully. The powerful force thrust him backwards as wave upon wave of heat and fire engulfed the surroundings. He scarcely managed to expel his essence to create a barrier to shield them from the scalding heat as the windows shattered, blowing outward across the length of the building as the fire feasted, hungrily devouring the air. Groaning, Alex pulled himself to his feet, his ears ringing. They were too late. Grasping

Conrad's arm, he pulled him up with a grimace, all too aware of the barrier half shattering while the rest became a torrent of icy rain.

"Change of plan," Alex gasped, clutching his midriff. Sweat streamed from his body, mingling with the water as his strengthened barrier became nothing but a frost-lined mist. He dared not shift his form fully as the fire was too intense, and to do so would be a death sentence. At least this way, the fire's blaze would be diluted, giving them a chance. But time would not be on their side, not against this heat. "We go right, get out who we can."

Orange and white flames rose from the left, feasting hungrily on the building. Walls collapsed in flashes of silver shards and molten metals, as what remained of the ceiling sagged. As he moved to advance further through the mounting smoke, Conrad grasped his arm.

"What about Ashley?" he demanded, his gaze straying to the left, to the devastation of the ruined building that was engulfed in a cloak of flames and smouldering embers.

"No one will get close to her, she'll burn out." He couldn't hold Conrad's gaze, it was too flooded with emotion.

Taking another step into the sweltering heat made his every movement feel sluggish. He pushed more energy towards his essence, parting the smoke around his failing protection as it began to steam. He couldn't keep this up for long; with every second the temperature rose, his sister's power would become greater and she could not survive fire's kiss for long. He needed to reach the Tabus, get as many to safety as he could. Retrieving his sister was no longer an option. He grimaced, biting back the rising pain and disorientation as his frozen core began to warm up. They needed to get out of here, quickly.

"I'm not leaving her."

"Even you can't survive Phoenix fire," he cautioned Conrad. "We go this way."

Grasping his side, Alex tried to suppress the cough, his eyes fixed ahead where the heat had started to shatter the remaining walls. He could tell from the way they glowed and resisted that, unlike the windows, they were not made of simple glass. They had been forged to withstand magic and the fact they now began to crumble despite the fire not yet igniting here, only showed they were being consumed by Ashley's aura. She was berserk, and her aura would spread, consume, and grow until her essence burned itself out. She lacked the training, the knowledge to draw her aura back, to preserve herself. The energy was simply wild, unleashed. He focused on transferring the water from his sweat back into the barrier while trying to draw water from any source he dared.

'*Lex, this is Bindu, we're in position.*' Alex grimaced at the interruption, knowing how taxing it would have been for her to link him into their web without being physically near. Through his panting breaths he sent a thought, hoping it didn't feel as weak as he did.

'*Targets were in the banquet hall. Estimation fifteen Vampires. Watch your six.*'

'*Guards?*'

'*None. Tess found no additional life signatures when she hacked the sensors on their systems.*'

'*Ah, so that's Tess.*' Bindu's mental tone suggested their paths had crossed. '*Okay, we're coming in. Do you need any help? It's looking pretty hot up there.*'

'*I have six Tabus close. We'll be bringing them through the front door, assuming the staircase is still standing. Be careful, Bindu, this isn't ordinary fire.*'

'*You don't need to tell me, Lex. Holler if you need anything.*'

Alex turned his focus back towards Conrad, noticing that at some point his grip had released. He glanced over his shoulder, a curse weakly playing upon his lips, to see nothing behind him but fire and smoke. There was nothing he could do now but press on. Conrad had made his choice.

Flames licked his arms, leaving blisters that caused his essence to stir. Glowing shards of distorted and bubbled mirrors lined the broken and shattered hallway, casting back haunting reflections as his other-self fought to emerge. He knew he had no choice, not if he had any hope of reaching her. The flames were too hot, too hungry. Even for an ifrit, this fire was unbearable, but not as much as the thought steeling his mind. If he didn't reach her, she too would be consumed.

He cried out in anguish as the heat became too much, causing his blood to burn and his other-self to emerge in response to his need. The sweat cascading down his blistered skin turned molten as the air surrounding him became saturated with the scent of sulphur. Vibrant blue flames licked the air around his growing aura as his essence expanded in a visually mesmerising display. Vibrant oranges, yellows, and reds erupted from within, pouring from his essence as every part of him became aflame. It was a display that put the majesty of a volcanic eruption to shame. The lava flowed, mingling with the fires of Phlegethon that spewed forth from his very being, coating his every fibre and building upon him, forging him into his other-self. His shell grew and pools of vibrant colours swirled tumultuously below the darkening skin, as his once-toned body became the enormous form of an ifrit, a being forged from fire and Phlegethon.

Seeing himself within the shattered shards of mirrors as he advanced, his monstrous claws swiped angrily, fracturing horrific images, sending another glass wall crumbling to the ground only for several more reflections to taunt him with his grotesque appearance. His enormous horns rose like jagged thunderbolts, cutting the air with their blazing brilliance, making him appear like a demon stepping straight through the gates of Hell. The heat was suffocating, causing beads of blazing magma to force their way free, creating minute eruptions upon the surface of his flesh, their intense shades tracking his form like sweat until finally cooling and becoming part of his darker shell.

His alteration was a thing to behold. He, like all elementals, did not change and alter like shifters. His ifrit essence simply bled from him, building a new body upon his old one like a protective covering, and yet every fibre remained him. Every part resonated within; they were *his* giant clawed hands, *his* monstrous features and enormous torso, they were just another aspect of who he was. This form held his true power and he needed every ounce of it to reach Ashley. '*I'm coming,*' he thought, begging her to hold on, to be strong, to wait for him.

His resolve almost faltered as he recalled how Rei had reacted to his form—how, after seeing it, the only looks he received from her were those of hatred and fear. But his vanity didn't matter now. All that was important was making sure Ashley survived. At the rate she was consuming her magical essence, she would burn out too quickly. '*Hold on, I'm here, I'm coming.*'

He hurried, his thundering steps grinding the glass to dust beneath his massive clawed feet. He could hear her screaming, two voices, a woman and a bird, shrieking and crying as one. Minute volcanoes continued to erupt upon his flesh, sealing and renewing at speed, a warning his core was becoming too hot, that there was no protection from the damage he still endured. There were but two fires hotter than his own and both had been forged from the eternal flame. The first was the fiery breath bestowed by the gods to the dragons, and the second was the Phoenix, whose form was first born from the fire itself.

He could see her now, across the collapsed floor. She was magnificent. Her body was nothing more than a humanoid sea of fire, her arms outstretched with phantom wings of flame extending behind her. The heat roiling from her was unbearable, even to him. Each breath he drew was laboured, unsatisfying, unbearable. But bear it he would. He would save her, even if it cost his life. Her survival was all that mattered.

He fought through, avoiding the licking, hungry blaze as he picked his way across partially devoured supports, aware of their damaged structure trembling beneath his hulking weight until finally he set foot upon the only place still untouched by the fire's hunger, the plinth on which she stood. He could feel the agony of each footstep as the unbearable heat scalded his feet. The air was just as searing, and yet it was as though it was also protected from the damage in some semblance of self-preservation.

His skin was still a mass of molten eruptions but, not fearing he could damage her, he did the only thing he could when his voice went unheard. Sinking to his knees, he wrapped his terrifying arms around her, bringing her into his embrace as he called her name. The contact was excruciating, the worst agony he had ever endured, and yet nothing compared to how he knew he would feel should he lose her. He held her close, hoping the sound of his desperate pleas would somehow wake her enough to drive back the berserker fury. If not, he could think of far worse ways to die than with her in his arms.

Emily stood statue-still, a quizzical expression upon her face as the unfamiliar figure she had been looking at began to melt before her gaze. The electric blue clothes seemed to bubble upon the figure and, for a moment, she thought her dreams had turned to nightmares once again as horrific growths appeared upon the person's flesh, distorting their gaunt features into ghastly disfigurements. Seconds later, a splintering crack pierced her ears as the world around her shattered into nothingness. Silver rain cascaded around her, its touch like razorblades upon her skin. But when its downfall ended, reality had been made anew, becoming an open space littered with miniature worlds trapped within the mirrored fragments and lit by fire. She remained still, her gaze focusing ahead just as the master had asked. She was to wait until her new master made themselves known, and serve them in any way they desired. Covering her mouth, she heard herself cry out as her coughs caused pain to swell through her torso.

Her hand rose to the throbbing pain in her side, causing her to suck a breath through bared teeth as her touch caused it to burn and the flow of the warm, sticky fluid to quicken. She dared a glance down, and hoped the master would not be too disappointed that one of the mirrored fragments had buried itself within her flesh. She looked down upon herself carefully. The Master had said she needed to look appealing, yet the red scratches oozing ruby fluid across her skin were ruining the pretty clothes she had been given. She tried to wipe them, succeeding only in worsening the smears.

She glanced around, hoping to find help, hoping she could fix the damage before her new master came for her. Through the smoke, she saw a figure emerging, and tried her best to straighten up despite the intense pain in her side. Behind him were five other shadows. She marvelled as the smoke appeared to part for him, as if he had the right to pass. Before he could reach her, she grasped the fragment, hoping to remove the imperfection, but merely touching it sent her crumpling to her knees, where further shards sunk deep into her legs.

She cried in pain and frustration. The Master would be so disappointed in her. She flinched, expecting punishment when the hand of the man reached down towards her.

"Come, you are mine now," he whispered. She looked at his hand again, lifting hers into his. His gentleness stirred warmth within her as he lifted her to her feet and the oppressive heat surrounded her lessened just a fracture.

"I'm sorry, Master," she whispered, doubling over as the pain from her side caused darkened spots to swim before her gaze. She gasped as his arm encircled her waist, helping to support her as they walked. Glancing behind her, she saw the world behind her being devoured, the floor sinking into a gaping mouth of nothingness.

"We need to move faster!" he commanded, and a string of voices, including her own, all echoed their obedience.

Rubble rained down from above, the ceiling parting to send plumes of billowing smoke into the darkened sky as the groans and complaints of overburdened supports sought release from their load.

Emily felt herself become weightless, gasping as she was lifted into her new master's arms, his pace increasing as the collapsed rubble of the enormous doorway came into sight. She clung to him tightly as he guided her and the others outside into the cold, refreshing air.

Breathing deeply, she cringed at the burning pain, but the air tasted so fresh, so rejuvenating, that she just had to do it again. The coolness on her flesh, the openness of the sky, it was all so large, so overwhelming. She felt herself begin to tremble as people rushed forwards to greet them as her feet once more found the floor. It was soft, cushioning her feet as her heels sank into the earthy texture of the grass. Her hand clutched her side firmly as coughs escaped her sore throat. She backed away from the approaching swarm, their shouts and voices too loud, too many. Without thinking, she grasped her master's arm as they tried to take her, praying he wouldn't punish her as she choked out her words, "I'm sorry,"

"It's okay, go with them. You are free now, they will help you," he encouraged, gently removing her tight grip from his arm. The words seemed strange to her ears. How could she be free when it was her duty to serve him? She felt the hands of a medic upon her. Her gaze turned back to her new master and she was just in time to see his sad smile as he gave an encouraging nod, before sinking to his knees and becoming lost in the swarm of medics.

~

Ashley had known who stood before her the instant she had seen the mirror shatter through the distant smoke to reveal his magnificent form. She was frozen, paralysed within an ever-expanding aura of magic she could not restrain, yet her soul cried to him, asking why he thought he had needed to hide something so magnificent! He was no shifter, he was something so much more, something truly striking. The way his fiery essence pulsed and flowed beneath the darkness of his molten flesh was hypnotic, mesmerising, like gazing deep into the night sky, or watching the power of a thunderstorm. He was a thing of raw and powerful beauty. She was glad to be able to gaze upon him, to know him so completely if only for a moment.

If she'd had control of her body, she would have reached out to touch him. But instead, she stood silently, crying unheard for him to leave as he dropped to his knees before her, his powerful arms folding around her with gentle strength, to cover her almost completely.

Through his touch, she somehow sensed his shame, a shame scarcely concealed over the torrent of his thoughts assailing her mind. He was in pain, dying. He held onto her knowing it was killing him. He clung to her desperately, willing to sacrifice everything in the hope of saving her. Her core grew hotter, her essence reaching out to embrace his even as she screamed for it to stop. She heard its claim, its song within her mind as it embraced him with her power. *'Mine.'*

She wanted to warn him away, to have him retreat while he still could. She already knew nothing could survive her touch. Her otherself spoke to her, its voice so loud, offering apologies because it could no longer rein in its power. The dam restraining it had broken, and all that could happen now was for its power to flood out until nothing more was left. It screamed and cried with her as the man she loved held her and the jagged edges of their essences melded together into one smooth connection. She could feel his pain, and yet he clung to her desperately, whispering softly, confessing his love, offering words of comfort as if he could quell the rising tide. But she had already burnt too hot, too fast.

United as one, both parts of her knew there was no recovering from what had happened and so she closed her eyes, relishing the sensations of being held within his firm embrace. To let go now would be to offer him salvation. Fatigue washed over her. She had tried to fight the draining energy, to hold on, but now her release would save him. *Please save him*—she thought.

At that moment, she felt so safe, so serene, as if everything in the world was how it should be. As if recognising her surrender, her knees weakened, her weight supported by his strong arms as her energy waned and her breathing slowed. A sudden alarm coursed through her as she realised what was happening. She wanted this, but now she realised she wasn't ready to leave him; not yet, not without telling him loved him. She struggled for a breath, trying to push her final words through her failing body, but the only sound that escaped her was a whimper as the darkness embraced her and her fire died.

CHAPTER 17

Alex stood outside, the P.T.F. blanket that was draped over his shoulders sending small waves of cold energy from the enchantments woven within. His skin felt raw and tight, his face red from the burns, but as his essence cooled, their effect would lessen. His small squadron gathered close as the building continued to burn. The occasional thought through Bindu's connection reached out to him, offering support as he stood transfixed by the scene before him.

Loud rumblings could be heard from within as supporting walls continued to collapse in exasperated sighs as they finally relinquished their burdens, sending dust and embers into the sky. The fire was insatiable, burning hotter and more vibrantly than anything he had seen before. The balcony they had used to enter had become nothing more than flaming rubble as the entire right side of the house crumbled down to its foundations. The roof to the left, where his sister would have stood, had been blown clear from the property, landing in a smouldering heap at the forest's edge. The walls still stood, but reports from his team confirmed the ceiling of the banquet hall was almost completely destroyed.

He watched with a hollow emptiness building inside him, his

thoughts turning to Conrad as he saw Tess approach with her arm slung under Jack's shoulder as she half-dragged his hobbling body towards them. The medics rushed to meet them lifting Jack from her support to guide him towards one of the waiting ambulances. Alex could hear his weak protest, and sent Bindu a quick instruction. His sister's friends would be treated at his base, including the healer. If he ever woke, he would answer for his crimes. Healers were rare; he would be indentured to the base until such a time as his debt had been paid. Bindu sent back a quick acknowledgement, dispatching one of the other team members to retrieve William and Jack.

Alex realised his face must have shed the indifferent expression he tried to maintain when present in an official capacity, because he saw the tears start to form in Tess's eyes before she even spoke, as her grasp tightened on the sketchbook in her hands.

"You didn't find her?" Tess asked, the light from the fires causing her damp cheeks to sparkle.

He reached out, cupping her face in his hands as the blanket slid from his shoulders. "It's not that we couldn't find her. We know exactly where she is, it's just impossible for anyone to get close."

"And Conrad?" Tess questioned. Alex shook his head. "You mean to tell me that *he* went in there, he went after her, but none of you can?"

He looked at her regretfully. What was he meant to say? Was he meant to tell her that he had made the only decision possible? That there was no hope of anyone reaching her... that he had decided to let his little sister burn out because, now that her abilities were unrestrained, there was no way she could rein the fire in, no way she could stop it from harming those in its path. How could he tell her they had come too late; that there was nothing anyone could do, not even himself, her big brother, the one who should have protected her, prepared her. He was powerless to do anything but watch her burn.

He felt Bindu's hand on his shoulder and hung his head as he realised he had just voiced his monologue to anyone still linked to him, being too exhausted to guard his thoughts. Wiping his hands down his face, he sighed, his vision returning to the devastation before him. As Bindu tried to explain to his sister's closest friend all the things he could not voice, he turned away, his gaze fixed upon the fire, watching it burn.

The dark backdrop of the night sky made the vibrancy of the flames even more intense than their ethereal shades. There was something hypnotic about the way they swayed as if in a dance, while destroying everything in their wake. Fire engines with silenced sirens arrived, their lights meshing momentarily with those of the departing ambulances containing the rescued Tabus. The lawn was overcrowded, two ambulances still waiting while the fire trucks drew closer to the blaze and the firefighters emerged to do heroic battle against the hungry beast. Shoots of water sent mist into the air, but the fire burnt through the water, seeming to ignite it as if it were oil feeding its flame.

Swearing, Alex ran towards them, his arms waving frantically. To a fire like this, everything was fuel, even water. It would burn with the power of the eternal flame until his sister's life faded. Only when her own fire died would this one return to its mortal nature.

He sank to his knees as he saw the water begin to gain ground, vanquishing its foe as the first plume of smoke altered in shade beneath the barrage of water. Tess approached him slowly, holding Jack's latest sketch before his gaze. It took a moment to realise what he was seeing, but when he did, he found the faintest of smiles. He studied the image for a long time, lifting it from her hands to absorb the lifelike details of a formidable ifrit embracing a Phoenix as the world around them burned.

∼

Conrad felt her heat begin to wane. The fire surrounding her flesh became fine wisps of vibrant orange which peeled back to reveal her ivory skin beneath. She felt limp in his arms as he sank to the fractured floor, cradling her. His clawed hands combed through her hair frantically, his vision desperately seeking out any sign that she still held breath within her body.

"Ashley," he whispered, pulling her close as he held her protectively, no longer fearing the effect his heat would have upon her. All along, she had been naturally resistant, immune to the blistering heat of his essence and able to withstand the touch of his rawest form. His soul had been right all along; she was his, she had always been his. "Please," he begged.

There was so much he wanted to say... feelings so powerful that the only thing they could become was tears. He searched inside himself for the right words—the words that, if spoken, would somehow reach across time and space, across the realms and draw her back to him. But no such words existed, not in this world or any other.

The world crashed down around him, yet still he sat. His own world had already been destroyed beyond any recognition. He understood the tether now, why she sang to his soul. She had been part of him, the missing piece, his soul mate. Now she was gone. Without her, without her smile, the sound of her voice, the touch of her hand, life no longer held meaning. Now she was gone, nothing would be the same. Part of him would remain forever lost, dead and grieving.

He placed his lips to her forehead as he rocked her lifeless form. He had known her such a short time and, despite him fighting it at every step, he had known the truth. She was his soul mate, the very breath in his lungs, his reason for living, and now she was gone. He had spent so long fearing what his love would do to her, so long denying what he felt, but now it was too late to tell her. Too late to say he loved her, too late to place his lips upon hers and lose himself in the sweet promise of her kiss.

He placed his forehead to hers, pulling her closer still, gathering her in his embrace as if sheltering her tiny frame would somehow save her. But she was gone. Everything she was, everything she could have been, was gone. Her magic had burnt out, consuming her in the process. He stroked her jaw with his claw, placing his lips to hers, wishing her safe passage to the other realm. Her lips were as soft as they had promised to be, their coolness gaining heat as he refused to end this final parting. Heat engulfed him as he closed his eyes, his lips still on hers, using the connection to seek her spirit in the other realm, praying she had not burned out so completely that her very soul had been destroyed. He pulled away, feeling only emptiness. She was gone. He pulled her close again then gasped as her eyes flickered open.

"Conrad," she croaked, lifting her hand to cradle his face. He leaned into her touch, relishing the coolness of her flesh upon him.

"I thought you were lost, I couldn't find your spirit." He looked upon her in wonder, his claws tracing her with desperate gentleness, his eyes not willing to believe what he was seeing, before even questioning how she could have possibly known it was him through his monstrous visage.

"I'm a Phoenix," she whispered. "We don't die from our fire, we burn out and are reborn." She reached out to grasp his hand, her fingers clasping around just one of his enormous talons. "Thank you for coming."

He cringed, realising her tiny form was cradled within the arms of a beast. He looked away, attempting to ensure she couldn't gaze upon him any longer.

"Don't," she whispered. "Don't hide something so spectacular." Her voice was weak and he could tell it was taking everything she had not to sink into unconsciousness.

"I'm sorry you had to see me like this," he apologised. He hadn't registered the praise she had spoken, because the hateful, mocking words from the past overpowered her whisper. He flinched as her arm curled around his neck, pulling herself up until their noses almost touched. He searched her eyes, expecting to see revulsion and disgust, but instead he saw something which caused his heart to flutter. Despite his bestial appearance, she looked at him now with the same desire she'd had all those times they had almost kissed. As if reading his thoughts, her lips pressed to his muzzle with weak hunger.

He closed his eyes, no longer fearing the stirring of heat she caused in his core. The elation of her acceptance enveloped him and his blood burned for her. This one kiss did everything he feared it would. The fire of his essence consumed them both, but hers simply answered in kind, creating harmony. She pulled away, sucking her bottom lip as if to taste him for a moment longer. With a smile on her lips, her eyes flickered shut as she once more grew heavy in his arms.

Through the hole above them, the damp mist from the rescue services' hoses began to cascade down upon them. "Let's get you out of here," he whispered, his form shedding around him as the fiery essence that created it was reabsorbed back into himself, along with an overwhelming sense of fatigue. His clothes had fused to his skin, causing him to cry out as he peeled his jacket from his blistered flesh in order to wrap it around her naked body. The ifrit part of him was something which grew from within, a living shell, and as such, anything in his possession was normally shielded, but her fire had been too much, even for him.

Pain radiated from his core as his arms grew heavy. He stood, scooping her into his protective grasp, staggering slightly as a feeling of weakness began to consume him. With a growl, he gripped her tightly and an overwhelming feeling of protectiveness encompassed his very being as he forced himself beyond the pain, beyond the exhaustion. He pushed them away to a place in his mind he could return to later. For now, the only thing that mattered was Ashley. He gritted his teeth. He was getting her out of here, getting her to safety. Nothing, no one would harm her again. Not so long as he drew breath.

∽

Tess watched with emptiness as the remaining frame of the building started to collapse in on itself. The firefighters were doing their best, but the flames were aggressive. She had listened with numbness as Alex spoke to his team and they recounted the quick and easy execution of all involved parties, many being trapped by the collapsing ceiling and unforgiving fire. A name kept circling in her mind as she listened. They spoke of numbers, of the clans they identified. But it seemed to Tess that people were missing. They had shielded and diverted their chip location data so it appeared they were in other places. A nearly impossible feat, but Tess had the skills to isolate who had been present, and if their numbers were correct, at least two people were unaccounted for. One was a figure known as Thaddeus. The other, however, she was certain was the person responsible for everything that had happened.

"Vincent Masters," she whispered finally. Alex crouched down beside her, giving her his full attention. "The Taphouse and this mansion both belonged to his clan. Please tell me he was amongst the dead. Tell me you got the bastard who killed my friends!" Tears streamed down her face as she watched the building with a growing sense of emptiness.

"The wronged have been avenged." Detective Mendel's voice startled her. She hadn't even noticed his arrival on site but, from the ash and debris clinging to him, he must have been here for sometime. "We apprehended him trying to flee. Justice was swift."

"Detective Mendel," Alex acknowledged gravely.

"Did my son go in there?" he questioned, already seeming to know the answer.

"He did."

"So your sister was a Phoenix. I guess I was worried over nothing." He placed his hand on Alex's shoulder.

"Worried over nothing?" Tess sniffled, wondering how he could possibly think that, given both his son and her best friend were dead.

"About his feelings. We thought she was ice-aligned like the rest of the Ciele family," he explained to her. She saw confusion cross his face as he looked upon her. Almost as if the pain she was feeling, that she wore upon her stained cheeks, somehow didn't make sense.

"Why would that mean anything? What good does that do now?" she demanded, casting a brief glance towards Jack who was seated in one of the P.T.F. vehicles. Bindu had said they would take everyone to their base. She knew they were waiting for her, but she couldn't bring herself to move.

"She turned his eyes gold. We thought he'd destroy her, but it turns out..."

"She destroyed him instead," Alex finished.

"Now, why'd you go and say something like that?" Reuben Mendel demanded, as Tess heard the horrific sounds of her sobs. "Didn't you hear me? She turned his eyes gold."

Alex looked at him, bewildered.

"Ah, so you don't know *everything*. An ifrit's eyes only turn gold when they've found the one they need to protect. A calling beyond the voices of the wronged, a calling of the soul, and that is a powerful thing. There's nothing quite like it."

"What does that have to do with anything? Nothing can survive a Phoenix's flame, especially not when its magic turns berserk," Alex interjected.

"Nothing, except their soul mate." Reuben nodded towards the smouldering remains, where a dark figure could be seen emerging from the flames.

Tess cupped her hands over her mouth as shouts echoed from the medics who rushed forward.

∼

Alex watched as the orange hue of the fire seemed to part around the dark figure emerging from within. Conrad's pace was slow, his feet barely clearing the debris he navigated, yet his focus never faltered. In his scalded arms, barely covered by a jacket, was his sister, her limp body pressed tightly to his chest. Medics, hovering on standby, began to stir, watching his difficult progression to the grass garden. As soon as he was clear of the ruined and crumbling building, it was as though his strength faded. His legs grew weak and he dropped to his knees, still cradling Ashley closely. This was the signal the gathering medics had been waiting for. A signal they had fatally misread.

The medics crowded around him, attempted to advance, to take Ashley from his protective grasp. The look in his eyes should have warned them of their error. Even Alex could see the fierce protectiveness in his gaze. They should have known he wouldn't let them take her away. Fire curled around them, drawn from the building to encompass them in its protective storm. Alex had only seen this manner of reaction twice before, and in both instances a preternatural had been wounded to the extent they had to draw strength from their origin, and this power was anything but rational. It knew only the desire of its child, and Conrad's sole focus was on defending Ashley.

"I thought you said the flame wouldn't hurt him," Alex whispered, as Reuben drew level with him to watch the unfolding events.

"No, I said it wouldn't kill him, but even with their connection it probably took everything he had to withstand. He probably didn't even realise how hurt he was until he reverted to human form."

Alex stepped forward, quickly shrugging free of Reuben's touch as he reached out to restrain him, as if he knew what he had in mind. When he reached the group of medics, he saw two of them were now armed with tranquiliser darts, their hushed tones discussing a tag and snatch retrieval while their comrades took aim, their rifles steaming from the cold enchantment shielding the darts to ensure they would reach its target. The pink hue of the fletching sung of their second mistake—they were already greatly underestimating his strength. Those darts would be about as useful as sending a docile mouse to fell a serpent. It would simply bait him.

"*Mine*," Conrad growled, his vision snapping towards one of the medics who had dared to take a step forward, his dart gun raised, ready to fire.

"Sir, please calm down, we're here to help." The medic tried to placate him, his trigger finger twitching as he lined up the shot. The dart released, striking the ground with a dull thump to discharge its contents. The medic looked up at Alex, whose fingers still rested on the barrel of the lowered weapon.

"I'll take it from here," Alex stated. "Be grateful. If you'd hit him with that, we'd all be dead. Use your common sense and do as the man asked. They'll not be coming with you in any scenario, so you may leave." His voice was firm, holding an authority he hoped they dared not ignore.

"But, sir!" the medic in charge began, only to be silenced by his cold interruption.

"That's P.T.F. alpha Ciele," Alex announced, tapping his charred jacket to bring their attention to his rank, "and the young lady there is under our protection."

"But—"

"Dismissed." The medics exchanged a look of bewilderment, before silently deciding it was better to keep their distance.

Once they had departed, Alex crouched level with Conrad, amazed to see the golden embers of his eyes burning possessively. "Conrad." Alex raised his hand placatingly as Conrad's grip tightened on Ashley, shielding her. "I need you to let me see my sister so I can check her." He kept his voice soft, non-threatening, as he slowly slid his feet forwards, closing a little more distance between himself and the barrier of swirling flames.

"I know you need to keep her safe. That's my job, too, as her big brother." Alex edged forward again, sweat beading his brow as he reached out tentatively. The fire surrounding them dissipated into a fine cyclone of smoke, granting Alex permission to approach. Carefully, with slow, smooth movements, he placed his hand on Ashley. He saw Conrad's muscles tense, but the soft reassurances leaving Alex's lips seemed to be working. Pulling a small light from his pocket, he knelt forwards, shining the beam into her eyes, watching for the dilation of her pupils.

"Conrad, did my sister regain consciousness after the burn-out?" He kept diverting his vision from Ashley to look into Conrad's eyes, using his name and reinforcing his relationship to the figure he was protecting.

"Yes," Conrad whispered, earning a quick smile before Alex continued his examination. Alex could see him relaxing as the understanding that they were safe began to register. Sensing the alteration, he touched Conrad's hand gently, feeling the strong tremors of exhaustion. The more aware he became of the world beyond Ashley, the harder it would become for him to push aside his exhaustion.

"We need to get my sister somewhere safe now, so can you help me to move her?" Even despite his returning cognisance, Alex knew better than to try to take her from him, as doing so could undo everything he had just achieved. He held his gaze, watching, waiting for his response.

Conrad gently lowered Ashley to the ground, tucking her hair carefully behind her ear in a gesture that even alone would have sung of this man's feelings for his sister. Then he moved his hands away. "I don't think I can stand," he whispered weakly. "How'd we get out here?"

Conrad's hands moved to steady himself, but it was a futile effort. Seeing his eyes roll backwards, Alex reached forwards, catching him before he struck the ground.

CHAPTER 18

'*You're mine now, understand?*' Ashley's eyes opened as she sucked in a panicked breath and her arms flailed as she screamed, trying to fend off her attacker. Panic consumed her as two hands restrained her, pushing her back towards the bed. She screamed again, heat expanding outward from her chest as the hands released her.

"Whoa, Ashley, calm down. It's okay."

The voice sent relief flooding through her and, for the first time, she noticed her surroundings. In her panicked state, her eyes had instinctively been drawn towards the exit, a large wooden door, propped open by a stone doorstop. Her mouth felt dry, pulling her longing gaze towards the small washbasin just to the side of the door. She licked her lips, hoping to return moisture to some part of her body. The gentle pressure of a hand upon her arm drew her focus from her overwhelming thirst to her brother. He looked older than she had ever seen him, worn out and dishevelled. His red, burned face was littered with white flakes of peeling skin, his brow was creased with concern and the telltale signs of exhaustion darkened his eyes.

"Alex, where... what?" She raised a hand to her throat, hearing the raspy sound that had been her voice. Her vision once more scanned her surroundings, recognising the room for what it was, a hospital room. Her fingers grasped the sheets as she forced herself to breathe. Her brother was here, she was safe, yet still she looked for all possible exits.

The glare from the window hurt her eyes, its vibrancy casting rainbow shadows through the empty glass jug upon the table. "Water?" She moistened her lips again, finally finding a measure of relief as saliva coated her dry tongue. Her brother gestured towards the drip in her arm, causing her to frown. She still felt thirsty. Her dry throat burnt with need.

"You're at my base camp. What's the last thing you remember?"

"Conrad," she whispered, feeling a blush rise to her cheeks as she recalled their first kiss, a kiss which had brought her back from the brink of death—or at least that was how she would remember it, even if it wasn't quite accurate.

"Good." There was a pregnant silence as she continued to examine the room. Blankets had been gathered into a large recliner in the corner of the room, as if someone had been staying with her. The discarded sandwich wrappers and crisp packets in the small waste paper bin earned another frown.

"How long?" she rasped, her discomfort easing just a little now her throat wasn't quite as dry.

"Just over a week. Aside from being severely dehydrated and a little malnourished, you're doing well."

Seeing the heavy emotions in her brother's gaze, she gave him a questioning look.

"I never would have forgiven myself if..." She watched her brother's eyes mist with tears, an emotional response so alien, it seemed to transform his entire features. He looked so vulnerable. She placed her hand on his, noticing the fine layer of ice-enchanted bandages for the first time and realised how severely he must have been injured. Her gaze returned to his face, to the peeling skin and at once she realised how he must have received such burns. "I know I have some explaining to do, but—"

"It's alright, I already know. I understand why you couldn't tell me." She massaged her throat, her gaze travelling longingly back to the empty water jug.

"How?"

"When I burnt out, my mother told me everything." She remembered the feeling of death crushing the breath from her body, and her heart slowing to a stop. For a few moments, she could hear Conrad, his voice pleading for her to open her eyes, to return to him, and then there was silence and she was in another place. Her ethereal form was forged of fire, and before her stood a person she thought she would never see in any place beyond her dreams—her mother—and beside her was another being, a creature sharing the same fiery radiance as herself, and they had told her everything they could. About how she had left her to lead away those who were hunting them, sealing her gifts so no one could uncover the truth of what she was. It was then that her father spoke, telling her of her origin and the choice she had. She could choose to remain with them, or fully combine with her other-self and be reborn.

It was then she began to feel her body, the phantom tingle of her flesh, the warm pressure upon her lips as Conrad reached out through the realms in search of her. She felt his burning tears upon her skin and the regret of so many things left unsaid and undone. The phantom pressure became a real sensation, sending heat throughout her body. As he pulled away, removing her lips from hers, she felt colder than she had ever felt before.

"Your mother entrusted you to my father," Alex explained, "knowing that when you became old enough, we could ensure your safety. The plan was to keep you hidden until your third cycle, when your inner strength would surpass that of the seal. At which point we could train you to understand your gift and register you as a Perennial, a protected species. For some reason, you awoke early."

"My mother told me I was born in March, not May. Apparently, I always used to get the two confused." Ashley glanced around again, before pursing her lips into a slight pout. "Maybe we can keep that between ourselves. No one likes to find out they are older than they thought!" Her brother's chuckle brought a smile to her face as she saw him shed most of the burden he seemed to be carrying since she had awoke. "How did I end up here?"

"Conrad," he answered simply. A wash of concern and shame overwhelmed her. She hadn't even asked how he was. As if seeing this, her brother smiled again. "He's fine. We had to monitor him for a few days as he was badly burned, but he recovered quickly, given his nature and your bond. Now we can't get rid of him. He refused to leave and trust me when I say he's a force to be reckoned with! You actually just missed him. I sent him to get some food. He's been a fixture in that chair for a week," Alex said, gesturing towards the corner. "We let him stay on the condition he took care of himself."

The clattering sound of a cup on the floor drew their attention to the door, just in time to see the water Conrad had been carrying cascade across the floor. Ashley's heart quickened at the sight of him. His hair looked unkempt, his blue eyes were ringed with circles as dark as the t-shirt he wore, and yet he had never looked more perfect. The surprise on his features morphed into the most brilliant smile she had ever witnessed, a smile that caused her heart to flutter. He closed the distance between them and her breath hitched as he took her tenderly in his arms as if he were fearful she might break. Pulling back, he ran his hands desperately through her hair, his vision searching hers to make sure she was truly awake, that his mind was not playing tricks on him.

Reaching up, she wove her fingers through his tangled hair, pulling his lips to hers. A smile played on his lips as he rested his forehead against hers. Closing her eyes, she savoured their closeness, the energy shared between them.

"I love you," she whispered, determined not to miss the opportunity to tell him again. She saw the elation her words had brought before he once more pressed his lips to hers. In that moment, as he held her close, she knew that everything would be okay.

<<<<>>>>

Dear reader,

We hope you enjoyed reading *Salvation's Kiss*. Please take a moment to leave a review, even if it's a short one. Your opinion is important to us.

Discover more books by Kathryn Jayne at https://www.nextchapter.pub/authors/kathryn-jayne

Want to know when one of our books is free or discounted? Join the newsletter at http://eepurl.com/bqqB3H

Best regards,

Kathryn Jayne and the Next Chapter Team

You could also like:
Familiar Ties by Kathryn Jayne
To read the first chapter for free, please head to:
https://www.nextchapter.pub/books/familiar-ties

Lightning Source UK Ltd.
Milton Keynes UK
UKHW012003261120
374146UK00001B/129